THE

BANE

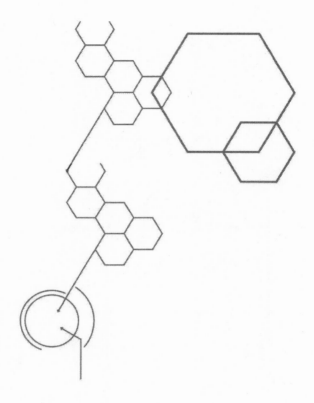

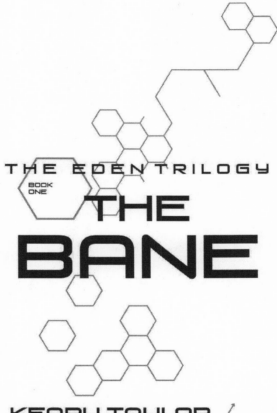

THE EDEN TRILOGY

BOOK ONE

THE
BANE

KEARY TAYLOR

First Print Edition: March 2013

Taylor, Keary, 1987-
The Bane : a novel / by Keary Taylor. – 1st ed.

ISBN 978-0615769806

KEARY
TAYLOR
BOOKS

ALSO BY KEARY TAYLOR

THE EDEN TRILOGY
The Ashes: An Eden Prequel
The Raid: An Eden Short Story

FALL OF ANGELS
Branded
Forsaken
Vindicated
Afterlife: the novelette companion to Vindicated

What I Didn't Say

BANE – noun

1. A person or thing that ruins or spoils.
2. A deadly poison.
3. Death; destruction; ruin.
4. Obsolete: that which causes death or destroys life.

ONE

"Good-bye my friend," Avian whispered. His eyes closed with silent words of regret that echoed through the rest of us.

We all shut our eyes as Avian pressed the device to Tye's arm. The back of my throat tightened when I heard the sharp hiss of the cybernetics under his skin short out and die. Agonizing seconds later, he took his last gasping breath.

Avian set down the one piece of technology that existed in Eden on the wooden table. I finally opened my eyes again when I heard his suppressed sob. Bill and Graye bowed out of the medical tent silently, unable to deal with Avian's grief in addition to their own.

I couldn't keep my eyes away from Tye.

His body lay limp on the table, one of his legs about to slip off. His left arm rested at his side, the skin shredded and torn where he had tried to rip it off. The dirty, bloody wires and metal bones shone from underneath. His head lolled to one side, staring emptily at me with one still-human eye and one cybernetic one.

I wished Avian would stop sobbing. I should have tried to comfort him, but what do you say to the man who had just killed his own cousin?

Avian looked up at me from where he stood with his hands braced on the table next to the body. "Thank you for bringing him back, Eve."

I bit my lower lip and managed a small nod. He held my eyes for a long moment, each of us knowing what the other was thinking. We would never hear Tye's hesitant laughter again, never urge him to take a break from his post to eat a few bites. He would never hunt in the woods or go on a raid again.

"I don't understand," Avian said quietly. "They don't attack at night. We're supposed to be safe when it's dark."

"I don't understand either," I replied. There were certain rules when it came to the Bane. Inactivity during the night was one of them. Night time was the one advantage we had over them.

"Let me help you," I offered as Avian started picking up the body. He graciously accepted, his entire frame trembling as we carried what was left of Tye to the furnace. We couldn't even bury our fellow men and women in the ground after they were infected – which meant we could never visit their graves. Even destroyed cybernetics were too dangerous to keep around. They were melted down and transported away.

Avian collapsed to the ground as we slid the heavy door closed. Another round of tears consumed him as I lit the fire beneath it. I sank to the ground next to him, hugging my knees as I watched the flames grow in intensity and consume Tye.

All it had taken was one brief touch from the Bane. Tye had tried ripping his own arm off before the infection it carried could spread any further. It was useless. Less than an hour after being touched, Tye's eye started changing. He'd turned on us within three hours and tried to return to the city. It had taken the entire unit to drag him back to Avian. Bill had to knock him unconscious so he wouldn't try to kill us all.

"Why don't you go to bed?" I said quietly as I stared at the flames. "I can take care of things."

"No," Avian said as he shook his head, wiping a few tears away with the back of his hand. "I can handle it."

2

"You don't have to," I tried to argue, but only half-heartedly.

"Go home, Eve. You've done your job."

I stood and walked out of the tent.

Small fires glowed in the darkness, scattered about in the village of tents. I avoided eye contact and pushed the flap of my own tent aside and stepped into the darkness. My worn-out cot felt more uncomfortable than ever as I collapsed onto it. I stared up at the blackness above me, my arms resting above my head. The sound of Sarah's breathing a few feet away let me know she was still awake.

We lay silently for a few minutes. Tye's death would be as hard on Sarah as it was on Avian, brother and sister in painful loss.

"How's Avian?" she finally spoke.

"I helped him with the furnace but he sent me back," I forced the words out of my mouth. All I wanted to do now was sleep.

Sarah was silent again and I knew there would be tears rolling down her pale cheeks. I understood why she had not come to the farewell. It killed a little piece of us all whenever we attended one.

I faintly heard her roll away from me before I fell off the cliff of consciousness into the dark.

TWO

My eyes slid open to meet the darkness above, adrenaline and relief flooding my system at the same time. We all occasionally screamed in our sleep, every one of us still haunted by nightmares. At night your mind can turn against you and show you cybernetic-infested friends, make you feel your cells harden and turn you against everything that made you who you were.

I pulled myself up, listening for sounds outside. It was early, the sun still struggling to make its way above the mountaintops. Everything was silent.

Wearing the same clothes I had worn yesterday on the raid, Tye's blood still dried on them, I grabbed my pack from off the floor. I slid my handgun into my belt and stepped outside, leaving Sarah sleeping. I headed for the tree line.

My boots darkened, dampened by the heavy morning dew. My ears strained for any sounds that didn't belong, searching for any warning hums of an ATV or the faint chop of a helicopter. The morning was quiet, but that did not mean I dropped my guard. With danger a constant, dropping your guard meant getting killed, or worse.

The trees dropped away in an abrupt line, giving way to the ten-foot tall wire fence. Five acres of garden lay before me. We were each required to work a minimum of two, five-hour shifts per week in the garden. We were all responsible for keeping Eden alive in one way or another.

I geared up with a pair of worn gloves and a religiously cared for hoe. I pushed back my dirtied sleeves and fastened my pack tighter to my back. It never left my back, other than when I slept. To be separated from it could mean the difference between life and death. It had everything I needed to survive in the wilderness for nearly a month.

As I worked my way to the southeast corner of the garden, I saw I wasn't alone. A figure in dirty rags was kneeling on the ground, working steadily on a row of slowly growing potatoes. It was Terrif, the oldest member of Eden. He was mute and growing frail. He knew the most about gardening though. Without him, our harvest would be half of what it was.

A person's value shifts greatly when the world comes to an end.

Terrif looked up at me briefly as I went to work on a new area that would be planted later that afternoon. His eyes met mine for just a moment, oddly grey orbs that were starting to slowly lose their sight, and went back to his work.

The garden was in its fifth year and gaining maturity. The fruit trees had produced well the previous year and we were hoping the late start of spring was not going to hurt production this year. It was agonizing, having so little control over something so vital to our survival.

Within a year of the Evloution, people started realizing they weren't the only ones on the run and began to band together. As this colony of thirty-four formed, they knew we were going to have to provide food for all these people or everyone was going to starve. And so the garden had been planted. Eden itself might be constantly moving for safety reasons, but the garden was the center, the anchor of which we revolved around.

5

Each of us had reached Eden in our own way. Those who had survived the Evolution had figured out that it wasn't safe to be in the cities anymore. With so much electricity and other mechanical resources available, the Bane flocked to them like addicts. If you were smart you ran as fast as you could toward the mountains or to the open country.

I didn't remember much of my arrival at Eden. Only that I arrived alone, a thirteen-year-old girl, mostly naked, covered in blood, but without a scratch on me. I had no memory prior to that time, no recollection of my parents or of where I had come from. I could only recall one word that might have something to do with my past: Eve. And so that was what I was called.

I insisted on training with all the older men, learning to handle a weapon and survive out in the wild. By fourteen I was going on raids and helping to protect those around me. Avian and Sarah had helped me when I needed, despite how determined I had been that I could take care of myself.

Avian had just escaped from the Army that was tearing itself apart, just as the world was falling to ruin. He'd rescued his sister Sarah, hiding in the garage after their parents had been infected. He'd had to shoot both of them to get her out. He next went after his cousin Tye, who'd locked his infected mother in their trailer home, and stood guard outside the door with a rifle. Together they fled into the mountains. They were some of the first to arrive in Eden, only twenty-one, twenty, and nineteen-years-old.

As the sun started graying the sky, others trickled in to the garden, those assigned to work the morning shift while the others guarded camp. Not many words were spoken, each person working in silent grief. I saw eyes flicker to my face, questions forming in their heads. They wanted to know how our elite team had finally failed to bring someone home. I may have only been seventeen but they didn't expect any less from me than they did Bill or Graye. Or Tye.

I wanted to tell them it was Graye they should be questioning, but I would never betray him like that. If he wanted them to know what he had done to Tye, he could tell them himself. It wasn't my place.

Just as the sun broke above the tree line, Sarah joined at my side. She carried a sack of seeds, dropping them in a shallow trench. I raked the damp dirt over them.

"How is Avian this morning?" I asked, keeping my voice down.

"He looked like he hadn't slept all night," she said as she dropped seeds. She gave a small cough, covering her mouth with a fist. "He wouldn't eat this morning but said he was fine."

"I'll talk to him when I get back." I sighed as I continued to rake.

Avian was the one person who never left Eden. He never went on raids, never even worked in the gardens. He couldn't leave his supplies and the CDU, the one sure device that protected us from the Bane. All too often he was needed. Even though he had only two and a half years' worth of medical training, he knew more than the rest of us.

"People are wondering what happened last night," Sarah said, looking around to make sure no one was listening. "I heard them talking at breakfast this morning. They're starting to lose trust in Graye."

"Why?"

"They overheard someone talking to Avian about how Graye had something to do with Tye's infection. We all know he can be selfish and sloppy."

I straightened slightly and looked over my shoulder where Graye was working. He was alone, his head hanging low. I

7

would never say it aloud, but Sarah was right. Graye always tried to grab just a few more things, one more treasure to take home for himself. He hadn't noticed the Bane creeping up on him. Tye had gotten Graye out before it was too late but it had cost him his life.

"We can't afford to turn against ourselves," I said, getting back to work before anyone could notice my stiff behavior. "We all know better than that."

"They're upset," Sarah said simply. She coughed again, just once.

"They're going to have to move on," I said, more bluntly than I had meant it. "We need him. We need everyone."

Sarah didn't say anything else as she continued her work. It wasn't until a few minutes later that I realized she was vocalizing not only the thoughts of others in Eden, but her own.

I worked a longer shift than required, in a way anxious to prove my devotion to Eden. It was unnecessary, but I seemed to be feeling the guilt Graye wasn't. The afternoon shift started trickling in, the post in the watchtower shifting. As I handed off my tools and gloves to someone else, I realized that Graye and I were the last of the morning crew to head back.

I hesitated, unnerved at having to walk back with him, but I wasn't stupid. It was safer to travel with a companion, even if it was just between the gardens and home.

We walked in silence. We'd known each other for four years now and had been going on raids together for almost three. He was a good fighter and when push came to shove, I would want him on my side.

Graye had come to Eden when I was fourteen. He was twenty at the time. He had been recently married and had a baby girl, both lost to the infection. It was hard to condemn him for his selfish actions; he had lost everything that ever meant anything to him. He was just trying to take something back from the world that had stolen everything from him.

We were almost back to Eden, our journey nearly successfully silent, when he finally spoke.

"I didn't mean it you know," he said in his gravelly voice. "I never wanted Tye to get hurt."

"I know," I said as we stepped into the perimeter of camp. That was as close to an apology as anyone would ever get from Graye.

We went our separate ways.

THREE

I hadn't expected anyone but Avian to be inside the medical tent but found him hunched over, working on a skin and bones foot. Wix lay on the table, propped up on his elbows, watching as Avian worked.

"Hey, Eve," Wix said with a bright smile on his narrow face. "Look what I got on the way home!" He held up one of the fattest snakes I had ever seen.

"Looks like it got you too," I said, raising my eyebrows.

"Eh, it's nothing," he said with a grin again, watching as Avian treated the bite.

I just shook my head as I sat on a stump that served as a seat. Despite being two years older than me, Wix was the skinniest person I had ever met but made up for his small size with personality. Even all the tough scouts like Bill couldn't tease him about his build. It was impossible to dislike the green-eyed, red-haired kid.

"Well, that's all I can do," Avian said as he finished wrapping a bandage around Wix's ankle and foot. "Let me know if it starts oozing or turns black. I want to check on it before you go to sleep tonight."

"Well that doesn't sound pleasant," Wix said as he sat up, his twiggish legs hanging off the table. "Thanks for fixing me up, Doc."

He limped out of the tent, his prize and dinner swinging at his side.

"Snake is actually pretty good," I said as I watched Avian clean up.

"What are you doing here, Eve?" he asked.

"Making sure you're okay," I said, taking the quick and honest approach. I took a good look at him. His lean but toned frame was stiff, his brow pinched together, his intense blue eyes dark.

"I'm fine. Did Sarah say otherwise?" he said with a sigh, throwing a few used rags into a basket.

I shrugged, picking at a piece of bark that was peeling off the stump I sat on.

"You don't need to worry," he said, placing his hands on the table, staring at it. I had little doubt he was seeing the body of his cousin and hearing the volts course through it. It was the same thing I was seeing.

"I wanted to talk to you and Gabriel, together. I'm worried about people turning on Graye," I said, ignoring Avian's downfallen attitude.

He looked up at me, and after several long moments, still didn't say anything. I was worried that I knew what he was thinking: that maybe they should.

"You know we can't afford to lose him," I said quietly, but keeping my voice firm.

His eyes hardened for a moment. "Gabriel is on scouting duty right now. He will be back this evening."

"We need to talk about it," I said as I stood. I hesitated at the opening to the tent, wanting to argue. But keeping my mouth closed, I walked out. I would make my argument later, when both Avian and Gabriel were there.

I missed the serving of lunch. I hadn't bothered to eat breakfast that morning so I was suddenly starving. I walked to the far end of camp and yanked up the door to the cellar. The room that stored the majority of the food in Eden smelled like earth. It was a comforting place, it felt protected, like Mother Earth wouldn't ever let anything happen to you there. I helped myself to a couple of carrots and a few hard rolls that were left over from that morning.

It spoke volumes about the character of the people in Eden that there was no need for a guard at the food stores. Most people who made their way here were starving, living only on what they could find in the wild. Here everyone could come and go as they pleased, take what they needed. We all lived by that rule: take what you *need*. We knew how to ration, no one would starve.

I ate as I made my way back to my tent. Finding it empty, I threw my few items of clothing and my bedding in a sack and slung it over my back.

Eden moved every two months or so for safety reasons. The Bane were starting to use helicopters. They scouted too. For humans. We couldn't risk them seeing us or pinpointing our exact location. The two limitations we had were the gardens and water. We always had to be within walking distance of water.

I walked to the south bend of the river, finding myself alone with only the birds for obnoxiously loud company. Kneeling next to the water, I scrubbed my clothing. All of it was barely more than rags anymore. I washed out my blankets and hung it all on the line to dry. My clothes felt hardened and caked with grime as I peeled them off. Dirt clouded the water momentarily as I soaked them and scrubbed furiously. But as hard as I tried, I couldn't get Tye's blood out.

The water was freezing, freshly melted snow from the mountains. Bumps rose on my skin as soon as I stepped into the water, my stomach quivering. Closing my eyes, I took a short breath and let myself sink into the river.

I let the flow of the water wash my hair, letting it take the dirt away from my skin. I kept my eyes closed as I settled onto the smooth rocks at the river bottom, listening to the noises I couldn't discern in the water. It felt peaceful down here. There was no one but me. There was no one else to think about; no worries about supplies, food, or of being infected. The cybernetics couldn't survive in the water, everything shorted out.

Down here there was just Eve.

When I finally rose from the water I shivered, the air around me brisk. Goosebumps flashed over my bare skin. I climbed out and onto the boulder that my clothes sat on. I wrapped my arms around my legs tightly, huddling against the cold while my clothes continued to dry.

I hoped Gabriel wouldn't take too long. As leader of Eden, he was never away for long. He would never call himself the leader, but that's what he was. He had never been elected, never asked to be such. But he was the most evenhanded, the one who always seemed to have the answers when no one else did. He and his family formed Eden. Terrif was his father-in-law. Together they had started the gardens that had saved us all from starvation.

He was as much of a father as I'd ever had.

My clothes were still damp when I pulled them on and started the walk back. I passed several other women on the way, heading to do their own laundry. Two of them wouldn't look at me, the third tried very hard to form a polite smile. I just kept my eyes glued to the ground.

I found the morning scouting group depositing their weapons in the armory, and was relieved to find Gabriel among them.

"I need to talk to you," I said.

"Yes, Avian informed me of that," he said as he came to my side and watched as the rest of the men walked out of the small building. He scratched at his graying beard, his thick brows furrowing.

"Can we talk now?" I asked, feeling impatient. The distress that was hanging in the air agitated me, making everything seem urgent.

"Fine," he said, and we set out for the medical tent to find Avian. We retrieved him and made our way to Gabriel's tent.

We each took a seat and I could tell both the men were irritated to be there. They would both hear me out though.

"What Graye did was wrong but you both know we can't afford to turn on him. We need him, especially now that Tye is gone. You both need to talk to everyone." It all came out in a desperate rush.

Gabriel and Avian looked at each other with a knowing glance. Avian gave a tired sigh as he looked back at me. "We know that. Everyone does. They aren't going to turn on Graye. They all love him too, despite his faults. We lose people every year."

I sat there, feeling stunned for a while. I had read everyone wrong? "Then what is happening? Everyone is about to explode out there!"

"They're grieving, Eve," Gabriel said, his expression a mix of annoyance and disbelief as his eyebrows furrowed together. "It's a natural process. They want someone to blame, to shove it all off on and Graye is that man."

My eyes slid from Gabriel's face to Avian's, whose expression reflected what Gabriel had just said.

"No one is going to force Graye out. No one is planning revenge. They're just trying to deal with Tye's death," Avian said, his voice catching on his last two words.

14

We were quiet for a few moments, my eyes studying theirs, making sure they weren't lying to me.

I felt stupid for missing the mark so completely.

Once they saw that I believed them they moved on.

"We have found signs of something moving in the southern forest," Gabriel said. "We found shoe prints and traces of waste. We don't think they're Bane but we need to be careful. If they're human we may watch them for a few days, see if we want to invite them in."

"How many?" I asked, my interest piqued.

"It looks like three, two older and a smaller child."

"Where are they headed?" I asked.

"We're not sure. If they are headed out this way, they are probably just running. We will try and contact them soon. We could use each other, I am sure."

"Don't act too soon though," I said a bit too quickly. "We have to be careful."

"Of course," Gabriel said with a nod.

I didn't know what to say for a minute. I had come in here, prepared for an argument, to state my case. Instead I had made a fool of myself.

"Take the day off, Eve. Try and relax," Avian said, looking concerned.

"Take the day off?" I questioned. I could no sooner take the day off than I could stop breathing.

"Yes, take the day off," Gabriel said, he eyes sternly set on my face. "I'm ordering you to take a break from your duties. I don't want you scouting today. You're too wound up."

"But Gabriel, I…"

"I mean it, Eve!" he suddenly shouted. He shook his head at me, his brow furrowed. "Go home."

My jaw set, I stood and walked out.

Home. I didn't even know what that was.

I threw the flap of my tent aside, finding it empty. I grabbed my bow and my quiver out of the corner and walked back out. They may have ordered me to keep away from my duties but I couldn't sit around idle.

The woods were both silent and full of sound. Noise didn't travel far, absorbed by the towering trees that surrounded us, by the earth and moss that covered the ground. And yet the birds never stopped chirping, the insects never ceased their harmonious singing. If they ever did it was too late.

I watched for the signs: trails in the grass, the droppings on the ground. I had to push farther and farther out from the perimeter of Eden to find anything these days. I wasn't the only one that hunted in Eden but I was persistent.

Goosebumps rose on my skin as I caught a glimpse of movement to the south. I pulled the arrow back, holding my breath. Two seconds later the buck stepped into view.

The next second it jerked violently, the tip of an arrow appearing in the side of its neck. It took a few staggering steps forward.

My arrow was still nocked in my bow.

A figure leapt out of the underbrush, knife in hand, and slit the thrashing animal's throat. Just as the animal fell still, the boy looked up and my gray-blue eyes met his wide brown ones.

It took me a fraction of a second to react. I leapt over the boulder I had been hiding behind in one bound. That was all it took for the boy to leap back into the brush and take off at a sprint.

I heard him crashing through the maze of the forest, leaving a wake of fallen grasses and trampled moss behind him. Every time I thought I was gaining on him though the sound of his retreat would get farther away. And then it just stopped.

I was persistent, and I searched, but the boy had vanished.

I climbed out of the tree where I had made a desperate attempt to gain some ground and catch a glimpse of movement. I dropped to the ground with a gentle stirring of the dirt and took off in the direction of Eden.

When I stepped away from the tree line and into camp, I found things in a state of unease. Several scouts were gathered around Gabriel talking quickly in hushed tones. Others stood on the perimeter looking nervous and anxious.

"What's going on?" I asked as I came to Sarah's side.

She barely glanced at me. "The scouts saw someone in the woods again. They're getting closer."

"Yeah," I said as I started walking toward Gabriel and his group. "I saw one of them."

Gabriel caught sight of me as I approached them, his brow creasing. "I told you to take the day off, Eve."

"I saw him, in the woods," I said, ignoring his protests.

"You saw him?" he questioned doubtfully.

"Yes, I chased him but he hid. He got away."

Gabriel gave the scouts a disapproving look. "I suppose that explains the fourth body."

I gave Gabriel a questioning look.

"They found evidence of the three unknowns in the woods. Eli saw a fourth one, running through the trees."

A smile tugged at the corner of my mouth. "I was out hunting. He killed my buck. I tried to capture him but he got away."

Gabriel glared at the two men in front of him. "Pay a little closer attention next time," he said, then waved them off.

"It's not safe wandering in the woods alone," Gabriel said as he watched the crowd disband.

17

I only stared at him, waiting for the moment of false fatherly chiding to pass.

"Even for you," he added, his tone less scolding now.

"I am going to need two people to help me collect the buck. He was a big one."

FOUR

The smell of steel was something I would recognize anywhere and it was strong in the air. Low, hurried voices spoke behind me, using words I couldn't understand.

My heart hammered, the only part of my body that seemed able to move. I lay on my stomach, my face resting in a hole cut into the cold, medal table.

The voices approached through the dark, excitement and nerves tangible in the air. I was suddenly afraid. I wanted to run, to hide so the people in the dark could never find me. I didn't want to know what they were going to do to me.

A gloved hand touched my head. It was so cold because all of my hair had been shaved off.

They gathered around me and even though I couldn't see them, I felt half a dozen pairs of eyes settle onto the back of my exposed head.

The sound of a drill was the last thing I heard.

I jerked awake, my hands flashing to my head. I slumped back, relieved to find that my straight blond hair was still on my head. I closed my eyes again, the smell of steel still burning my nose.

Something stirred the dirt outside my tent, immediately drawing my attention from the nightmare. It was still hours from dawn, no one should have been awake at this hour, much less outside their tents.

Silently, I sprang from my bed, slinging my pack on in the same movement. I grabbed a knife and a handgun from my own stash of weapons and went to the opening of the tent.

The moon cast a faint glow on Eden, just enough light to enable me to see the figure that was retreating to the tree line.

I stayed out of sight as I slid between tents, careful to keep my cover. The outline looked vaguely familiar. It moved with sure, deliberate strides, quieter than I would expect. He must have dropped something or tripped just outside of my tent for me to have heard him.

He kept watch as he moved through camp but held his pace quick and straight. He was in a hurry to get out of there.

I followed him to the edge of the forest, hiding behind Wix's tent as I watched the figure dart into the trees. He glanced back once before he dropped into the trees.

I darted into the forest ten yards to the west of where he entered. My footsteps fell silently on the damp earth as I regained footing. When I heard more than one set of footsteps I took to the trees, being careful not to rustle the leaves as I crossed from one bough to the other.

It wasn't difficult to keep up with them. One of the figures moved with a limp, all the while trying to keep a small figure close to her side. The small group didn't seem dangerous.

I dropped from a limb directly in front of them, my blade just inches away from the man's chest.

"We don't tolerate theft in Eden," I said, my voice calm.

"Then point that knife back around," a male voice said, filled with forced confidence. "I believe you stole my buck."

I had been right, this was the same person I had seen in the forest earlier.

My eyes flickered to the figures that stood behind him. A woman who looked to be just a year or so older than myself stared at me with wide green eyes that shone brightly in the moonlight, her brilliantly red hair draping around her face in curls. She had her arms around a small boy with similarly curly blond hair.

"I couldn't let them starve," the man before me said simply.

He carried a cloth in his arms and I could see several food items sticking out of it. The small child held a piece of bread possessively in his hands, ready to protect it with his life.

"It's dangerous coming here and taking what isn't yours," I said as I held his eyes.

"We haven't eaten in days," he said, his voice sounding tired. I wasn't sure if I should think of him as a man or a boy. It was difficult to tell his age. "We've been running for a week, maybe longer. So I guess either you kill us or starvation will."

My eyes scanned them carefully, checking for any signs. Their eyes looked normal but it was difficult to tell in the minimal light. I was fairly certain the woman was organic, considering her wound. The Bane could heal themselves as long as the injury wasn't fatal. The cybernetic molecules would spread to the damaged area, stealing more of their humanity as the injured flesh was replaced with mechanical components.

The boy seemed likely organic as well. Bane children didn't know how to hide their true nature.

So the only one I had to question was the man. He moved with skill, he had shot with deadly accuracy. He hadn't earned a clearing yet.

I observed him for a moment. He was lean and well-muscled. A survivor's body. His shaggy brown hair fell across

21

similarly brown eyes. There was a rough scar that ran across his throat and down toward the neck line of his shirt. Claw marks.

"You are going to have to come with me," I said finally, keeping the mans tired but determined stare.

He held my eyes for a moment before looking back at his companions. The woman actually looked slightly relieved. The child only bit into his bread, devouring it with a speed that left half of the food on his face.

"Alright," he finally said, as if he actually had a choice. I nodded my head in the opposite direction and they started walking. As we moved through the trees, their leader kept glancing over his shoulder at me.

Camp was still silent when we entered its perimeters, as it should have been. Pressing a finger to my lips, I urged them toward Gabriel's tent. I assumed by the lack of alert that the guard in the tower had fallen asleep. I took a mental note to request that Gabriel add night watches to my list of duties.

I went to the east wall of Gabriel's tent, the one I knew he slept on.

"Gabriel," I whispered in attempt to not wake everyone nearby. "Gabriel!"

I heard a grunt and a shift of movement. At the same time an alarmed looking Avian stumbled out of his tent.

"Eve?" he questioned as he squinted through the darkness. "Whoa...what...?" He struggled to make his brain work, realizing I wasn't alone.

"I found them out in the woods nearby. After *he* stole from the stores," I gave a hushed explanation. "Gabriel," I hissed again.

This seemed to finally rouse him. I heard a curse and two seconds later Gabriel half tripped out of the entrance.

"What the devil…?" he said angrily and stopped short when he took in the growing group outside his tent. "Who are they?"

"The ones we saw in the woods," I repeated.

"You caught them?" Gabriel said stupidly.

"No, he's forcing me to point the blade at them." I rolled my eyes.

Gabriel glared at me for a moment before he turned his attention to Avian. "Get the CDU," he said.

With a nod, Avian turned and jogged toward the medical tent.

"Where did you come from?" Gabriel demanded as he turned to the older boy.

"We were just outside a city, a few days south of here. There were thirteen of us. We're all that's left."

"The city?" Gabriel said, surprise evident in his voice. Everyone avoided the cities these days.

He nodded. "Our camp moved around but we were always within walking distance. We needed to be able to get to supplies. The Bane found us though."

That was explanation enough for us. While food was becoming scarce in the city as things passed their expiration dates, other supplies were still to be found; clothing, medical supplies, weapons occasionally. We went on our own raids when the need arose.

The sound of Avian's quiet jogging announced his return. His expression was grim as he rejoined the group. We were all quiet as he charged up the CDU and calibrated it.

"What is it?" the young child asked as he pressed himself against the woman, eyeing the device with uncertainty.

"This," Avian said as he finished pushing buttons, his tone careful for the child. "Is called a Cybernetic Diffusion Unit. Or a CDU for short. It protects us from the bad things."

23

"What are you going to do with it?"

"I'm just going to touch you with it. It will give you a little shock but shouldn't hurt."

"This isn't necessary," the older boy said as he watched the child. "We're not infected."

Even as Avian touched the CDU to the young boy's arm I knew nothing would happen. They weren't pretending. A Bane would never let the situation get this far before it tried to infect the entire camp.

The child jumped as the electricity leapt though his system. He buried his face in the woman's skirts, not wanting to watch as Avian looked into the woman's eyes with polite apologies. She barely flinched as she was shocked.

With more uncertainty, Avian turned to the boy, his expression not so kind anymore.

If the CDU was used on a Bane they would be shorted out and killed instantly, including their human parts. The cybernetics saturated every part of your body once you were infected, even if your skin stayed intact, your muscles, your hair. This was the device that had saved us from Tye once he had been infected.

The thief did not take his eyes from Avian as he approached. He rolled up his sleeves, almost in a challenging way. As if daring Avian to prove him not organic.

I didn't even realize I had been holding my breath for over a minute until Avian had taken the CDU away from the boys arm. He hadn't even flinched.

"Satisfied?" the boy asked in a flat voice.

"No," Gabriel said, his thick brows drawing together. "You've stolen from us."

"We needed food," the woman spoke for the first time. "The boy, he had to eat."

Gabriel turned his dark blue eyes on her, his hands on his hips. While his face was stern he looked almost comical, standing in the moonlight in his nightgown. With his gray beard he looked almost like a picture I had seen of Santa Claus long ago.

"What are your names?" Gabriel demanded.

"This is Victoria," the older boy said, indicating the woman. "And Brady. And my name is West."

"Are you going to cause any trouble here?" Gabriel asked.

West shook his head, his eyes meeting mine. "I'd rather not have her knife me, so no." The woman and the child both shook their heads as well.

"We were going to approach your camp in the morning," West said, his tone less sarcastic. "Brady couldn't wait to eat."

Gabriel looked at the group for a long moment. I could see the gears turning in his finally awake head. The decision to let them stay was a gravely important one. On the one hand it was risky. We knew nothing of their past and there was the chance they could be being tracked by the Bane. On the other hand we could use more bodies, especially West, considering the recent loss of Tye. And besides that, they were human. We owed it to them to take them in. We were becoming a dying race.

"You," Gabriel finally said, indicating West. "You may stay with Avian for the time being. There is an extra tent close to his, used for storage at the moment, that the two of you can stay in," he said, meaning the woman and child.

Avian and West eyed each other warily but I could tell West was too tired to fight anything.

"Thank you," Victoria said gratefully.

"Are you alright until morning?" Avian asked, looking at Victoria. "I have medical training."

She seemed embarrassed to have his attention on her, her face flushing scarlet, visible even in the moonlight. "I will be alright, thank you."

"Don't try and run off in the night," I said as everyone started to disband. "It's not safe."

West met my eyes for a moment and I thought I saw a hit of a smile tug at his lips.

"I want to talk to you at day break," Gabriel said as he lifted the flap of his tent. "All of you."

Avian and I nodded, and the newcomers followed Avian. Alone again, I started the walk to the watchtower. It wasn't my night but I climbed the ladder anyway. I woke the guard who was on duty. He was immensely apologetic, embarrassed that he had fallen asleep. More embarrassed that he had been caught. He would feel ten times worse come morning when he learned three people had raided camp while he had dreams of television and air conditioning.

The distant sound of awkward helpfulness drifted up to the tower for a few minutes and then the night was quiet again, just as it should be.

I sat on the hard wooden bench, pulling my jacket tighter around me. The air felt suddenly cold now that the adrenaline that had been saturating my muscles had ebbed.

I rubbed my eyes, which suddenly felt heavy. I hated sleep. Idleness made me irritable and frustrated. Sleep was about as idle as one could be. It wasn't like it came as a relief to me. Others in Eden dreamt of times before the Evolution. Of families, of homes with electricity and running water. Of what life should have been like.

I couldn't remember what it was like before the Evolution. Even though I was thirteen when the world ended, my very first memory was of Avian's burning blue eyes.

For years, technology had been evolving. Robotic prosthetics helped people live, artificial hearts kept people alive. Nanorobotics and cybernetic technology evolved faster than the media could even keep up with. It started out so harmless. There was nothing but good intensions. It was difficult to find faults in the people who had created the infection.

And then the company NovaTor Biotics created a new breed of technology, manufactured a product that was going to save millions of people's lives, improve a few million more. They called it TorBane. Tor to claim it as their own, Bane to tell you what it did. It stood for Biological And Nanorobotic Enhancement. Bane. They created technology that infused human DNA with cybernetic molecules. TorBane had the ability to generate new limbs, organs, and just about any other human part. The machine was a part of you, just like your feet or your eyes. It was a perfect blend of machine and man.

NovaTor and its scientists became legends overnight. People were put on waiting lists, crying with joy that their lost leg was going to be regenerated, that their little sister who had been waiting for a liver transplant was going to live.

The unconfirmed question hung in the air. TorBane had the ability to regenerate any body part. When your heart, liver, lungs began to wear out you could simply buy new cybernetic hybrid ones. If you could afford it. Could people now live forever?

Fifteen-hundred implants were given in the beginning. Those who were treated came from every corner of the world, were observed for a few weeks after the procedure to make sure the implants grew as they were programmed to, and then sent home. For three months the world seemed like a better place to live in.

But the technology kept trying to improve the human body. Side effects started showing up. The people who had undergone the procedures were having other parts of their bodies change. A cybernetic lung was joined by a mechanical kidney, an enhanced, metallic eye. TorBane was evolving on its own, slowly taking over the human's bodies. Much like a virus, it morphed into something stronger, more deadly.

Then it wasn't just the patients that were starting to lose themselves. It was their families, their close friends. The nanorobotic molecules weren't stopping where they were supposed to. The technology was dubbed as "the infection" and could be spread as easily as touching an infected person. And the later generations claimed the human body within hours instead of weeks.

The soulless, human-looking machines were born. The Bane.

They were fast, they were aggressive. And they were hell-bent on infecting us all.

A war broke out between those still left, splitting the world. There were those who wanted to build an electromagnetic pulse, to wipe the infection out completely. But the rest of them cried there had to be another way. Setting off that kind of an EMP would wipe out every computer, every car, every water heater, and backup generator – it would send the world back into the dark ages.

They waited too long to come to an agreement.

By month four, ninety-eight percent of the world's population was infected, not even human anymore. More machine than man. We, mankind, were a dying race.

This was the age of the Evolution. Of the Bane

It hadn't mattered, wondering if mankind could now live forever. They lost their humanity instead and were worse than dead. Those that had survived fled into the country and the world was plunged back into the dark ages anyway.

FIVE

As the first hints of light started to faze into the sky a man named Tuck came to replace me. He seemed surprised to see me instead of his comrade whom I had relieved. I climbed down from the tower with stiff legs and headed back toward the tents.

I caught a glimpse of the red-haired woman and the small child walking with Avian toward the medical tent. Just as I walked past it, Gabriel stepped out of his tent. He gave me a knowing look and walked with me after Avian. A few moments later I heard someone step out of another tent and looked back to see West following us.

The air in the medical tent was sharp, smelling faintly of blood and stolen bleach. Victoria was already sitting on Avian's table, pulling her skirt up to her knee as Avian pulled on a pair of precious latex gloves. It was disheartening how something that had been so mundane just a few years ago had become so precious.

"I trust you got some rest last night?" Avian asked as he inspected her foot, the boy standing close by. The skin on her foot was swollen and red, puss begging to be let out.

"Yes, thank you," she answered quietly, her expression timid and uncomfortable, as if the thought of a man touching any part of her body scandalized her.

Gabriel sat on a stump, his fingers scratching at his grayed beard. I could tell he was searching for words, unsure of what his actions were going to be.

"What are your intentions?" he finally asked, directing his question to West. "What is your goal right now?"

"Stay alive, just like all of you," West answered simply. He glanced over at me, his eyes lingering for a few seconds.

"And where had you been heading, when Eve found you?"

"Just away from the city. We didn't know if we would ever find anyone else. As far as we knew, our little group could be the only humans left. And then there were only three of us after we got separated from our group."

Gabriel considered his words. Emptiness filled me as I thought about what West had said. The possibility of no one else being out there felt like final defeat. No wonder they had looked so tired last night. They'd had the weight of the world on their shoulders.

"We could use you," Gabriel said, having seemingly made up his mind. "We lost someone recently; his absence will be felt, in more ways than one." Avian's eyes flickered toward Gabriel's face for a moment. I didn't miss the pain that filled them. "We invite you to stay with us, if you can be trusted. We won't hesitate to dispose of you if we find otherwise."

"We won't be trouble," Victoria said, her voice desperate. "Please, we just want to stop running."

Our attention turned to West. Even though it hadn't been stated, and even though Victoria seemed to be the same age, he was obviously the one who had taken care of everyone, the one who made the decisions.

He nodded.

"I will have some of the extra tents set up," Gabriel said. Avian looked relieved to hear that he wouldn't have to share his quarters again with a stranger he didn't know if he could trust. "How does she look Avian?"

He didn't even look up as he scrubbed at her skin. Victoria's face looked pained. "The cut was bad. It's amazing you didn't bleed to death. Even more amazing this infection hasn't killed you. I wish we had some antibiotics but if we keep it clean it should heal up fine. I suggest she stay off her feet for at least a few days."

Gabriel nodded, looking momentarily at Brady. I knew it hurt him to see another child. Gabriel had lost a son to the infection in the beginning.

"You will go with Eve to the fields this morning," he said, taking his eyes away from the boy and looking at West. "This is important. The gardens keep us alive. Eve, if he acts suspicious, if you fear any betrayal, kill him."

West glanced at me briefly, his eyes slightly wide with surprise at Gabriel's bold words. He then looked back at Gabriel and gave the smallest nod of understanding.

"Come on," I said as I went to the flap of the tent. "I am already late." I didn't wait to see if he followed me.

He walked a few steps to the side of me. I watched him for any wrong movements. I kept my hand on the knife that was fixed in my belt, ready to use it on him if he tried to attack. He only followed me, his eyes taking in the forest around us.

"How many are there here?" he finally asked.

"Thirty-four," I said automatically. "I mean, thirty-three. There are thirty-three of us in Eden." It felt like a rock had just formed in my chest as the image of Tye's lifeless metallic eye staring at me came back.

"And your leader, his name is?"

"He's not exactly our leader. He didn't ask to be one but we all trust him. His name is Gabriel. And the other one is Avian. He is as close to a doctor as there is anymore."

"And your name is Eve." It wasn't really formed as a question, but there was a curious sense of doubt in his words. "Where do you come from, Eve?"

My stomach knotted up, my hand gripped tighter on my knife. "You ask a lot of questions."

"I'm just trying to figure things out."

He didn't say anything else after that and I made sure I didn't let him see my face, picking up my pace just a bit. Everyone had come from somewhere in Eden. But I had no clue where I had been before Eden. All I had were broken images from nightmares that didn't link together, a shattered mirror that would never be put together again.

We walked in hardened silence the rest of the way to the gardens. When we arrived it felt as if every pair of eyes fell upon us, growing wide with fear and curiosity. I couldn't raise my gaze to meet theirs. The attention made me want to run. I had raised myself to keep out of sight and in the shadows.

Pretending like we weren't being scrutinized, I led West to the storage shed and grabbed a wheelbarrow. "This way," I said, keeping my gaze down.

West was well aware of all the looks he was getting but he didn't hide from them like I did. He met their eyes, his face showing no emotion as he followed me through the gate and down a path. Despite the questions everyone was practically screaming with their eyes, no one said a word as we passed.

We stopped in the western field where hints of corn were starting to sprout. Tufts of green rose in perfect rows. Spring brought hope every year. Every row echoed our victory over the infection, against the Bane. We were still here. While we were still here, there was still some form of hope.

I dropped to my hands and knees and started on a row, picking out the rebellious weeds that insisted in cropping up.

Seeing what I did, West dropped a few rows away from me and started pulling too.

My hands worked swiftly but I kept looking back at West's form. His back was turned to me, his head bent low as he worked dutifully. He looked able to take care of himself. His frame was well-muscled. His dark hair fell across his eyes, left shaggy and longer like the majority of the males in the world. The only man in Eden who kept his hair short was Avian, who shaved his head completely every other week or so.

Tangled in my own thoughts, I suddenly realized that West had looked over at me. He had paused in his work, his hand a few inches above the ground, holding a weed. I felt frozen for a moment, unable to look away.

The small smile that tugged on his lips was all I needed to snap back into reality.

"How long have you been here, Eve?" he asked, turning back to his task. He threw the weed into the wheelbarrow.

"For as long as I can remember," I replied without thinking. I felt oddly disarmed, as if he had tipped over a wall in me that I didn't really realize was there. I didn't really want that wall tipped.

"Since before the Evolution?" His voice sounded slightly surprised.

"No, just after it."

He paused for a moment, as if considering my reply. "How old are you?" he asked.

"How old are you?" I shot back.

"Eighteen."

We were both quiet for a few moments, only the soft sound of earth being worked disturbing the silence.

"I'm seventeen," I said quietly to the dirt. "I think."

"You think?"

"I think," I said sharply, making sure not to look into his face.

I saw little of the newcomers the rest of the afternoon. They stayed close to Gabriel's side, getting settled in. Word was spreading fast about them, it would be impossible for it not to. Emotions were mixed. Some were elated to have three new members come into our family. There was obvious excitement about Brady. There weren't many children anymore. Other's felt like I did, not sure if trust was to be automatically given just because they were human.

The sun started to set, an orange haze peppered with stars. I sat on the rocky hill that protected Eden on the north side, watching as everyone went about their evening routine. Some made trips to the outhouses, others to take an evening bath, some heading to bed early. I watched them, feeling a sense of pride for them yet feeling disconnected and distant. I was one of them but I didn't really understand them.

I heard rubble being disturbed on the trail and a moment later Avian climbed up over the ledge, giving me a half tight-lipped smile as he joined at my side.

The silence between us was comfortable as we saw the fires being lit below us. Trails of smoke drifted into the sky before they faded into the darkening light. The sound of Avian's breathing comforted me. It was so familiar. If anything was home in this wreck of a world it was Avian.

"What do you think of them?" I finally broke the silence, my eyes never leaving the tents below us. I picked West out, walking hesitantly to a fire. He didn't sit to warm his hands, just stood back from the group and watched.

"I don't know," Avian mused, observing. The glow of the fires cast an orange haze to his face that highlighted his sharp brow, the line of his cheek bones. "The woman and child seem

35

harmless. I don't know what to think of West though. There's something about him."

I nodded in agreement. West had history to him. Some people were just like that. You just looked at them and could tell there was a story behind their face. "He's keeping a secret."

"Like what?" Avian asked.

I shook my head. "I'm not sure. He knows something."

Avian was quiet, unsure of what to say, echoing my own hesitation. I didn't like being uncertain about people, especially when those people could end the lives of the others around me.

"Happy birthday, Eve," Avian said quietly. He extended a hand to me, a small box in his palm.

A smile tugged at my lips. "My birthday."

It probably wasn't my real birthday. Having no memory of anything when I came to Eden, Sarah insisted we pick a day as my birthday. Some date to mark the years of my life as they passed. I had no idea the date had come.

"There was once a time when turning eighteen meant something. It used to be a big deal."

I took the box from his hand. It was simple, nothing special to it. I pulled it open and something light and shiny fell into my palm. I held it up to the light. It was a silver necklace, attached to it was a tiny set of wings, carved out of a soft black stone.

I took the wings gently in my fingers. They seemed so delicate, yet hard at the same time. I knew I must be gentle with it or it would break. It was the most elegant piece of craftsmanship I had seen.

I smiled as I recalled the conversation Avian and I had had when I was about fourteen. I had asked him what his name meant. He explained that his father had been a pilot and his

36

mother had loved birds. Avian related to things to do with birds and flight. To give remembrance his parents he had gotten two small birds tattooed onto his left breast, just above his heart. I had loved Avian's name ever since.

"May I?" he asked.

I only nodded. He took the necklace and fastened the clasp behind my neck. His hands felt warm as they brushed my skin, causing goosebumps to rise on my flesh. He sat back and observed where it lay on my chest.

"You made it," I stated, picking it up again to observe the flawless details. The feathers looked so soft I brushed my fingers over them, expecting soft plume instead of hard stone.

He only nodded, his eyes still looking at his creation. "I didn't want your birthday to go by without some notice. It's an important day for you."

"It doesn't feel important," I said as I lowered the necklace to my chest again.

"It is," Avian said, his eyes going back to Eden.

And we sat there on the hard earth, our shoulders barely brushing, until the sky went black and the stars shone with burning intensity.

SIX

I cinched my pack tighter as I walked out of the armory. A blade was strapped to each of my legs, a handgun secured in my belt, and a rifle rested in my left hand. I stood to the side of the entryway as Graye looked at me with serious eyes and ducked inside. Bill joined us a few moments later.

"Same as always?" I asked as they both looked to me. They nodded their heads, Graye shifting a gun into his other hand, Bill strapping a blade to his arm.

"Just a minute, Eve." I turned to see Gabriel walking toward us, West following two steps behind. "I want you to take him with you."

"We can handle it, Gabriel," I said as I turned back to my scouting partners.

"I'm not asking, Eve," he said sternly as he joined our small circle. "With Tye's loss we need him. I won't leave us unprotected because of your pride."

"Fine," I said as I stalked into the armory. I grabbed a rifle and walked back out. I raised my eyebrows slightly at West as I handed it over. "Keep up."

I headed toward the tree line. West kept just two steps behind me.

Graye took to the northern border, Bill to the west. We kept a constant circle around Eden. I was a little disappointed to see that West had not chosen to follow Bill or Graye.

I kept my eyes to the trees, my ears alert. Maybe I could just simply ignore West's presence. Maybe he'd get the message that I didn't want him there and go scout on his own.

"What have I done to make you hate me?" West suddenly demanded. His unexpected words stopped me in my tracks. "You don't... you don't even know me."

I whipped around, all of my defenses instantly bristling. "That's the point. I don't know you. I don't know if I can trust you."

"And how do I know if I can trust you?" he asked, his voice dropping low. "How do I know that you aren't just going to turn that blade on me out here where no one can see us?"

"You don't," I said. "But I wouldn't do that. We need you."

"Exactly," he said smugly.

My eyes hardened as I held his. I wanted to wipe the annoying little smile off his face with the butt of my gun.

"Just stay out of my way," I hissed as I turned and started walking east.

"Why do they treat you different?" he asked as he followed me. "Like you're some kind of leader?"

"Why don't you find out?" I said as I stopped suddenly, turning cold eyes on him again. When he didn't say anything, I started walking again.

"'Cause I know how to survive," I said as I scanned the trees, keeping my ears keen for any misplaced sounds. "Because I help keep them alive."

"Why are you any better than either of those other two guys?"

"Would you just shut up?!" I hissed as I glared back at him. "You're going to get us both killed!"

West threw both hands up in defense, his rifle pointing toward the blue skies. "There isn't anything anywhere near here. We haven't seen anything since the first day we left our camp."

I stared at him in disbelief for a second. Did he honestly think that meant he could let his guard down?

Finally, I just shook my head and kept walking.

The necklace Avian had given me bounced on my chest as I walked, its surface cool and hard. The light reflecting off it blinded my vision for a fraction of a second.

A memory stirred.

I'd seen this necklace before.

"Graye!" I screamed as we headed back into an alley. "Leave it! We've got to get out of here!"

"Hang on! I'll be right back. I've got to grab something!" The helicopter above our heads nearly drowned his voice out.

"Graye!" I screamed, but it was too late, he had already dashed back out into the street. At the same time, Tye jumped out from behind me, dropping his pack full of supplies beside me.

I was about to dart after them when a strong hand grabbed hold of my arm. I whipped around to see Bill shaking his head at me. "We don't all need to get caught."

I stared at him wide-eyed, yet knowing what he said was the truth. I wasn't thinking clearly. But what was Graye doing? We had everything we needed. What could he possibly be going back for?

A light shone overhead from the circling helicopter. We ducked behind a long unused Dumpster, dropping into the shadows. The faint sound of glass breaking was followed by the roar of a Bane's ATV.

Twenty seconds later we saw a flash of light from in front of the building as the Bane exploded and Graye and Tye came

running around the corner. The glint of the circling light
overhead reflected off an object in Graye's hand.
An hour later Tye's eye had hardened and turned metallic.

My breathing came in shallow breaths as I looked back
down at the necklace and my fingers encircled it. Avian had
asked Graye to grab it for me on the raid. Tye had saved him
from being touched but had been infected himself. Tye had
died to get Avian's gift for me.

"Why are we stopping?" I jumped when West's voice was
too close behind me. His eyes scanned the trees for the reason
for my hesitation.

"Nothing. Why don't you take the south trail? You don't
need me to babysit you," I said as my brow furrowed, my
fingers closing tighter around the pair of wings.

West gave me a concerned look but nodded and started
walking in the direction I had told him to.

My blood burned with fury. Why would Avian risk so
much for something so stupid? Something so unnecessary?
Tye's death was in no way worth the shiny bobble I wasn't
sure I even wanted anymore.

Taking two seconds to collect myself, I started off toward
the eastern border. I wouldn't let myself get distracted on
scouting duty. I wouldn't let a Bane slip past me because I was
regretting things I had no control over.

The terrain took a steady climb upward when I reached the
limits of our boundaries. I took two steps backward before
sprinting forward and then launching myself onto a branch of a
wide-leafed tree. I pulled myself higher into the branches,
twigs and leaves brushing my skin as I ascended. When the
branches began to thin and bow under my weight I settled.

Valleys and low mountains spread before me. At one time
this was a part of something, belonging to some state or city.

None of that mattered anymore. Once the infection got you, nothing mattered anymore, except for turning the rest of us into nothing too.

And beyond where I could see, there was an entire city of Bane. And more cities full of them beyond that.

There were a few rules when it came to the Bane:

A Bane will *always* try to infect you. They won't try and kill you, but they will be *very* aggressive in trying to immobilize you.

They sleep at night. If you're going to attempt a raid on a city, your best chance is during the night. For some reason they liked the sun. Maybe it charged them, made them more powerful. Maybe it was just an echo of their human selves.

They generally stick to the cities.

But the rules seemed to be changing. Tye wouldn't be dead if they weren't. They wouldn't have attacked us on the night he died. They wouldn't have been in that helicopter or on the ATV. And we wouldn't have to scout the woods if they weren't wandering away from the cities.

A movement below me caught my attention. It could have been nothing, a breeze I hadn't felt, an animal stalking through the forest. Nonetheless, I was down the tree in less than five seconds and moving through the woods on silent feet.

Something breathed a few yards away, a heavy sound, reverberating through a chest too big to be human. A musky smell floated in my direction, the scent of wet fur.

It saw me the same time I saw it. A recently woken brown bear.

Adrenaline shot through my system in an intoxicating way. I grabbed for my blade and the bear realized it was in danger. It took lumbering bounds toward me.

I leapt at my opponent, blade gleaming in the air, and swung. It connected with the bear's throat, though as I had expected, it wasn't enough to take it down. The beast gave a ferocious cry and swiped at me with a massive paw. I jumped out of its path, reaching to my belt for my handgun. At the same time another shot was fired from above my right shoulder.

I shouldn't have gotten distracted by the shot. I was a better hunter than that.

In the half-second I glanced back at West, the bear leapt at me, angry and fearful. Blood seeped into his fur from the bullet wound. That was all I noticed as his gigantic paws swiped at me.

I landed a good four feet from the creature and by the time I rolled over to spring back up, it was on top of me again, its teeth bared as it gave an irate growl in my face.

I pulled my handgun once again and fired one shot straight up into the bear's heart.

It collapsed on top of me with crushing force.

"Eve!" West's shout came from somewhere behind the mass of the bear. "I'm sorry, I didn't think it would keep coming at you after I shot it!"

Bracing my hands against the bulk of the beast, I shoved with everything I had. It was just enough to roll it off of me and wiggle out. I stood, wiping my hands, and noticed West's wide-eyed expression.

"What?" I asked, annoyance in my voice.

He blinked twice and then shook his head. "Nothing. Let's get this thing back to camp."

We hacked off what we could, packing as much of the eighteen-hundred-pound beast as we could manage and set off through the woods.

"What was it like?" West suddenly asked as we huffed from our loads, struggling through the forest. "Where you came from, before here?"

"You really ask too many questions," I said as I wiped my arm across my forehead quickly. When he didn't say anything in response, I shook my head, irritated. "I don't remember anything before I came here. Eden has taken care of me, Gabriel mostly, Sarah. Avian when I needed him."

He seemed to be mulling that information over. We were quiet for a while as we hauled our load. I was looking forward to eating the fatty meat of the bear tonight but at the same time I wished we hadn't wandered this far from Eden before finding it.

People buzzed with excitement as we dragged the pieces of bear through camp to the mess hall. I left them and West to take care of the meat that would feed us for days.

I walked toward my tent, passing by the newly set up tents. Just as I was about to slip by, a mass of red hair stepped out, followed by an explosion of Brady. The boy giggled as he raced out and hid behind another tent.

"Brady, stay here!" Victoria said, her voice alarmed.

I paused, feeling awkward just walking away when we stood in such close proximity, but not knowing what to say to this person I didn't know.

"I'm sorry if he startled you," she said apologetically as she grabbed Brady's hand and pulled him back to her side. "He's restless. We've been running so long, he's not sure what to do with himself now."

"He's an active boy," I tried to make conversation. "He needs that to be a survivor."

Victoria only gave a nod. "He's a good man you know," she said, her voice dropping a bit. "I mean West. I can tell you don't like him, but we wouldn't have survived out there without him."

I stiffened. Was my hesitancy about him so obvious? Feeling the awkwardness double, I gave a nod and continued on to my tent.

That night, after the rest of the bear had been retrieved and the other food had been cleared away, the stars started to wink into the sky. I sat beside the fire in front of my tent, staring into the flames.

I had avoided Avian all day. I didn't know how I was going to react to him when I had to face him. What he had asked Graye to do was stupid. I didn't need the necklace. It was just a silly little thing. It wasn't going to help me or anyone else survive. Why had he bothered?

My thoughts turned to Tye. He often joined me in my solitude, if he would leave his post. We shared that. Neither of us liked having to take time away from our duties. There were nights we would both sit here, staring into the flames in silence, wishing we could be scouting the woods, or keeping watch in the tower. Now he was gone, nothing but a pile of ashes thrown into the wind.

The ground crunched as someone walked toward me. I didn't look up from the flames, not really caring who it was that joined me. We sat in the darkening silence, two people lost in their own thoughts.

"She told me you saved them," I eventually said to the flames.

West didn't say anything.

"I'm sorry I've been so cold to you. I don't trust people easily."

He was quiet for a few moments. He shifted positions, sitting forward, his forearms resting on his knees. "He's her son, you know. Brady."

I wasn't completely surprised by this. Part of me had assumed he was but when I thought of how old Brady was and how young Victoria looked, the numbers didn't add up.

"Victoria was fifteen when a man forced himself on her. She joined our camp when Brady was only fourteen months old. He's four now and she's only nineteen. She's only a few months older than I am."

I shook my head, disgust filling my stomach. It explained why she reacted the way she did when Avian tried to fix her foot, like she couldn't stand the thought of him touching her.

My eyes remained glued to the flames, I couldn't think of anything to say. Conversation was something I wasn't good at. I was good at most of the things I did but talking wasn't one of them.

West checked something in the inside pocket of his jacket, securing it like it was something precious. I diverted my eyes when he glanced over at me to make sure I hadn't seen.

West kept secrets. In our wrecked world, secrets could be dangerous but weren't we each entitled to them?

SEVEN

I was woken in the early hours of the next morning by the sound of Sarah's wheezing coughs. I tried to ignore it at first. But as the sound of her coughing intensified I rolled onto my side to face her.

"Sarah, are you alright?" I asked quietly through the dark.

She didn't answer me but her coughing paused. It took me two full seconds before I realized what had happened, why she was suddenly so deathly quiet. She had stopped breathing.

"Sarah!" I said in a panicked whisper. I was out of my bed and across the tent. Through the dim morning light I could see that Sarah's skin was covered in sweat and her eyes looked sunken, her lips the wrong color. Without another second's hesitation, I scooped her up in my arms and barreled out the tent.

Sarah's head jostled around as I ran with her in my arms. Her eyes slid partially open. They were rolled into the back of her head, looking frighteningly gray. She still wasn't breathing and her lips were turning an ugly shade of purple.

"Avian!" I cried as I neared his tent. "Avian! Wake up!"

I didn't even hesitate as I plowed through the flaps of the tent and stumbled inside. My arms shook as Sarah's body limply lay in my arms. "Avian, wake up!"

He jerked up from his cot, his eyes wide but unfocused with sleep. "What... Eve...?"

"Sarah!" I cried, frustrated that he didn't understand what was happening. "She's not breathing!"

This seemed to finally shake the sleep from his brain as he jumped to his feet, taking Sarah from my arms and laying her on his cot. He held his fingers to her neck, sitting quiet for a moment.

"She was coughing and then all the sudden she stopped breathing," I explained as I watched him put his ear to her chest.

"Run to the medical tent, grab my kit," he said, his eyes wide with fear and adrenaline.

I dashed out of the tent and sprinted for the infirmary. People were poking their heads out of their tents, wondering what was going on, what all the shouting was about. I slipped inside the white tent. It only took me a moment to find the black, hard-sided kit.

It took me all of ten seconds to get back to Avian's tent. By this point a few people were standing outside, confusion and sleep filling their faces.

When I stepped back inside, I found Avian doing chest compressions and breathing air into Sarah's mouth. I handed the kit to him and stepped back.

He opened the kit and took a syringe out. He pulled the cap off and plunged the needle into her chest. Sitting back on his heels, he watched her.

A few seconds later, Sarah took a gasping breath, her entire chest surging off of the cot. Her eyes didn't open though. Suddenly her body went slack again and she lost consciousness. Thankfully her chest continued to rise and fall.

Avian sat back on his heels, his fist pressed into his pursed lips

"What's wrong with her?" I asked, my throat feeling tight.

He just shook his head, not saying anything for agonizing seconds. I wondered if he didn't dare speak yet. There were emotions just under the surface that were threatening to explode.

The flap of Avian's tent was opened and in stepped Gabriel, West silently following behind him.

"Sarah's sick," I said hoarsely, saving Avian from having to speak. "She stopped breathing but Avian helped her."

Gabriel gave a simple nod, his eyes fixed on Sarah. My eyes slid to West, his own meeting mine. They were reserved but I was surprised at the concern that I saw there.

"Is there anything I can do to help?" West asked, his voice sincere.

Avian gave a sniff, finally seeming to jerk out of his state of shock. "You can help me move her to the medical tent."

Each of them grabbed an end of the blanket Sarah was lying on, and being very careful not to jostle her, carried her from one tent to the other. By this time, most everyone had woken up. They watched with fear as she was transported to the medical tent. I knew what they were all thinking. We had just lost someone. We couldn't deal with that again, not so soon after.

The men laid Sarah softly on the examination table though I didn't think their tenderness was necessary. Sarah was still completely out. I helped Avian place pillows around her in a vain attempt to make her more comfortable.

"She was coughing the other day," I said. "When we were in the gardens."

Avian just nodded, placing his hands on his hips and watching Sarah.

"Eve," I was slightly startled when I heard Graye's voice from the entrance. "We need to leave for scouting duty. We're already late."

I looked from his face to Sarah's still form. I wasn't one to shirk my duties, ever. But how could I just leave right now?

"I'll go in her place," West spoke up. "I still haven't been assigned an official scouting party." I realized he had been watching my face. His eyes connected with mine for a brief moment. I couldn't make the words "thank you" form on my lips for some reason, but I hoped he felt my gratitude anyway.

Graye nodded once, and West followed him silently.

Avian had grabbed an array of well used but meticulously cared for medical equipment. He placed an instrument on her chest and listened. Next he pressed his fingers to her wrist, checking it to the one watch that existed in Eden. He wrote a few notes down.

"What's wrong with her Avian?" I asked again, standing along the edge of the tent, unsure of what to do with myself.

He shook his head, bracing his hands on the table next to Sarah. "I'm not sure. I might say an allergy attack, but this was too severe and Sarah's never suffered from allergies before. Pneumonia maybe? It could really be anything."

"Is she going to be okay?"

He didn't answer right away. "We'll do what we can. But until I can figure out exactly what this is there isn't going to be much I can do for her."

"But if she stops breathing again, you have more of those shots, right?"

"It was just adrenaline," he said as he sat on one of the stumps. "I have two more now."

I couldn't decide if two sounded like a lot or nothing at all. Avian used those shots for multiple things. Terrif's heart had stopped once and Avian's shots had got it started again. But what if something like that happened again? We'd be down to only one. What if Sarah stopped breathing again? What if it happened more than once?

50

"I'm going to go get us some food," I said, ducking out of the tent without saying anything else.

The scent of freshly baked bread wafted through the air as I made my way to the ovens. Half a dozen other people were gathered around the kitchen. A few women passed out the rolls. Another man was scooping a steaming mush into bowls and handing them to people.

As I stepped up to take Avian's portion and mine, everyone's eyes grew a little wider.

"Eve, is she okay? Is Sarah alright? What did Avian say?" I was bombarded with their questions. It didn't take long for news to travel in Eden.

"Avian thinks it might have been an allergy attack. She stopped breathing for a minute this morning. That's all I know."

I grabbed our food and made a hasty retreat back to the tent. I found Avian staring at Sarah's still form, his brow furrowed.

"Eat something," I commanded as I handed him the warm food.

"Thank you," he said, accepting the bowl and the rolls. For a brief moment, I saw the young man who had fled for his life five years ago, with fear in his eyes, not knowing what to do.

Avian had been a bright student. He had skipped grades and eventually got a scholarship to an accelerated private school. He had graduated high school at the age of fifteen and received a degree in biology by the time he was eighteen. Scholarships had been offered but it wasn't going to be enough to pay the hefty price of medical school. Just months after he came of age, Avian joined the Army with the offer that they would pay for all of his medical school. Along with his

51

military training, Avian had been put into an accelerated medical program specific for Army and survival training.

But only two and a half years into his training, he noticed how everyone was acting strange. Violent, disoriented. Savage. The world fell apart and Avian took what knowledge he had gained and fled with his sister and cousin into the mountains.

I picked at my food, not feeling like eating in the least. My stomach was a hard knot and I couldn't tear my eyes away from Sarah. I was sure at any minute she would open her eyes and complain about having to lay on the hard wooden table.

After we both pretended like we had eaten something, we watched her in silence. I was getting anxious. I didn't know how to handle just sitting. I debated internally what I could do that was close by, so that if I needed to, I could run right back in. Not that I could really do anything to help Avian. When it came to the body, I was just glad mine functioned. I didn't know how to fix it.

I was saved from idleness in a horrifying way.

Sarah started shaking violently. Her arms flailed and her legs shook. We both sprang to our feet, catching her just a fraction of a second before she fell off the table.

"She's having a seizure!" Avian said, panicked.

"What do we do?" I screamed.

"Help me roll her onto her side," he shouted as he ducked out of the way of her thrashing arm. With difficulty we maneuvered her onto her side, balancing her so she wouldn't shake her way off.

"That's it?" I asked.

"That's it," Avian said quietly, looking at me with fear in his eyes again.

The seizure lasted for just over a minute. Her limbs continued to swing violently, her arm beating against Avian's

52

side so hard I knew he would be bruised in a few hours. I could only stare at her for a moment when it was finally over, horror filling me.

Avian sank onto his seat again. His head dropped into his hands, rubbing his scalp with force. He really didn't know *what* was wrong with Sarah. I felt angry with him for a moment. Why didn't he know what to do? He always knew what to do with everyone else. Why couldn't he save his sister?

We paced around the tent, each pretending to do something productive. I rearranged the plastic aprons used for operating several times. He cleaned his tools until they shone.

We were both startled by the sound of Sarah coughing. We jumped to her side, Avian grabbing one of her hands in his.

"Mum... Avi... ahh," she tried to speak, her eyes struggling to open.

"We're here Sarah, me and Eve," Avian said as he pushed the hair back from her face with his free hand. "We're here."

She gave a soft sound of acknowledgment before her eyes closed fully and she fell asleep. Or into unconsciousness, I wasn't sure which.

Avian's body slouched as he stood next to me, his shoulder brushing mine. His hand fell away from her face. As it dropped to his side, his hand brushed mine. His fingers stretched out toward my own, curling around them until our fingers were intertwined securely.

My eyes shifted to our hands, my chest suddenly feeling strange. It was almost like a bunch of bees were buzzing inside my chest, making my breaths come in shallower swallows. And I felt like I should pull my hand away. People generally didn't touch me, I didn't touch people.

But I didn't. I left my hand in Avian's. The feeling of the bees buzzing in my chest didn't feel too bad. In fact, it felt kind of nice.

EIGHT

We waited. And waited.

Sarah's condition didn't improve. She continued to have seizures. She coughed in her sleep, so violently she started choking. On the second day we had to use another of the shots. After four days of watching Sarah waste away, Avian used his last one.

We were going to need more.

Something, maybe everything, in Sarah's body was breaking down and I wasn't sure how we were supposed to fix it in a world that had forced us out into the backcountry.

As if Sarah's illness wasn't enough, there was a lot of anxiety flowing through Eden. A Bane had been spotted twenty miles away and a helicopter had been heard, though not seen. We needed to move camp but Avian begged Gabriel to wait. He didn't dare move Sarah, especially since he was out of the adrenaline.

Camp was quiet as I rose and strapped my pack to my back. There was barely enough light to see by as I pulled my boots on. I pulled the shiny silver handgun from under my cot and tucked it under my belt. I grabbed a box of ammunition as well, dumping a heaping handful into the side pocket of my pants. I secured my favorite rifle to the side of my pack.

I surveyed the tent carefully, making sure there was nothing I was going to leave behind that I would need later.

Last night had been one of panic. Sarah had started coughing again, so violently it left blood on her lips when she finally stopped. As I helped Avian, Bill had come into the medical tent informing us that there were now two Bane that had been spotted. We had no way of knowing if there were more out there. They were getting closer.

Gabriel was ordering everyone to pack up. Eden was to move in two days. Those who could leave sooner were encouraged to do so.

"We can't move her," Avian said, panicked. "She won't make the trip."

"You don't have a choice," Bill said quietly. "If we stay here, we'll all die."

"If Sarah had the right medicine, would she be okay?" I asked as I hesitantly placed a hand on Avian's shoulder in an attempt to comfort him. I felt awkward. I wasn't good at that kind of thing.

"She'd stand a chance. But it's all gone. I don't have anything left."

So there I was, walking out of my tent, ready to take the two-day journey to the city by myself. I wasn't going to let Sarah die.

I had just gotten to the outskirts of the tents when I heard footsteps coming up behind me. I turned and West met my eyes as he cinched his backpack.

"Let's go," he said quietly as he looked away from me into the woods.

I hesitated for just a moment before we took off.

We jogged through the trees silently for nearly an hour as the sun crawled up into the sky. I had to remind myself frequently to keep my pace slower. West was in good shape and he was by no means slow, but few people were able to keep up with what was my normal speed.

"Why did you come with me?" I finally asked. "You don't even know where I'm going."

"I figured it must be important if you were willing to head into the woods by yourself with Bane in the area," he said. "I felt like I needed to do something, even if I'm not sure where I'm going."

"I'm going to the city. There are a few pharmacies that should have the medication Sarah needs," I said as I jumped over a tree that had fallen across our path. "This is going to be really dangerous."

"I know," he said as he jumped over after me. "She's really important to you, isn't she?" West asked. "Both of them are."

I nodded. "Sarah has been like my big sister. She's taken care of me. I owe this to her."

We stopped briefly at mid-day to drink from a stream that looked clean and I shared some of the food rations I had taken the night before. We were going to have to be careful. I had only taken enough for myself. Now it was going to have to keep the two of us going for the next five days. Maybe we'd get lucky and find something non-perishable in the city.

The sun was hot as it started toward the western horizon. Spring was finally starting to warm up into summer. This was exactly what the gardens needed.

I explained the layout of the city to West as we walked. There were certain hideout spots we knew were safe, places the Bane would never think to look. There were three pharmacies in the city, each on opposite ends. It would take us nearly a full day to get to all three, *if* there were no complications.

A few weeks ago I would never have tried a raid in the day time, but Tye's death proved the night was becoming just as dangerous.

As the light faded away, we found a place to make camp.

I caught a decent-sized rabbit and was lucky to find a large handful of wild, though not nearly ripe, blackberries. When I came back to our camp, I found West had built a fire and slung a hammock high up in a tree.

"Where did you get that?" I asked as I set to skinning and gutting the rabbit.

"I found it in my old camp. Someone left it. It will be a lot safer sleeping up in that than it will be on the ground," he said as I gave him the rabbit. He drove a narrow, sharp stick through it, then set it over the fire to cook.

I gave a nod, pretending like the fact that we were going to be sleeping right next to each other didn't make me uncomfortable.

It felt good to get food in my system. While none of us in Eden were starving, we had to be careful through the winter to make sure our stores would last until spring. It was nice to get my share. I licked my fingers and threw the bones as far as I could to keep the wolves away.

The heat of the day faded away and the chill of evening started to set in. We both huddled closer to the fire, palms raised to the flames.

"What do you remember from before the Evolution?" I asked, my voice quiet.

West glanced at me for a brief moment, taken off-guard by my sudden, very serious question.

"I lived with my father and my grandfather. My mother left when I was really little. My grandfather was a scientist, my dad was a doctor."

"What kind of a scientist?" I asked. Just the word scientist brought up all kinds of hateful feelings in all of us. It was the scientists at NovaTor that had ruined our world, our race.

"He did experimental stuff," he said as he rubbed his tired eyes. "It was weird; I was always around other adults. I never even really knew any other kids. We lived in this unit that was attached to where they worked. A woman came to take care of me during the day while they were at work. When she couldn't come they would take me with them."

"I bet that wasn't too fun for you," I said as I stared into the flames.

"It was all I really knew. It might have been harder if I'd ever lived any different," he said with a shrug. "And you don't remember anything?" he asked. "Nothing before you came to Eden?"

I shook my head.

"No parents? No childhood friends?"

"Nothing," I said. "I know everyone has lost someone, but I don't even remember there being anyone. People talk about electricity and running water in houses, but it's just a story to me. A myth even. The world in Eden, the world of raids and running, it's all I've ever known."

West looked over at me and I looked back at him, watched the flames dance in his eyes. "Maybe it's better you don't remember. Not everyone has a happy childhood."

I wasn't sure how to respond to that so I looked back into the fire. Even though I didn't feel cold often, the wind that gusted through suddenly shook me with a shiver. West draped an arm across my shoulders, squeezing me to his side. As he did, I felt something square and flat press into my side.

"What is that?" I asked.

"Nothing," he said, tensing up. "Just…a connection to my past."

I looked at his face for a moment. More secrets.

"We should probably get some sleep," I finally said as I looked away from him.

"Good idea." West stood. We both kicked dirt over the dying fire until it was smothered.

West helped hoist me up into the hammock and I pulled him in after me. Despite how uncomfortable I felt, we wrapped our arms around each other to keep warm.

West quickly drifted off to sleep. I considered the fact that I was going to be sleeping in the arms of the boy I wasn't sure if I could trust and could hardly stand just a week or two ago. The fact that he had chosen to take off with me into dangerous woods with no hesitation spoke pretty loudly though. Maybe I had judged him too harshly.

I didn't sleep more than a total of three hours. Every little sound made me jump, ready to pull my handgun out and unload it.

West slept like the dead.

We got moving long before the sun came up. We were quiet as we moved, feeling the seriousness of what was coming.

We managed to keep out of sight of any Bane that day and made camp far back in a cave that night. We didn't say much and I silently wondered if West was regretting his decision to come with me. Maybe he finally understood just how dangerous this really was.

I doubted either of us slept that night.

It was always haunting, walking among the houses, feeling the pavement underfoot. This may as well have been an alien world to me. I preferred my canvas tent to the brick walls. The houses seemed too much like a prison.

The suburbs eventually gave way to the rise of apartment buildings and offices.

We crouched behind a long abandoned car as we came to an intersection. After I checked to make sure nothing was watching, I signaled West, and we darted across the street to the pharmacy. Hugging the wall, we made our way around to the back of the building. As we stepped inside, I heard the whooshing of helicopter blades off in the distance. Gray color started to creep into the city.

The door had been busted in by Bill a few years ago. We'd cleared out the items we needed, things to reduce fevers, things to clean out wounds. I just hoped I would recognize the syringes Avian needed.

"Hurry," I whispered as I looked around the building to make sure there wasn't any sleeping Bane inside.

"What are we looking for?" he asked as he hopped over the counter and started searching through shelves. I climbed over as well and started searching with him.

"The adrenaline was in a syringe," I said as I headed to look toward the back. I noticed the fridges and opened one. It seemed a miracle that the electricity still ran in the building. The fridge was cold. Row after row of vials and syringes greeted me. "Got it!"

We both scoured the labels, searching for any indicator of what we needed. I didn't even understand what most of it was supposed to be. My heart started pounding faster as the room lightened. They would all be waking soon.

"This is it!" West suddenly gave an excited hiss. "There's… one, two, two of them."

"That's all?" I asked, feeling my stomach sink into my knees.

"Yeah, I'm pretty sure," he said, checking again.

I grabbed the syringes from him and wrapped them in the cleanest shirt I had, packed exactly for that purpose. "Check for aspirin, cough medicine, anything that looks like we could use it. And hurry, we haven't got much time."

We picked our way through everything. I wished I could load up one of those long-forgotten cars outside and just dump the entire store into it. Even if everything was expired by several years, it could still help us.

"Come on," West said as we double checked to be sure there was nothing left we might need.

We slipped out the back door. As we did, I picked up on the sound of the chopper blades again, this time sounding further away than earlier. They were heading out to scan the outskirts of the city.

The other pharmacy was five blocks to the east, all city with nothing but abandoned cars for cover.

I bit my lip, scanning the road for any signs of activity. "Let's go," I said.

I bolted toward a bus that was tipped over in the middle of the road. West's footsteps pounded softly behind me. My own adrenaline raced in my system, propelling me all the faster as I peeked around the bus, saw that the coast was clear and sprinted along the side of a building.

"You okay?" I asked as I stole a brief glance at West as we pressed against the side of the building.

He only nodded as he stared wide-eyed back at me.

I looked around the corner, keeping my body pressed to the cool surface of the side of the building. I caught sight of a woman walking in the opposite direction from us. Only half her head was covered with red hair that trailed to her waist. The other half of her head was shiny metal. Her left hand had no flesh, only cybernetic skeletal fingers poked out of her long-sleeved shirt.

I glanced at West, pressed a finger to my lips, then motioned for him to follow me. We sprinted silently across the street.

There was only one block to go. I could see the pharmacy when something inside the bottom floor of a building caught my eye.

There were Bane, just standing inside.   Frozen. Motionless. Staring out at us.

"Why are they like that?" I asked, my head turning as we continued to jog toward the pharmacy. "Why do some of them try to infect us when others just stand there? They look like they're waiting for something."

"Let's not find out what for," West said, shaking his head.

We reached the pharmacy and stepped through the large broken window. We went to the fridge first this time. The electricity was still working in this building as well.

"Here we go," West said. "Four... five... six. There's six of them here."

"Great," I said as I wrapped them with the others. I stuffed the shirt back in my bag and set it down on the ground as I went to scour the shelves. "That's got to be enough. I don't think we'll have to go to the other pharmacy. We probably couldn't make it anyway with it getting this light. It's across the city. Six or seven miles."

There were bottles and bottles of aspirin, cases of allergy medication I hoped might have a chance of helping Sarah. There was probably something here for seizures as well, but I wouldn't know what it was.

"Does it smell funny in here to you?" I asked as I followed the source of the strange scent.

"Just like an old abandoned building with breaking down chemicals," West said as he stuffed his pack full of life-saving medication.

I wandered to the back of the building, into a utility room. A rusty looking water heater dominated the cramped space. Electric cables and lines ran in different directions, disappearing into the wall. This was where the smell was coming from.

A movement outside the small window to my left caught my eye.

The glass shattered as the Bane outside fired. The bullet brushed past my left shoulder, embedding itself into the thick metal side of the water heater. It was just enough to cause an explosion.

"West!" I screamed, ducking as the flames billowed out at me. "Get out of here!"

I could feel the oxygen being quickly sucked out of the building as the flames ate it up. I scrambled along the floor toward my pack.

"Eve!" I heard West screaming toward the front of the building.

"Run!" I shouted as I came to his side, grabbed his hand in mine, and bolted out the door.

The sun had broken over the buildings and the morning rays were charging the enemy. I heard the rev of an engine come from behind the building and the screeching of tires against asphalt.

We were only two blocks away from where the forest butted up against the city but we weren't as fast as an ATV.

The Bane shot across the street behind us. The sound of the engine was the only thing I could concentrate on as we ran for our lives.

The pile of metal that slammed into me from the side and knocked me to my back wasn't the one I expected.

Neither of us had noticed the other Bane hiding in the shadows of another building. He had launched himself in my direction, tackling me to the asphalt, immobilizing and choking the life out of me with one bare flesh hand and another cybernetic one.

As I stared into his metallic eyes, I couldn't believe this was how my end was finally going to come.

The Bane suddenly jerked to the side as a metal rod dented its head in. It collapsed with a hiss of dying electric sounds. I looked up to see West holding a five foot long broken street sign, looking quite pleased with himself. A half-smile tugged at his lips despite the terror in his eyes.

I climbed to my feet and pulled my pack tighter as we started running again, praying none of the syringes had broken during my fall.

As the screech of tires against pavement assaulted my ears again, I turned and pulled my handgun out.

In one shot, I embedded the bullet into the gas tank and the ATV exploded in a ball of blazing glory for humanity.

Somehow we made it to the edge of the city and back into the trees. West wheezed as we ran further into the forest, falling several steps behind me.

"Holy..." he gasped. "Eve."

I slowed and turned to him as we stopped. "What?"

"Your shoulder," he said, his eyes filled with horror.

My stomach knotted instantly and I almost didn't dare look. With all the adrenaline coursing through my system I didn't consider two very important things that had just happened.

I looked down at my shoulder and realized half my shirt had been burned away. So had my flesh. The skin from the top of my right shoulder down as far as I could see on my back was a charred, black, smoking mess.

"Oh my ga... Eve," West said, his voice a horrified whisper that choked off. "Are you...?" I knew he was going to ask me if I was okay but it was obvious I wasn't.

And then it hit me. "I don't feel anything. I didn't even know it was there."

West continued to look at me with that horrified expression. I could only stare back for a moment.

"It touched you." I could barely even hear his words as they escaped his throat.

My blood froze in my veins and it felt like all my internal organs had suddenly disappeared. One touch was all it took. The Bane had been all over me.

"I have to go back to the city," I said as I locked eyes with him. "You have to run, West. Don't look back."

I took two steps back where we had come from when he grabbed my wrist. "No," he growled and shook his head. "No."

"I have to West," I hissed, angry with him. He knew how our world worked now. "I only have a few hours. Then I'll be trying to kill you too."

"No," he said again, his jaw clenched as his eyes burned into mine. There was moisture brimming in them. "I'm taking you with me. If you start to turn, I'll shoot you myself and run."

"It's not a question of *if*, West," I said, my voice low and husky sounding. I shook his hand off and started back again.

West grabbed my wrist again, this time yanking me back toward him with much more force. His other hand encircled my waist pulling me against his body. "No," he said again.

And then he crushed his lips to mine. I could have sworn I was back in the middle of that explosion in that moment.

I didn't even realize for several seconds after that I was being dragged through the forest again, West's hand securely around my wrist. I couldn't think straight enough to resist.

Finally, I yanked the gun from the belt of my pants and forced it into West's other hand. "Here," I said, my eyes daring him to fight me. "You're going to need this soon."

He tucked it into his own pants and continued to pull me through the trees.

NINE

The chill of the morning air shook West in an obvious way, his teeth chattering as we ran through the forest. His hand was still clenched around mine, his fingers a frozen color of purple. Our breath caused clouds to bloom around us in the chilly morning air.

As we pounded our way through the woods, I could only think one thing, over and over. What was happening? Or more accurately: what *wasn't* happening?

We had run through the entire day after I had been tackled by the Bane, and had continued through the night. I kept waiting for the sensation of my cells hardening, waiting for my vision to sharpen and for data to start flashing across my eyes, or something. It shouldn't have taken more than two or three hours for the changes to start. It had now been just short of twenty-four and still nothing had happened.

The terrain became familiar and I felt both relief and panic. Perhaps Avian could give me some answers and I now had the medication Sarah needed. Yet I was infected. I couldn't bring it into Eden. That was the very thing we had fought all these years to keep out.

I was startled to see how Eden had changed since I left it. There were only a few tents still standing and the place that was my home looked deserted. I remembered that Gabriel had told everyone to leave.

The few people who were left looked busy packing and preparing for departure. But they stopped and stared at West and I as we walked swiftly toward the medical tent.

"Avian!" I half shouted before we were even inside the tent. "Avian!"

"Eve?" I heard his excited yet panicked shout as we burst into the tent.

I froze as I got inside, seeing nothing but Avian, standing there looking back at me. All the years watching him work, the hours we had spent by campfires, the feeling of his hand in mine, the sound of his breathing rushed through my head. Everything I was going to lose by turning into a Bane was standing in this tent.

"Eve," he finally whispered as he closed the gap between us and wrapped me in his arms. His entire frame was trembling.

He took a step back, placing his hands on my shoulders, and took a good look at me. He then realized what was under his right hand.

"Eve!" he nearly shouted as he whipped his hand away. "You're fried! How are you not writhing in pain?" He grabbed me and maneuvered me onto the table.

Sarah wasn't lying on it anymore.

Was I too late?

"I can't feel it," I said, my voice sounding dead. "There was an explosion."

"It's a good thing you can't," Avian said as he poured some water onto a rag. "Burns are some of the most painful injuries. This would really, really hurt."

Avian cut away the rest of my charred shirt and I clung to the tattered pieces to keep myself covered. I stole a glance at West who stood in the doorway and watched with fearful eyes. Avian started scrubbing my charred skin.

"When did this happen?" Avian asked, his voice oddly tight.

"Yesterday morning," West answered.

"This looks a week old," Avian said quietly, shaking his head. "It's already started to heal."

I tried to swallow the rock in my throat but it wouldn't go down. "A Bane touched me, Avian. It was all over me. It happened just after the explosion."

Avian suddenly froze. He stopped breathing for a moment and I felt him automatically withdraw his hand just slightly.

"I haven't changed. Nothing's happened, except that I can't feel this," I said as I nodded my head toward my shoulder.

He paused for a while longer before hesitantly placing the rag back to my shoulder and slowly started scrubbing again.

"What does this mean, Avian?" I asked quietly. "Why haven't I changed?"

He didn't say anything for a little bit. It nearly drove me insane.

"I don't know," he said, his voice tight again.

"This doesn't happen. They all ch...chan...ange."

I blacked out.

There were wires attached to every exposed surface of my body. And I was running. It felt like I'd been running forever. The belt turned under my feet, creating an endless four-foot section of road.

"Increase the speed," a voice said.

The belt started spinning faster under my small bare feet. My pace picked up so I wouldn't fall.

"Doesn't she get tired?" a young voice asked.

"That's what we're trying to find out," the first voice replied.

69

I turned my head toward the window where they watched me. A pair of curious eyes stared back at me.

I opened my eyes, only to squint them back closed. Light streamed in, momentarily blinding me. My left shoulder felt stiff, and as I reached a hand to it, I found it covered in layers of bandages. I was also wearing a shirt that I recognized as Avian's.

"Try not to move too much," a voice said kindly.

Ignoring the voice, I pulled myself into a sitting position. I blinked my eyes several times, willing them to focus.

I was still on the medical table but found Gabriel had joined us. I wondered when he had come back. He should have been with the others at the new location.

"What happened?" I asked as I rubbed my eyes.

"You passed out from the pain," Avian said, his voice stiff again.

"But I didn't feel it," I said, my voice sounding a little more annoyed than I had meant it to. "I still don't feel it."

Avian and Gabriel exchanged looks. West just stared at me with a blank expression.

"We need to have a talk, Eve," Gabriel said as he looked at me. "In private."

West seemed to realize this last part was directed at him. "I'm not leaving her," he said, his voice stubborn.

"I'm not giving you a choice," Gabriel said, his eyes hard. I then heard someone shift position outside and recognized Bill's shadow through the wall of the tent.

"Go," I said quietly to West. "I can take care of myself."

He gave me a hard look. He didn't like this but after a moment he walked out. Bill walked away with him.

Once I was sure West was out of earshot I looked back at Avian and Gabriel. "What is happening to me?" I asked, my eyes daring them to not answer me. "I can't feel the pain. I didn't change."

"You still feel the pain," Avian said, swallowing hard on the rock that seemed to have moved into his own throat. "Your brain just doesn't tell you it's feeling it. That's why you passed out this morning. Your body couldn't handle the pain once I started cleaning the injury."

"But I didn't feel it," I insisted.

The two of them exchanged looks again. That was really starting to annoy me.

"What do you know?" I snapped. "What aren't you two telling me?"

Avian bit his lower lip, his eyes dropping to the floor. Gabriel took this as an indicator to take the lead. "When you came to us, Avian and I knew right away that something was different about you, Eve. You shouldn't have survived out there on your own. You were only a thirteen-year-old girl for heaven's sake," he said, shaking his head, his eyes dark with remembrance.

"We didn't know what it was. We watched you for weeks, looking for any signs that you were a Bane, sent to spy on us or something. We kept the CDU with us at all times, ready to use it should you show any indicator that you might turn on us.

"You started training with the scouts. You were nearly as strong as any of the grown men. You never got tired. You were so blasted tough and solid. But you never seemed to notice that you were any different. You lived among us. You didn't turn against us. So Avian and I kept your secret. We never told the others in Eden, to protect you, and to protect them."

"You've been injured before, Eve," Avian spoke. "Never anything as serious as this, but you never even realized you

71

were hurt. And I never had to fix anything. Your body just fixes itself."

My heart pounded as I listened to Gabriel. I recalled everything he was saying, remembered the way the two of them had hovered over me at all times when I was younger. I had thought they were trying to protect me. They had been protecting themselves though. They had been ready to short me out at any moment.

Apparently there had been reason to.

I was still too strong, still too fast. And apparently my brain didn't register pain.

"What the hell am I?" I said in a raged hiss.

"We don't know," Avian finally said as he looked up. "You're human but part of you is cybernetic. You've been enhanced in a way we've never even heard of before.

"That's why you didn't change when the Bane touched you. You're *already* part Bane."

My breathing increased as my eyes dropped to the floor. It suddenly rushed up at me as I fell off the table and landed roughly on my hands and knees. Avian jumped to help me up but I pushed him away.

"No," I said as I shook my head and stumbled to my feet. "Get away from me!"

I bolted out of the tent and stumbled through what was left of Eden without seeing or caring where I was going.

My tent felt safe and frightening all at the same time. This was my space, a place where I could be alone and try to think. And yet it was wrong. Sarah still wasn't here. While I hid in my tent, Avian had come to tell me that she was starting to recover but was staying in his tent so he could watch her.

Eden was too quiet as darkness fell. It felt strange to have our colony split up like this.

The dirt stirred outside my tent as someone approached.

"Go away, Avian! I don't want to talk to you right now!" I shouted as I lay in my bed and pulled my blanket up over my head.

"Good thing I'm not Avian," a voice said as it entered my tent.

"What are you doing here, West?" I asked as I glared at him, pulling the blanket back down.

He stood there, staring back at me, refusing to be intimidated. He held something bulky and black in one arm.

"I brought something I hope might make you feel better," he said as he shrugged.

"I just found out I'm the enemy I've been fighting against for the last five years. I don't think there's anything you can do to make me feel better."

West rolled his eyes. "You could try *not* biting my head off. Get up," he said.

"What?" I asked, my voice annoyed again.

"Get up so I can lay this down," he said as he raised his eyebrows at me.

I didn't know what he was talking about, but I did as he asked. He then rolled out the black mass and I realized it was a hide.

"The bear?" I asked as I rubbed my hand over the soft fur.

"Yeah," he said as he looked at it on my bed with a half-smile. "I asked Bill if he could tan it for me. I wanted to give it to you as an apology for stealing your kills."

"Well, I did take your buck that one time. I was the one who technically stole it."

West looked up at me, a half smile coming to his lips. "See, it made you feel better."

I realized that I was smiling too.

"Thank you," I said, really meaning it.

West nodded then stood there uncomfortably as if he wasn't sure what to do with himself.

"They asked you to watch me tonight, didn't they?" I asked as I narrowed my eyes at him.

"And you're not going to give me trouble about that, are you?" he shot back at me.

I just glared at him for a minute. I hadn't forgotten the fact that we had spent two nights together, a little more intimately than I would have cared to remember, or the fact that in the moment he thought I was as good as dead, he had kissed me.

"You can sleep in Sarah's bed, then. Don't oversleep though; I'm packing up early in the morning."

"Good," he said as he went to lie on the other bed. "I've already packed up all my things. I would have been sleeping in the dirt if you kicked me out."

I crawled into my new bed, surprised at how much of a difference the hide made. I balled my pillow up under my head and pulled the covers up to my chin.

"Goodnight, Eve," West said quietly through the now dark tent.

"Goodnight, West," I half whispered as I turned away from him onto my side.

TEN

The stiffness in my arm woke me as I tried to roll over. The bandaging had loosened up during the night but still prevented me from having full movement.

It was already very light outside. I must have been asleep for nearly nine hours. I then remembered what Avian had said about my body feeling pain, even if my brain didn't register it. Apparently all of me had needed rest.

A soft snore reminded me that I wasn't alone and I rolled over to see West sprawled across Sarah's bed. He lay on his back, his arms spread out, his head lolling to the side facing me. I suddenly wondered where he'd gotten the scar on his neck from.

I noticed something on the floor that didn't belong and reached across the cramped space for it. It was a notebook, its edges tattered and frayed. The cover had all kinds of writing on it, but most prominent were big bold letters that had worn down to just ATOR BIOT. I opened to somewhere in the middle of it, evaluating its shape and size, and realized this was the object West always carried on him.

I wasn't one to invade another's privacy and was about to close the notebook when some of the writing caught my eye.

Block capabilities of chip X73I implanted in project Eve seem to be successful.

I read the line twice to be sure I had read it correctly.

Quickly, I looked up at West to make sure he was still asleep.

Suddenly I had to reevaluate everything I had ever known or thought about him.

Unable to keep from doing so, I turned my eyes back to the pages. I continued from the line I had started with.

> *Subject Eve I was tested on treadmill for two hours straight with no indicators of tiredness. Vitals remained stable, peaking little during fastest speed. Tests have yielded similar results for the past five days.*

> *Eve continues to show lessened need for sleep. After close monitoring for the past four months, we have recorded subject sleeps for little more than five hours a night, at times less.*

> *Tomorrow weight endurance testing will begin.*

I stared at the scribbled words for a full two minutes when I came to the end of the page. My stomach knotted. I realized I had been holding my breath.

My eyes focused on the page again and I noted the date written in the top right corner. I would have been roughly seven years old at the time.

I flipped through the pages, seeing words and equations and endless things I couldn't comprehend, but taking nothing in really. All I saw was my name. *Subject Eve, tests done to Eve, problems with Eve.*

"What are you doing?!"

The notebook was suddenly ripped out of my hands and I looked up to see West glaring at me with burning eyes.

"What is that?" I asked as I stared at the notebook in his hand. "Where did you get it?"

He didn't say anything for a second, just continued to look at me. An internal debate warred behind his eyes.

"Don't you dare lie to me, West," I said, my voice turning cold. "I will *hurt* you if you lie to me."

He continued to look at me for a minute. A mix of emotions played out behind his eyes: fear, agony, regret, among other things I wasn't so sure about.

"I told you my grandfather was a scientist," he said, his voice hoarse sounding. "Those are some of his personal notes. About a third of them are about you."

I couldn't make my throat form my loss of words. My chest felt oddly hard as West confirmed what I had had assumed.

"He experimented on me," I finally managed. "For how long?"

"I remember you always being there. Since you were a baby."

"You remember me?" I said slowly, my eyes never breaking from his.

"Like I told you, my grandfather was the scientist. My father was the doctor who monitored you. We lived at the testing facility. Sometimes they would let us play together." His voice trembled a little as he spoke.

"I don't remember you." I forced myself to speak. "I don't remember any of it."

"Someone released you after the infection started. I think they wiped your memory."

"Why didn't you tell me?" I asked, my voice suddenly shaking with rage. "Why didn't you tell me right away? I had no idea who I was, but you knew!"

"I wasn't sure," he said, the tone of his voice picking up with defense. "It's been nearly six years since I've seen you, Eve! You're a woman now, not a girl with a shaved head! And I thought you must have died a long time ago! It wasn't easy for me to think you were dead. You were my best friend! My only friend!"

I glared at West. I wished he hadn't said that. I wanted to be angry with him. I wanted to throw him out and to tell him to leave Eden and never come back. But a part of me wondered if what he was saying was the truth. Maybe West had been my friend at one time.

But I couldn't remember any of it.

"I trusted you," I whispered as I glared at him. "You should have told me sooner. Were you ever going to tell me?"

He was quiet for a second as he looked back at me. "I don't know."

"Well at least you're being honest about that," I said coldly. "You should leave now. I have to get ready to move."

"Eve, I'm..."

"Get out!" I shouted.

He stood and went to the flap of the tent. "I'm sorry," he said quietly as he walked out.

I set to packing my things.

I had just finished putting my clothes away when the flap of the tent was pushed aside. Avian stood there, his expression open, waiting for me to attack him again.

I just kept gathering all of my stuff.

"Sarah told me to come get her things. She's strong enough now we can move her. The allergy pills that you brought back are what finally did it I think. Maybe."

I just glanced at him so he would know that I had heard him. I rolled the bear hide up, vowing to give it back to West later. I didn't want it anymore.

Avian set to gathering Sarah's belongings, stuffing them in a bag the same way I did. Within a few minutes we had everything cleared out of the tent.

"I can get this myself," I said as we stepped out and Avian started taking down the tent.

"I know," he said simply as he untied a tether.

We worked quietly as the tent came down. We then packed the poles into their bag and set to rolling the canvas up.

"We wanted to thank you for what you did," Avian said as he worked at my side. "*I* wanted to thank you. It was incredibly dangerous but you did it anyway."

I just held the bag open and Avian slid the bulk of the tent in. I tied the opening after the poles went in and set it on the ground.

"The wagon should be back in just a few minutes," Avian said as he looked out to the east. "Sarah went this morning with Bill. West set out on his own a little while ago. It's just the two of us now and our things."

I allowed Avian to help me carry the three bags that had once been mine and Sarah's tent toward the pile that was his belongings and the medical supplies and tent.

"I don't want you to be angry with me forever," Avian said as we stood there, side by side. "You have no idea how many times I wanted to tell you, how many times I knew I should have told you. I'm sorry, Eve. It was wrong."

I gave a nod, as close as I could get to accepting his apology at the moment. Right then, it felt like everyone I knew had betrayed or lied to me.

The sound of wheels on the hard ground alerted us to the return of the wagon.

There had been two horses kept in Eden, until about eight months ago. The older of the two had broken its leg and Gabriel had to put him down. We managed with the smaller wagon with just one horse.

A woman by the name of Morgan and her husband, Eli, drove the wagon and helped us to load our things into the small space. With everything that had to be hauled, there was no room for anything else. Avian and I would be walking.

That was fine with me. I would have walked anyway.

Little was said as we finished loading. The couple told us that no one had seen any signs of Bane and that the new location for Eden was the best we'd had yet, located right next to a lake. Everyone was getting settled in just fine.

The wagon made good pace and we let them go ahead of us. It didn't take long before it was out of sight, leaving Avian and I alone.

We walked silently for the first few minutes. But Avian kept glancing over at me with this look like he just knew something was wrong.

"He knew who I was," I finally said. "West. He knew me before I came here. His grandfather experimented on me. He's the reason I can do the things I can do."

"He told you this?" Avian asked, his brow furrowed.

I shook my head. "No, I found a notebook filled with the things he did to me. West said I had been at this facility for as long as he could remember. Since I was a baby. He told me we used to play together as children sometimes."

"I have a hard time imagining you playing anything," Avian said. I noticed a smile tugging on his lips.

"I can't imagine I was very good at it."

A chuckle suddenly broke from Avian's chest. I couldn't help smiling too.

We walked quietly again for a while. My ears listened to the sounds of the woods around us, searching for any sign of alert. My eyes scanned the trees. I even smelled at the air, being alert for any scent of exhaust from an ATV or a helicopter.

I kept the handgun West had given back to me tucked into the back of my pants. I was ready to pull it out at any moment and unload it, grab Avian, and run for our lives.

"Why did you ask Graye to get the necklace for me?" I asked as I searched the trees with my eyes.

Avian hesitated for a few moments. "I wanted you to have something special for your birthday," he said as he looked at me briefly. He stiffened slightly. "I thought you should have something a woman would normally have. I hoped you would like it."

I looked away from him, fixing my eyes on the trail. I couldn't think of anything that seemed less fit for me as a gift. I'd never owned any other piece of jewelry nor had I ever had the desire to own any.

"You shouldn't have asked him to," I said quietly. "It wasn't worth it."

"I know," he answered me even more quietly.

I regretted my words instantly. Tye's death had been hardest on Avian and I kept bringing it up. Now I was pointing it out that in a way it had been Avian's fault he was dead.

Not really knowing what I was doing, I reached over and took Avian's hand in mine. I wasn't sure if it was an apology,

81

an attempt at comfort, or just what exactly. But it seemed to work. He squeezed my fingers, his shoulder brushing mine.

"I was out of my mind," Avian said, his voice tight as he looked down at his feet. "When you left. I didn't know what happened to you, what was going to happen to you. You're tough, but you're not indestructible. If it hadn't have been for Sarah I would have come after you."

"You can't do that," I said as I furrowed my brows, looking back up at him. "They need you here."

Avian slowed, pulling me to a stop with him, our hands still clasped together. "Don't do that again, Eve. Don't run off on me."

I looked up into Avian's face, surprised at the intensity that burned in his eyes. His face was closer than I expected it to be.

"I'll do what I have to," I finally managed to say. My heart was pounding in my chest in a way that was foreign. "I'll protect them, always."

He continued to look at me for a long, intense moment. He brought his other hand and softly brushed a thumb across my cheek for just a moment. My skin tingled as his hand went back to his side. He started walking back down the path, my hand still in his.

"Tell me what it was like, what it would have been like, if the world hadn't fallen apart," I said, moving on when I wasn't sure how to handle Avian's intensity or the intensity that was building up inside of me. "What would my life have been like right now, if I wasn't a cybernetic human hybrid?"

That brought a sad little smile to his face. "Let's see, it's early May. You would have been in your last year of high school. You'd be dying to get out of school. The last few months of your senior year are agony. All you want is for it to be over.

"Prom would probably be around this time. You would have had a dozen different guys ask you to go with them. You would have had your pick."

"What's prom?" I asked.

Avian laughed. "It's a dance. It's probably the biggest event of the school year. Girls buy fancy dresses and guys wear tuxedos. People rent expensive cars and pick up their dates. Then they go to the dance and just have fun."

The things Avian told me about seemed so foreign. It was like he was reading to me out of a fairy tale book and I barely even understood the terminology he used. I would never go to a prom.

"You might have had a boyfriend. The two of you would go on special outings, just the two of you or with friends. You might try and sneak out of your parent's house to try and see him. Boys always get girls into trouble."

"I can't imagine you getting me into trouble," I said as I glanced over at him. "Is that what you were like?"

Avian smiled and looked at the ground. "I was the guy that couldn't get up the nerve to ask the girl I wanted out. I would have stayed home by myself, burying my head in my latest medical book.

"I would have wanted to ask you but you would have said no."

I looked over at Avian and really *looked* at him. He was tall, at least six feet. He wasn't built as big as Bill or even West, but he wasn't small. He had the lean frame of a man who worked hard and had lived on a rations diet for the last five years. His dark, short hair accented the tanned color of his skin, his surprisingly blue eyes piercing. "I highly doubt that."

He smiled and squeezed my hand.

"Problem would have been that while you would still be in high school, I would have still been in the Army, hopefully going through real medical school. People wouldn't have liked the age difference. You would have barely even been legal."

There was meaning and weight behind Avian's words that I didn't really understand. I pushed the feeling aside.

I considered what I might have been like if I hadn't grown up the way I did. I was as mature as any of the other women in Eden, at least I thought so. They didn't look down on me and I didn't consider any of the others superior to myself. But maybe if I hadn't been experimented on and grown up in a world of running and raids I wouldn't have been that way. Maybe all I would have cared about would have been jewelry and what boy was asking me to the prom or what dress I was going to wear.

The world we lived in made me grow up. I didn't know what it was like to be a real teenager.

We walked at a swift pace for another two hours before signs of life were detected. We stopped at the tree line, looking out over the tents and bustling people. I glanced at Avian. He gave a weak smile, the smile of knowing the tiring, endless work that was before the both of us. I returned his smile, let go of his hand, and went to help reassemble Eden.

ELEVEN

With as little as we possessed it didn't take long to put everything back together. Everyone helped, no one was left in distress about what needed to be done. We were a family, a unit that worked as one.

Things were different though. With Sarah's newfound medical condition, she had moved into Avian's tent permanently. The seizures were infrequent but happened enough that Avian insisted. I was on my own now.

The sun shone down on us as we worked on the rows of vegetables in the gardens the next day, the temperature rising slowly. Graye worked silently two rows behind me. We had talked little since I realized what he had done for Avian. In a strange way, I felt like I should apologize to him but at the same time, it wasn't me that had asked him to grab the necklace.

Terrif directed people soundlessly to the areas they should work on. I could tell he was getting flustered with Wix, who had pulled up a section of carrots, thinking they were weeds. It was hard to stay mad at him though when he started eating the green stems as a way of apology.

West worked in the opposite corner, never looking up as he weeded in the potato patch. We had kept up a careful pattern of avoidance ever since I had discovered the notebook.

I had a million questions, but I wasn't ready to face him and ask them.

I pulled a massive weed out of the patch of peas I was working on, and tossed it into a wheelbarrow. My eyes scanned the tree line for the fiftieth time since we had arrived. Even though all the scouting parties, including my own, had found no signs of the Bane, I felt uneasy. They had to still be out there somewhere. The Bane were persistent.

The afternoon shift arrived and I bolted out of the garden as soon as I handed my gloves off. I wasn't ready to have to talk to West yet. I wasn't sure what I should say or how I would even react. Apparently he wasn't ready to talk to me either since he never made any attempts. That was just fine with me.

Upon arriving back at camp, I looked for Sarah. I'd had little chance to talk to her since she had gotten sick. I didn't want her to feel like I was avoiding her.

Just as I was about step inside their tent, Avian came out, our bodies bumping into each other unexpectedly. He grabbed my shoulders to steady the both of us and his vivid blue eyes looked down at me, a small smile coming to his lips. A hint of a smile crept into the corner of my lips as well.

"Sorry," I said. "I just came to see Sarah."

"She's inside resting," he said. "She had another seizure a few minutes ago."

"Is she going to be alright?" I asked.

"I think so," he said as he smiled at me again, warmth spreading through his eyes.

"I'm not deaf, you know," Sarah called from inside the tent.

Avian chuckled, placing a hand on my arm again. "I've got to go. Victoria is having troubles with her foot again."

"Bye," I said as he walked away.

I stepped inside Avian and Sarah's tent. It was dark, the air stuffy and warm.

"Tie it back, would you?" Sarah said through the darkness as I entered. "I think he's trying to suffocate me. I feel like I'm living in a cave these days."

I tied the flap of the tent back as she asked, light flooding the cramped space. I then sat on Avian's bed.

Sarah's hair was tousled, her dark curls sticking out in every direction. Her eyes were reddened and tired looking.

"How are you feeling?" I asked, hoping she didn't notice the way I scrutinized every inch of her.

"I'd be better if everyone would stop asking me that question," she said with a tired tone.

"Everyone is concerned."

"I know," she sighed as she lay back down. "I'm just tired of being the frail, sick one. I'm as fine as I can be I guess. I'm handling it. Whatever this is."

"There's nothing he can do?" I asked.

"If he had access to an MRI machine, a pharmacy full of drugs, and a neurologist, maybe. But we just have to be careful now."

"We can get drugs," I said. "I can go on another raid. I got the shots Avian needed before. If he tells me what you need I can get it."

Sarah shook her head, a smile creeping onto her face. "He would never ask you to do that, to go into danger like that again."

"He wouldn't need to ask me," I said as my brow furrowed, my blood boiling just a little.

"He wouldn't tell you what to look for to prevent you from trying. You're too important to him."

An awkward silence hung in the air after she stopped talking. Something was changing between Avian and me.

"Don't be angry with him for keeping the secret from you," she said softly, her eyes hesitating to meet mine.

"You knew too?" I asked, my voice accusing.

"No, but Avian told me after you came back. How are you handling that information?"

"The fact that I'm a robotic-human hybrid?" I said. "Just great."

"I'm serious, Eve."

I didn't say anything for a second as I looked down at my weathered hands. "I'm trying not to think about it too much. The fact that my shoulder has already healed up isn't helping that much though."

"He said you were hurt pretty badly."

"You should see the scar," I joked half-heartedly. "I didn't feel anything. I didn't even know it was there until West told me."

I felt it before I even saw the sly grin that crept onto Sarah's face. "Running off to the city with the new man in Eden, huh? Never would have pegged you for that type."

"What?" I asked. "What are you talking about? He just…came with me."

"And you had no desire to get a little close and cozy along the way with a face and body like that?"

"I'm going to go now," I said as I suddenly stood. "Take it easy."

Sarah just chuckled as I stepped outside.

Evening settled and the camp started to grow quiet. The stars seemed more intense than usual as they reflected off the surface of the lake.

I had tried to insist on taking the night guard but apparently Bill had already beaten me to it. A new watchtower had been erected and everything was nearly back to business as

88

usual. With nothing else to do, I found myself around the fire with Avian and Sarah. Recalling Sarah's comments earlier, I made a new resolve to not be distracted by anything or any*one*. I sat as far away from Avian as I could.

"Is Victoria alright?" Sarah asked, pulling her blanket tighter around her shrinking frame.

"It's a small infection. It just needed a little cleaning out," Avian replied.

I heard someone walk up from behind us and turned to see West hesitantly approaching. "Do you mind if I join you?" he asked to no one in particular.

Avian shook his head.

With little elsewhere to sit, he sat just to the right of me. He was close enough I could smell the earthy scent of him.

"Have they seen any more signs of the Bane?" Sarah asked. I was grateful for her insight and tactic to keep awkward silences away.

I shook my head. "Not since we left our last site."

"Maybe they're giving up," she said as she gazed into the flames.

"I doubt that," Avian said as he stared at the fire.

"Will they ever?"

No one said anything for a moment. That was what we had all wondered for the last five years.

"It's something in their engineering," West suddenly spoke. "The infection craves more human flesh. It mutated to spread. It's trying to keep reproducing."

"That's why the Bane keep looking," Avian said, neither a statement nor a question exactly.

West nodded. "It's looking to assimilate more."

"There's got to be a way to stop them," Sarah said as she shook her head. "Like making a large CDU. Why haven't we done that, Avian?"

"We don't have the resources," he said as he too shook his head. I knew he'd thought about this idea before. We all had. "Everything we need is in the city. And we can't just take the materials and bring it back here. We'd need massive amounts of electricity to make it work. And besides, none of us know how exactly the CDU even works, how it's engineered. It's some very complex technology."

"So basically, we're all just waiting around to be infected," Sarah said, her voice falling. "As long as there are still people out there, the Bane will keep coming."

"And we'll keep fighting," I said harshly, my tone coming out more sharply than I meant it to.

Sarah looked at me with cold eyes that surprised me. Without her even saying it, I knew what she was thinking. *I didn't have to worry about being infected. I was already immune by essentially being one of them.*

"Maybe we should all get some rest," Avian suggested, feeling the tension that was building around the fire.

Without saying anything, Sarah stood and walked back inside the tent.

"Goodnight," Avian said.

I stood, pushing my hands into my pockets as I stared into the fire. West stood too, and together we slowly walked away from Avian and Sarah's tent.

"I want to look through the notebook," I blurted out and stopped walking not ten seconds later. West took a few more steps before stopping. I stood watching his back, my hands still pushed into my pockets against the cold.

He didn't say anything for a while as he stood with his back to me. I could almost see the gears in his head turning as he considered my request and what it would mean.

Slowly, he turned and took three steps toward me to close the gap. He stared into my eyes, intensity burning in his own.

He reached his right hand into his jacket and pulled the tattered notebook out.

"The pages in the middle are the ones about you," he said, keeping his voice quiet. "And don't lose it. If you do…" he squeezed his eyes closed, his lips forming a thin line as he considered the horrifying possibility.

"I won't," I promised as I went to take it. West opened his eyes, holding onto the notebook for another heavy moment before finally letting go.

"Goodnight, West," I said as I stared back into his eyes.

"Goodnight," he whispered. He hesitated just a moment longer before he stepped away and ducked into his tent.

Armed with the answers to my past, I returned to my own.

TWELVE

The notebook lay on my chest, my fingers clenching it tightly. I looked up blankly at the dark ceiling. I hadn't been able to will myself to open it. All the things I couldn't remember, all the dreams that haunted me, the answers were all inside and I couldn't make myself look at them.

I squeezed my eyes closed as I remembered smelling the steel beneath me, of hearing the drill. Feeling my head and realizing all my hair had been shaved off. I had dreamed of running endlessly. Dreamed of a pair of earthy eyes watching me through an observation window. It was West, I knew that now. He had seen everything they had done to me. The only person I had actually known my whole life, and I couldn't remember him.

I didn't sleep that night. I just stared up at the ceiling, trying to dredge up memories I couldn't recall, memories that were recorded by someone else's hand on the pages I held.

Morning came, casting a grey hue to the space around me. I didn't leave my tent, couldn't make myself even get out of my bed. But it was one of those very rare days I didn't have any duties.

As I heard Eden begin to stir, a plate of food was pushed under the flap of my tent and then I heard footsteps retreating. I reached for it, eating what was there without realizing what it even was.

The food in my system seemed to boost my commitment to unlock the past and I finally opened the pages.

The notebook seemed thinner than it should have been, like there were pages missing. It was in pretty poor shape though, many of the pages barely clinging to the metal spiral that kept them all bound together.

West was right, the pages about me were located in the middle. The notes in the beginning of the notebook may as well have been written in another language. It was scientific and talked about a lot of different alloys, programming, words I didn't understand. I could only guess that they were about the design for making me what I was.

The first entry was dated from when I would have been roughly four-years-old.

> *It feels so impossible that my last entry was only six months ago. Given last week's visit from the military, it seems the past few years were so distant and so much easier.*

I assumed this was where the pages went missing from. The pages previous to this entry were of the mathematical, formula type.

> *NovaTor has been approached by a branch of the military to develop some new technology. The government has been kept aware of what we have been researching in regards to TorBane the last few years. But no one is supposed to officially know about the Eve project.*

Last week three men came to us with a separate project. They themselves had been working on something to make soldiers stronger, faster. It is a chip. It would be implanted in the brain and it overrules tiredness, pain, and emotion. You couldn't ask for a better soldier if you could take out those factors. I suppose maybe the last one is debatable.

They have been doing human testing with the technology. They had five subjects. But they are running into complications. Where these soldiers don't feel pain and don't get tired, they either collapse from exhaustion because their bodies become depleted, because their body is still functioning normally, their brain just doesn't tell them to slow down, or they break and injure themselves and don't realize it until they are completely immobilized or dead.

But they heard about the Eve project. About the regenerative capabilities. About the ability to heal.

They want us to combine the two technologies.

And they're offering money that is hard to refuse.

What concerns me is the blocked emotion. I know what it could do to a young girl's development. And I question what a life without emotion would be like.

They don't want just one test subject. But how can I in good conscious give them more than that?

I never understood the concept of blackmail fully until recently. Such a dark, malevolent thing.

After digging around and questioning my staff, they discovered the full details about the Eve project. How it wasn't exactly approved or fully documented. They threatened to report us and get the entire TorBane project shut down. But they'll keep quiet if we do their testing.

I have no choice but to turn the Eve project over to them.

I was a blackmailed science project. I was a freak.

Had I been with my family before that? Had I even had one, ever? Maybe they had picked me out of an orphanage. They could have found me in the trash for all I knew.

The next entry was dated two months later.

Our entire team has been working with the military on the chip. The development and technology is good, but it isn't fully ready. It isn't quite fine-tuned. A person's emotions are bound to develop around their blocks and eventually the block will become undone. They need the ability to do adjustments without having to physically go back into the brain each time.

We've brought on Dr. Erik Beeson. He's young, just two years out of his doctorate program. But the boy is brilliant. I've read many of his papers over the years about the brain and wireless capabilities. And after speaking to him I have no doubt he is going to be the perfect addition to NovaTor Biotics.

He is currently fine tuning the chip.

I feel as if I'm turning into the devil. And I'm dragging the Eve project down into the fiery pits with me.

Three months later:

Surgery is scheduled for tomorrow.

Two days after surgery:

Operation was a success as far as we can tell. Chip was implanted and project Eve transferred to recovery room. Currently under observation. Being kept under sedation for the first three days and then we

96

shall see what happens. Under normal circumstances, recovery could take up to a month, maybe longer. But considering Eve's capabilities I expect less. Vitals are showing signs of recovery already. Brain activity is steadily increasing.

What he didn't know was that the sedation had taken longer than they had expected. I had relived those horrifying moments of paralysis in my dreams. I had heard the drill. Thankfully, I must have been finally pulled under before they bored into the back of my skull. Or if I hadn't, I didn't remember that part.

Seven days later:

Subject I began to awaken five days after surgery. Eve was sluggish at first, appearing confused and unsteady. Coordination was obviously thrown off. Things changed rapidly by the next day.

An assistant went to check on Eve and to give her the morning rations. Subject was startled awake and attacked the assistant. We heard the racket and opened the door to find Eve on top of the assistant, fingers gripped tightly around her neck. The assistant wasn't breathing. Upon seeing us enter the room, subject leapt at us, attacking with force far beyond what a normal five-year-old should be capable of. It took three of us to wrestle her onto the bed and secure her down.

Aggression was extreme for the next few days. We waited for things to even out. The fusion of the chip and the human brain is bound to be fought. The implant is placed in an area of the brain where emotion stems from. The brain is trying to attack itself, manifesting as aggression. Programming will be adjusted to fix the problem. I suppose this shouldn't be a surprise considering her previous condition.

Adjustments automatically given to II. No complications.

Problem. That was what my reaction to being altered was. It was a problem that I hadn't liked what they had done to me, that I had tried to fight back.

"Eve? Are you alright?"

I jumped violently when I heard the voice from outside my tent.

"Yes, Gabriel," I said, trying to steady my shaking voice. "I just needed some time to myself today." Was I lying? What counted more as time to yourself when you're learning what happened to you in the past that you can't remember?

He hesitated, catching my out-of-character response. "Okay," he said, drawing out the word. "Let me know if you need anything."

"Thank you," I said, shrinking into my bed. I listened hard until I heard his footsteps fade away.

My hands were shaking as I looked back at the notebook. I suddenly felt like I had to keep this a secret, as much as West had felt he had to. I didn't want anyone to know what was in here. The past it contained exposed what I was, what I was capable of. It exposed the fact that I wasn't completely human.

But West had read it all. He knew everything that was written here. And he hadn't been afraid of me. He hadn't run away.

I shook my head. West was a distraction I couldn't afford. I didn't like to admit it, but that's what he was. A distraction.

An entry from several months after the chip had been implanted:

> *Thus far the chip has been successful in overriding limitations as designed. Endurance has been increased. Exhaustion has been overruled. Tied to this is increased strength.*
>
> *Phase II of the experiment is progressing well. It has been fascinating to see the differences.*

The shock of reading what was continued on those pages should have worn off. It didn't. Things continued to get more twisted and terrifying.

> *And unexpected side effect of the chip implantation has occurred. I have been aware of the fact that everything project Eve is able to do should be impossible. The strength, speed, increased eyesight and hearing capacities. This has evolved beyond the capability of the military's chip and TorBane.*

The two technologies have intertwined with each other I believe. The chip has given the TorBane technology the ability to spread and evolve. After sedation and a full body scan, hints of cybernetic enhancements have been detected throughout Eve's body. It is not just the brain, lungs, and heart that have been altered now. It is the entire body.

Test's I and II yield duplicate results.

I stared at my hand, willing my eyes to see the metallic fingers I had seen on the Bane, searching for any signs of alloys bonded to my bones. My skin didn't look any different than Sarah's would have, no different than Gabriel's or Morgan's. It was all inside. That was the reason I was so much faster, so much stronger.

This just brought up a whole new slew of questions. There was a lot about these notes that I didn't really understand. I didn't speak scientist. But what had he meant by my brain, lungs, and heart being altered?

And that was when it finally hit me. West's grandfather was the one who had created TorBane. Those letters on the cover that were worn out had at one time spelled NOVATOR BIOTICS. It was his research and his creation that had led to the fall of humanity. And I had been a part of that. He must have given me the technology, and that was why the military wanted to use that chip on me. I must have been among the first to get TorBane. He had created the infection using the data he had collected from the experiments done on me.

I suddenly hated myself.

100

I forced myself to read through the rest of the pages. It didn't seem important to read them in detail anymore. I had been experimented upon as a child. And now here I was. I was the way I was and there was nothing I could do to change that.

There were pages and pages recording the endurance tests I had been put through. They continued to monitor my sleep habits. It seemed I had required little sleep my entire life. I didn't even require as much food as normal people.

An entry from when I was ten:

As Eve's brain has continued to develop and evolve, adjustments have been required in II. Her emotions have been changing. Fear and anger started to surface this last week, indicating our previous programming has been outdone. As she continues to grow we will need to make more adjustments.

I did the tuning myself. It is a complex procedure; the programming must be done precisely. Emotion is something not easily blocked. Modification must be dealt with carefully to not harm the brain and therefore, the body. After I had the programming correctly written, the adjustments were interfaced with the chip. The change was instantaneous. Amazing, the control that is exacted through remote programming.

Subject is again devoid of emotion.

I stared at the last line for a long time, my insides feeling hollow and empty. It was as if this man had reached through the pages and yanked all my insides out.

Subject is again devoid of emotion.

It explained a lot. How I didn't panic when others did. How I didn't understand what was happening to everyone after Tye had died, how I didn't recognize their grief. How I always felt so disconnected from everyone around me.

I forced myself to read the last page that referenced directly to me.

> *Apparently the money has run out. I'm finally being released from the military's hold. They want the Eve project maintained and will pay for that, but they are putting it on hiatus for a few years now. This finally frees me and my team up to finish the TorBane research. We should have the final strain ready for mass production within two years. Maybe less. It is time to move on from the Eve project. All data needed in regards to TorBane has been collected from experiments done to project Eve. Project is being handed off to Dr. Beeson for maintenance. The next phase of TorBane testing is ready.*

And that was the end of the entries about me.

The sun started to sink into the western horizon and I still had not left my tent. Another plate of food had been pushed under the entry flap as evening set but it remained untouched on the ground.

I imagined myself sinking through the ground, of burying myself into the earth and disappearing. I had helped cause the end of the world. Whether it was by my choice or not, I was a means to the end. I was now meaningless, an experiment forgotten about, no longer needed. I was a hollow vessel with no reason for still being. They had gotten what they needed out of me and moved on.

Eden fell quiet, slumber sweeping over its inhabitants. And still I lay there, my eyes staring up at the ceiling, yet seeing nothing. My mind was blank, my insides hollow. It felt better that way. Should I fill back in, everything would collapse in on me.

I barely even heard the sound of feet outside before a dark figure entered my tent. I knew who it was, even if my eyes couldn't see his face until he raised the lantern and closed the flap behind him.

I looked away from him and drew my eyes back to the ceiling.

West stepped closer to me, set the lantern on the ground by the wall and sat on the floor facing me.

"Here," I managed to make my throat work as I handed the notebook to him. "Please take it."

He accepted it. "I'm sorry," he whispered.

I should have told him that none of it was his fault. He had been a child after all. It was his father and grandfather, NovaTor, not him that had done this. But I couldn't do it.

"You still don't remember any of it?" he asked quietly.

I barely managed to shake my head.

"I've thought about it. Dr. Beeson, the one who took over your care and research, he was a kind man. He didn't approve of everything that was done to you. When things started getting out of control, when TorBane started taking everyone, I think he let you go. He made you forget somehow. Probably with the chip. He knew you would survive, that you could take care of yourself."

I gave the smallest of nods. "Why did he do it to me? Why did your grandfather give me TorBane?"

West was quiet for a moment, as if recalling the past. "I honestly don't know how you came to be at NovaTor. But I do know you were sick. You were a brand new baby and you were going to die. My grandpa wanted to do a human test with TorBane and he just went ahead and did it. He didn't tell anyone. And you got better. You were fine because of the technology. And I think that's why you can't infect anyone. You were given it at such a young age, it is just part of who you are. Everyone else was given it as an adult so it overtook them. But this is who you are, Eve."

I nodded. What had happened didn't matter. I was what I was. What had happened wasn't going to change, no matter the paths that had created it.

"Please say something," he said quietly.

I turned my head slightly to look at him. Tears traced patterns in the dirt on his face as they slid down his cheeks. "I don't think I can even do that," I said as I watched one of the tears drop into the dirt beneath him.

West wiped his thumb across his cheek, before slowly extending his hand to my face. His eyes burned and clouded at the same time as he wiped his damp thumb across my own cheek. Borrowed tears.

"I can't feel anything," I spoke quietly through the dim light. "I can't feel emotion. I'm hollow."

West shook his head. "You're not hollow. You feel things."

I shook my head. "He blocked it all. He made sure I didn't feel anything. It became a *problem*."

West scooted closer, shifting himself forward. He reached a hand toward me, placing his palm on my cheek, his thumb traveling from my cheek to my lips. I closed my eyes as heat tingled on the surface of my skin.

"You feel things," he whispered again. His hand trailed down the side of my neck, down my arm until his fingers intertwined with mine.

A quivering filled my stomach as I kept my eyes closed. My entire body felt like it hummed as I smelled West's presence, so close to me. It felt as if I could sense every surface of his body, so acutely aware of him it was as if he was an extension of my own being.

West shifted again, the one hand still intertwined with mine, his other one coming up to the side of my neck. And then his lips were on mine.

It wasn't crushing like the first unexpected one had been. This one saturated me slowly, hesitant in a way that consumed me. It smoldered at first, heat rising with every passing moment, eating me up from my stomach outward.

A tiny gasp escaped from my lips as they parted and I didn't even realize what I was doing as my free hand knotted in West's shaggy hair. He shifted again, most of his body lying on top of mine.

I burned from the inside out. My heart raced. I wanted more but felt totally consumed by West, getting everything I needed yet feeling that it was not even close to being enough.

He pulled away just a bit, resting his forehead against mine. His eyes were closed as he tried to slow his breathing. "You feel things." He said raggedly. "I know you felt that."

West fell asleep, his arms wrapped tightly around me. His face seemed so peaceful. He looked younger. In sleep he didn't have to worry about survival, feel guilt for the actions of his family.

It took me a while to understand how I was feeling that night. I was relaxed too. Sluggish almost. This was more than the fall of my defenses

I felt happy.

Maybe I did feel things after all.

Maybe I'd had my own evolution.

THIRTEEN

Sweat beaded between my shoulder blades and rolled down my back. I wiped my forehead and scanned the trees again. Maybe it was just the fact that I was out on scouting patrol by myself but I felt uneasy. Something was waiting to happen.

While on duty that morning, I happened upon the biggest elk I had ever seen. It had taken three shots to bring it down. Bill and Graye had taken it back to Eden to be prepared to eat that night. And now I was out here on my own.

Dead pine needles crunched softly underneath my feet as I circled around the lake. I smelled at the air, searching for any traces of something that didn't belong. I tried to keep my head in the task at hand but I'd been distracted the last few days.

Everything had changed and yet everything hadn't.

Despite all the truths I had learned about myself, everything had somehow gone back to normal. I was still who I was. *I* hadn't changed. I just knew how I had become the way I was. I was still Eve. As long as I was breathing, as long as I was still in control of my actions and the cybernetic side of me didn't turn me against myself, I would continue to protect Eden until I took my last breath.

I'd been away from the people of Eden for the most part since that day I had read the notebook. Maybe I'd needed some time alone to think things over, to come to terms or something. I'd been on scouting duty every day and then on watch tower nearly every night. I wanted to talk to Avian about everything I'd learned, to have him help me process it all, but I wasn't quite ready just yet.

Gauging by the position of the sun above me, I knew it was about time for the scouting switch. I headed back toward the lake. I took a quick bath and walked to Eden in the fading daylight.

I dragged my fingers through my tangled blond hair and stepped back into the mass of tents. The scent of something delicious wafted through the air. There was a sense of excitement buzzing around, almost a tangible thing.

"Eve!" Sarah called. "Come on!"

I made my way through our version of a city, watching as people bustled about. I was confused why everyone wore their nicest clothes; at least what passed for nice these days.

"What's going on?" I asked her as I observed several women cooking up a food frenzy in our makeshift kitchen area.

"We're having a party," Sarah said with a wide smile. "Today is Gabriel's sixtieth birthday!"

My eyes widened a bit at this and I gave a nod. It was impressive. Not many people lived to see that age anymore. Terrif was the only person older than Gabriel in Eden. Only the strong had survived the Evolution.

"Come with me," Sarah said excitedly as she grabbed hold of my wrist and pulled me in the direction of her tent. "We have to get you ready."

"What's wrong with the way I am now?"

"You may only be part human, Eve, but the woman inside of you needs some pampering."

I wasn't sure what Sarah was talking about and if I was being honest, I was a little wary of what she might mean. We stepped into the tent and found Avian, just pulling a shirt over his thin but toned frame.

"Out," Sarah commanded. "I have to get Eve ready."

For some reason Avian wouldn't meet my eyes. "Yes, ma'am," he said and ducked out without another word.

I stared at the place where he had disappeared with a strange feeling in my stomach. There had been a weird vibe between us the last few days. I had not been around anyone much but I had seen less of Avian than I had expected. He would hardly look at me. I realized then that he had been purposefully avoiding me.

"Put this on," Sarah said as she rummaged through a bag of things. She shoved a mass of light green material at me.

"What is this?" I asked, holding it away from me and inspecting it.

"A dress," Sarah said with a half-smile as she looked back at me. She herself held something similar, but in a red color.

"A dress?" I questioned as I held the folds up, looking through what must have been the top of it. "It looks more like a small tent."

Sarah chuckled. "Here, let me help you."

Despite my protests, Sarah soon had me undressed and into the light green dress. I felt half-naked. While it was long enough to cover even my ankles, the thin straps at the top of it felt like they would barely hold the dress on my frame. The front of it plunged far lower than felt appropriate, exposing what even I felt embarrassed to see.

"This is ridiculous," I said again as Sarah worked on my hair, twisting and pulling at it. But despite my protests, a small smile played on the edge of my lips.

"It's part of being human, of being a woman. Or at least it used to be. We're all clinging to anything we can. Trying not to forget what it used to be like."

We were quiet for a while as her fingers continued their swift work. I wondered if the fact that it had *never* been a part of my existence had crossed Sarah's mind.

"You have a birthmark on the back of your head," she said quietly, her fingers rubbing at a place on the back of my scalp. "Did you know that?"

I shook my head, not really thinking about what she was saying.

"Avian's been strange lately," I said, recalling the cold way he had left earlier. "He's been avoiding me."

Sarah paused for a moment. She gave the slightest of sighs before resuming. "He saw you and West the other night. He saw your shadows through the tent."

"He was watching?"

"He went to talk to you, to make sure you were alright. He was worried because you hadn't come out all day," her voice grew quiet, sad. "That's when he saw you and West kissing."

A knot formed in my chest. I wanted to explain, to talk to Avian. But what was there to say? West had kissed me, but I had kissed him back. More than that, I had liked it. I had felt *something*.

But why did I feel so guilty?

"You deserve to be happy, Eve," Sarah said with another sigh, her hands falling into her lap. "As much as anyone else here, maybe more after all you've been through and done for us. But just be careful. He has feelings for you, even if he won't be obvious about them."

My stomach felt empty, but not in the way of being hungry. That hollow feeling was pulling at me again.

I closed my eyes and hugged my arms into my chest. Life was getting too complicated.

"You've got feelings for both of them," Sarah said softly. Even though I wasn't looking at her I detected the small smile that was in the corner of her lips. "Love's a complex emotion, isn't it?"

"Love?" I said, my brow furrowing as I looked up at her. "There is no place for love in this world anymore. The luxury of love died with the rest of the world."

"If love dies, that's when we've all truly died. That's when the Bane will have won."

I didn't know what to say for a while, contemplating everything she had said.

"Thank you, Sarah," I said with a half-smile, trying to distract myself. "For all of this," I said as I indicated the hair and the dress.

"You look beautiful," Sarah said with a smile. "Now come on, let's go!"

We went back to the party and sat down at the table, surrounded by Morgan, Eli, Bill, and Wix. Piles of food had been placed on the table, a good chunk of our left over stores from the previous fall's harvest were put out. The elk I had killed earlier had been prepared in every way I could think possible. Gabriel sat at the head of the long table, his wife Leah next to him. I had never seen him look so happy. He deserved it.

I glanced down the table as I ate. Avian sat near Gabriel. He still wouldn't look at me. West was seated at the middle of the table, next to Graye. He on the other hand kept glancing down at me, the barest hint of a smile ever present on his face. The smile of a secret.

"I'd like to make a toast," Avian said halfway through the meal, standing up and holding his glass. "To Gabriel. To the man who has always kept us safe. The man who has willingly led us, for not having to be asked to do so. To the man who has built this place we call home. To Gabriel."

"To Gabriel," we echoed.

As the meal came to a close, an unfamiliar sound came from the head of the table. Wix and a few other people stood in a semi-circle, holding a mixture of instruments.

"What are those?" I asked Sarah as I observed them.

"Teresa is playing a guitar," Sarah said quietly to me. "Thereon is playing a drum. And Wix is playing his violin. He was something of a child protégé when he was young, before the Evolution. He got to play at all these world-class venues and with famous symphonies."

I watched them as they played. The sounds were beautiful, but so foreign and strange to me. I knew nothing of music but something told me these instruments were not normally played together. Still, it was the most beautiful thing I had heard.

When everyone was finished eating, the tables were cleared away and a bonfire was built in the middle of the clearing. People started dancing to the music.

I stood to the side along the tree line, watching how they moved. At first it had looked so strange, silly. But as I observed the way they moved in time with the music I understood why they did it. There was something about the music that spoke to a place inside of me. Dancing was a way to let the body and the music combine.

"You look beautiful tonight," a voice said from behind me. I turned to see Gabriel come to my side.

"Thank you," I said as my eyes dropped to my bare feet. "I feel so exposed."

Gabriel chuckled, his lips disappearing into the mass of his beard as they pressed together. "Not exactly what you're used to."

"I've never worn a dress before."

"It's good for you. A reminder of what you really are." When I didn't say anything in response Gabriel filled it in. "Human."

"Thank you, Gabriel," I said quietly as I looked back down at my feet. "Happy birthday."

He sighed but smiled. "I feel so old."

"That's a good thing," I reminded him. "Not too many get to feel old anymore."

Footsteps approached us and we both looked up to see West. He joined us, his hands stuffed in his pockets.

"Happy birthday, Gabriel," he said.

"Thank you. Well, I'd better get back to my party," Gabriel said with a grin that got lost in his beard again. He winked at me once and then wandered back into the crowd.

West and I stood there for a few moments, staring at the scene before us. The fire, the people dressed up, the music, and the laughter. It was almost as if the Evolution had never happened.

But in that case, we would probably be inside a building, not under the stars. There would be a heater warming the room, not a billowing fire that licked out at the night air.

I think I preferred it this way.

"You look beautiful," West finally broke the silence.

"Thank you," I said, feeling heat rush to my cheeks, both from his compliment and from the way our shoulders brushed. West slipped his hand out of his pocket and his fingers intertwined with mine. For a fraction of a second, the world died black. And then it was all back.

"Would you dance with me, Eve?" he said quietly as we both continued to watch the people move before us. I blinked once, my vision back to normal.

I shook my head. "I don't know how. I'll look ridiculous."

He took a step toward the woods, pulling me behind him.

We didn't go far, just through the trees enough that no one would see us. There was an old trailer rusting away at the water's edge that we stepped around. I was careful not to snag Sarah's dress on it. We stopped where the trees met the water's sandy edge.

"No one has to see you dance," he said quietly as we stood face to face. I could still faintly hear the music coming through the trees. West took one of my hands in his, wrapping his other hand around my waist. I placed my other hand on his shoulder since that seemed like the right place to put it. West pulled me closer and I let my head settle on his chest as we just rocked side to side in a small circle.

The sound of West's heart beating matched the slow rhythm of the music.

"So have you thought about what I said?" he asked quietly into my ear, his cheek resting on the top of my head. "I know you feel things. You've evolved past the blockers, I know it."

"I've never felt things like this before. It's overwhelming," I said quietly into the soft cloth of his shirt.

"Is it bad though?"

I considered that for half a moment and then shook my head. "No," I whispered. I didn't tell him how it terrified me more than anything else had terrified me though. I'd been through a lot in my life and developing feelings was the scariest thing I had ever faced.

West slowed to a stop and brought his hand to my chin. Slowly he tipped my face up to his, his eyes staring down at mine with intensity. In that moment, I thought I almost remembered them looking at me through a window, younger and more innocent.

Almost.

"I'm glad you don't remember," he said in a low voice, his eyes turning darker. "Even if that means you don't remember me."

He tipped his head down and his lips met mine, brushing them so softly they tingled with anticipation as if they'd never touched at all.

"What was that?" I hissed as I whipped my head toward the tree line. I stepped away from West and into a stance ready to spring. My ears strained, listening for the sound of a branch breaking again. I smelled at the air, searching for signs of life that shouldn't be there.

I took a few steps into the trees, West following quietly behind me. "I didn't hear anything besides the party."

"Shh," I hissed at him, my eyes straining to see through the dark. A figure stepped back into the clearing at the same time someone else stepped toward us.

"Eve?" Sarah's voice called through the dark. "Is that you?"

I sighed as I glanced back at West who had a very annoying smile on his face.

"A little paranoid?" he said quietly.

"Shut up," I said as I rolled my eyes and walked toward Sarah.

"Eve!" Sarah called excitedly as she saw me walking through the trees. "The guys are setting up a knife throwing contest. The prize is Terrif's old hunting blade. They were all hoping you'd stay gone so they'd have a chance at winning."

I stepped back into the clearing and saw the target set up across from where everyone was gathered. As soon as Bill and Graye saw me they groaned and threw up their hands in surrender.

"Come on, Sarah!" Graye moaned. "Why'd you have to go and tell her? We might as well not play!"

"Settle down, boys," I said with a smile as I shook my head. "Go ahead. I'll just watch."

Cheers erupted and the energy turned to teasing Wix for taking up a blade to enter. He kept up with the banter though, pretending to be the toughest of them all.

"I'll be back in a minute," West whispered into my ear. He then started walking in the direction of his tent.

Sarah caught my eye, flashing a knowing smile.

It was pretty comical, watching Wix try and keep up with our best scouts in Eden. I had to respect him for trying though. The kid wouldn't be bullied.

I looked up from my place by the food tent and searched for Sarah. I found her talking to Morgan. Her skin was covered in a glaze of sweat, flushed in a not-good way. She glanced over at me and as she did I felt my insides hollow out. Her eyes were suddenly glazed-over, her face blank. I bolted up from my seat and was across the clearing in five bounding steps. I caught her just as she collapsed.

Sarah's right arm flailed wildly as I carefully lowered her to the ground. Her eyes stared blankly up at the night sky, her body thrashing violently.

Everyone had been told of Sarah's newfound condition. It had been necessary should she be with someone and have a seizure, they needed to know how to help her. But everyone still gathered around her, watching in horror and sadness.

"Where's Avian?" I asked to no one in particular as Sarah's arm batted against my right shoulder.

"He went back to his tent a while ago," Morgan said as she crouched down next to us, Sarah's form starting to still.

"Stay with her," I instructed. Morgan sat next to me and pulled Sarah's head into her lap. "I'll go get him."

I jogged towards Avian's tent with silent feet. A sense of dread filled me as I approached. I pulled the flap back, finding him reading on his cot.

His eyes met mine, and for a second I forgot my reason for being there. The look in his eyes screamed pain. I'd never seen that look on Avian's face before, and now that it was directed at me I never wanted to see it again.

"Sarah had another seizure," I finally said, my voice almost too quiet.

He marked his place in the book and rose to his feet. He couldn't even look at me as he walked out of the tent without saying a word.

I took a few steps away from his tent before stopping to watch him walk away, back toward the clearing.

"Hey." West's voice surprised me from the side. His hand slipped into mine. "You want to go back to the party?"

I took a quick step away, slipping out of his hand. "I think I'm going to go to bed now," I said. I didn't even glance back as I walked swiftly toward my tent.

I wanted to turn everything inside of me off.

Not feeling was easier.

FOURTEEN

I deposited my pack in my tent, always a nearly painful thing to do, and made my way to the east side of the lake. The trees hung over the water in this section, providing a lot of privacy. I slipped out of my sticky clothes, washed them quickly, then hung them out to dry. Summer had finally arrived in full force. I jumped in the water, the cool water hitting my skin with a sharp slap. I gave a sigh as my head surfaced, pushing my hair out of my face. The sun was nearly blinding as it danced on the surface of the water.

I set out for the west side of the lake.

It took everything I had in me to not think about everything. To not think about West, to not think about Avian, not think about Sarah's illness or the truth about what I really was. But my stomach turned to knots every time I thought about any of it.

I reached the western shore of the lake and turned back.

I was nearly back to where my clothes hung to dry when I felt something splash against me, waves not created by my strokes. I pulled up short, my head popping out of the water at the same time Avian's did.

"Avian!" I gasped as my hands automatically clamped around my chest. "What are you doing here?!"

"Swimming!" he said in a shocked tone. "What are you doing here?"

"Swimming!" I answered, turning my back to him. The water was dark because of the shadowing of the trees, for which I was immensely grateful. But we were still nearly ten yards away from the shore. I noticed Avian's clothes hanging about twenty feet away from mine, dripping wet, just as mine were.

"Well, turn around," I commanded as I started swimming for the shore again. Avian did as I asked.

I debated what to pull on. Everything was still soaking. My cheeks flushed as I pulled on only my underthings. It was uncomfortable wearing wet clothes with the temperatures so warm. I turned my back as Avian came to shore and pulled on his pants.

We stood there, both unsure of what to say, not quite looking at each other. There was so much tension rolling off of Avian. I hated the way it made me feel inside.

"I don't want things to be like this between us," I finally said, looking up into his face. "I can't stand this. You mean more to me than anyone here in Eden."

"Don't say something you don't mean," he said, his voice tight.

I took a few steps toward him, stopping just a foot away from him. "What is that supposed to mean?"

Avian finally looked into my eyes, his blue ones filled with emotions I was starting to understand. "You mean everything to me, Eve. I know I haven't exactly come right out and said it yet, but you do. But if you have feelings for West, I…" he trailed off as his eyes again fell to the rough sand underneath our feet.

I bit my lower lip, my own eyes falling from his face. They settled onto the two birds tattooed on his chest. "Something is happening to me, Avian. There is something inside of me that is waking up and I don't know how to handle

119

it. I'm feeling things I've never felt before. Things I don't understand. I'm terrified, Avian."

His eyes met mine again, soft and sad looking at the same time. I wanted him to do something, to say something. Avian always had the answers for me, always sorted things out when I couldn't understand. "Is…" his voice faded as he tried to make himself vocalize what was on his mind. "Is there any way you could someday feel the same way that I feel about you?"

I held his eyes for a long time, not answering. Something inside of me felt like it grew, making my heart beat erratically.

It suddenly seemed like I was looking at a whole new Avian.

Everything instantly changed between us.

"Yes," I said.

A small smile spread on his face. But it didn't reach his eyes and there was pain in it. He closed his eyes for a moment. "Then you need to realize that you can't have both, Eve. It just doesn't work that way."

I felt like I was going to get swallowed up by myself again. Something inside of me reached out to Avian, wanting to pull him closer and never have to let go.

He reached up, taking in his hand the stone wings he had carved, his eyes studying its surface. "No matter what you choose, I'll still be here. Just don't expect me to not get hurt."

My lips were against his before I even allowed myself to consider what I was doing. My arms wrapped behind his neck at the same time that his wrapped around my waist. My insides surged in ways I didn't understand, and a feeling of what I could describe as nothing other than belonging settled into every corner of my being. Everything about his scent, his body, his presence brought on a flood of memories, sizzling with newness and anticipation.

And almost as soon as it started, Avian pulled away, resting his forehead against mine, one of his hands pressing softly against my bare stomach. He closed his eyes, his lips pursed together. "You can't have both," he said quietly. He pressed one more quick kiss to my forehead, then grabbed his clothes and walked back in the direction of Eden.

FIFTEEN

The floorboards creaked in protest as my booted feet walked across them. Dust swirled around my legs, the light catching their form, tracing patterns in the air. The air was stale with the heavy scent of abandonment.

While on scouting duty that morning, I had found a cabin in the woods. A roughhewn road led up to it, the forest pressing back in, trying to take the land back. I had watched silently from the trees for a full ten minutes before I dared move closer. Silently, I had peered into the windows, searching for any signs of life, enemy or friend. There were none.

I felt like I was stepping into another world. The world of houses, of flooring, running water and windows was from another age. The age of humanity, of mankind. We were in the age of the Bane now.

The front area was full of furniture. Pictures lined the walls, smiling faces staring back at me. Books were stacked on random surfaces, a yellowing newspaper lay casually on the kitchen table. I grabbed a handful of the books and stuffed them into my bag for Gabriel and Wix. A bedroom led off of the front room. It was a small space with little more than the bed in it, but it was still larger than my tent. I was tempted to lie down on the bed, just to see how soft it was, but my nerves were too on edge.

A small bathroom was attached to the bedroom. I lifted the handle of the faucet in the sink and a small smile crept onto my face as brown water sputtered out. It was true. Running water really was real. I left it on as I turned to explore the rest of the house.

The kitchen was small, but it may have served the king of the land for all I knew. It was glorious looking. I knew what the women who worked in our kitchen would give to have use of this. I opened a lower cupboard and pulled out bottles, not even knowing what they were for, but figuring Eden would appreciate anything I could bring back.

I was looking out the cracked window of the back door when I felt the boards under my feet wiggle. There was a cutout shape of a small door. It creaked as I pulled it open. The overpowering smell of spoiled food assaulted my senses. I pulled my shirt over my nose and dropped into the dark space below.

It took a moment for my eyes to adjust to the darkness. The air was damp, tasting like earth and humidity.

The area that had been dug out had to be nearly as big as the rest of the cabin. Rows and rows of shelves crowded the area. Canned goods were stacked everywhere, buckets of flour and sugar covered all of the bottom racks. Two entire shelves were filled with glass bottles of water. The source of the smell was a few sacks of rotting potatoes in one corner.

Whoever had lived here was preparing for something. Had they been found by Bane? Had they gone to the city for supplies, only to be infected there?

Pushing away the ghosts of the past, I climbed back up the ladder and closed the hatch behind me. I wandered back into the bathroom to where the water was still running. It was clear now and flowing steady. There was a glass stall in the bathroom with a drain disappearing into the floor. This must have been a shower. It seemed to fit Sarah's description. I turned the knobs in it and a minute or so later, it too was cascading clear water.

Checking again to make sure the house was still clear and that that there was nothing outside, I stripped down and climbed inside. The water was cold but not as cold as it was at the lake. I found a few bottles of liquid and sniffed at their contents. They smelled so *good*, I massaged them into every surface of my body. I couldn't stop smelling my skin.

A towel was hanging next to the shower and after flicking a spider off of it, I used it to dry myself off. A movement to my right caught my eye, causing adrenaline to flood my system. It had only been my reflection though.

I approached the mirror slowly, taking in the person who stared back at me. My grey-blue eyes looked washed out in the dim light. My cheek bones were bordering on gaunt looking, having spent all my remembered life on rations and scouting through the forest every day. My jaw line was sharp as well, all of my features pronounced.

I turned my back to the mirror, glancing over my shoulder at my bare shoulder. The skin was rippled and twisted looking. Even though it had healed completely in just a few days, the scar would be there forever.

Unease crept into my system at letting my defenses down for so long and I climbed back into my clothes and pulled my pack back on. I walked back outside and headed toward the back of the house.

There was a large outbuilding behind the cabin, no windows, just roughhewn wood siding. I pulled the doors open and my heart jumped into my throat.

I had never seen a vehicle this far from the city before.

It was large, with a big bed for cargo. Bill called this kind of vehicle a truck. I could tell it was old – even in the days when it would have been used it would have been old. I wished I knew how to drive to see if it still ran. I made a note to bring Bill here with me soon.

I gathered up what more I could fit into my pack and started back toward Eden.

The light was just starting to dim in the sky when I reached the halfway point. The sound of a branch breaking drove me up the nearest tree. I moved silently along the boughs, my eyes searching for the source of the noise. I saw West, walking back in the direction of Eden.

I picked the biggest pine cone I could find out of the tree I stood in and threw it at West with precision, hitting him square in the back of the head. His shoulders scrunched up towards his ears, whipping around violently, a knife clenched in one hand, a handgun in the other.

A sly smile crossed my face as I picked another, throwing it so it landed just behind him. He spun around again, his eyes scanning the trees, a curse slipping across his lips. I couldn't help it as the laugh slipped out.

West whipped around, the knife launching from his fingers. Instinct reaction took over as I caught the blade tightly in my hand; the tip of it just inches away from my chest.

"Geez, West," I said sharply as I threw it back down at him, burying the blade in the ground between his feet. "A bit paranoid?" As I looked back down at my hand, the skin was already closing up where it had been cut. I wiped the few drops of blood off on my pants.

His eyes finally found me and after picking his knife up, he scaled the tree, sitting next to me on the large branch. "I was wondering where you had wandered off to," he said, his eyes hesitant as they met mine.

"I found a house," I said, trying to drive away the awkward moment. "It had a cellar underneath it. It was stock

125

full of non-perishables. Enough for two people to live off of for a year. And they had a truck. I don't know if it runs though. I don't know how to work it."

"Me either," he said as he shook his head. His eyes grew in intensity as he looked at me and I saw his thoughts reeling. "Is everything okay? You've volunteered for night watch almost every night since the party. It feels a little like you've been avoiding me the last few days."

"I have been," I said honestly as my eyes dropped to the ground below us.

"Does this have anything to do with Avian?" West asked, his voice dropping in volume a bit.

I pressed my lips tightly together. Yes, it did have something to do with Avian. "I'm confused right now. I don't know how to handle all these feelings. Everything is so intense."

West's hand shifted, his fingers covering mine. I looked back at him. He stared back at me.

"It's normal," he said quietly. "You're supposed to feel this way."

"Not for me, it's not normal."

"Evolution, remember?" he said as he leaned forward.

I debated with myself for the briefest moment, whether or not to let him kiss me.

But before his lips could meet mine, someone screamed.

I leapt out of the tree and was sprinting through the forest before West could even open his eyes to look for the source of the scream. It hadn't been far away. Within ten seconds I saw Graye, lying on the ground, twitching and writhing in pain. Two metal barbs were embedded into the skin of his chest, a sharp hiss emanating from them as they shocked Graye, over and over.

I'd never seen a Bane use a weapon.

126

I felt the sharp shock of the electricity coursing through my body as I yanked the barbs out of Graye. As I stuffed them into my pocket, I saw it, sprinting towards us, with robotically enhanced speed.

I sprang though the air at the Bane. His eyes shown with a metallic glint, empty and cold. Two cybernetic hands stretched towards me and we collided with a heavy smack. His hands went straight for my throat, my hands pulling at every gear, wire, and cog I could get them on.

"Eve!" I heard the scream as we collided.

"Get out of here, West!" I tried to scream, my voice cut off as the Bane's hands tightened around my throat. "Run!"

Black spots started forming in my vision as my air supply was choked off. I clawed at the hands, gaining no breathing room. Its eyes stared at me, empty as ever.

I worked my hand into my pocket, the metal rods sizzling my skin as it shocked me over and over. My arm felt ridged as they forced the muscles in it to clench up. With every ounce of strength I had, I forced my arm to move. I jammed the rods into the Bane's eye with everything I had.

Even though I knew it couldn't feel pain, it jerked away, its hands reaching up to its destroyed eye. It was just enough for me to wiggle my hand free and pull my handgun out and blast its head open.

At the same time, another shot was fired from behind me, hitting the Bane square in the chest.

I fell back to the ground, my breath coming in sharp gasps. The Bane collapsed to the earth with a hiss of electric death, its form falling still. I stared up at the blood red sky and tried to steady my breathing.

"Eve!" West yelled as he half fell to my side. "Are you alright?"

127

I was about to say yes when I raised my hand to look at it, the one I had grabbed the rods with. The skin of my fingers had been burned away, muscle, bone, and metallic parts gleaming in the fading light.

"Holy..." I breathed as I took it in. There was the proof. It was more than my lungs and heart that were cybernetic. It looked as if the cybernetics had bonded to my bones.

"Come on," West said as he yanked me to my feet. "We've got to get Graye to Avian. Whatever those things were, they burned some nice sized holes into his chest."

I stumbled to my feet and back toward Graye. His form was limp as I picked him up and slung him across my shoulders. We were both running through the forest moments later, desperation propelling us faster and faster.

"Since when do the Bane use weapons like that?" West huffed.

"They don't," I said, recalling every time I'd ever encountered a Bane. They *never* used weapons, other than their own two hands and the infection.

"Avian!" West started shouting as we reached the edge of the tents. "Avian!"

We barreled into the clearing and ran straight for the medical tent. Avian burst out of his tent, stepping aside when he saw my load, and followed us in.

"A Bane shot him with these electric rods," I explained as I laid Graye's still form on the table. "They hurt."

"What?!" Avian shouted as he grabbed a piece of medical equipment and pressed it to Graye's chest, listening to the other end. "He's still breathing but his heart beat is erratic. How long were they in him?" Avian started compressions to Graye's chest.

"Not more than fifteen seconds. I wasn't far away," I paced the small space of the tent, passing West as he stood in one corner, watching Graye as Avian worked on him.

"The Bane?" Avian huffed as he worked on Graye. He stopped and listened to Graye's chest again.

"I shot it," I said through clenched teeth. "I don't know if there are any more."

"You've got to get back out there," Avian said as he ripped away the remains of Graye's shirt, exposing the burned flesh underneath. "You've got to check."

"Come on," I said to West, stepping out of the tent. Gabriel and Bill came running up to us just as we exited.

"Is Graye with you?" Bill asked as he stopped before us. "I couldn't find him."

"A Bane shot him," I said, knowing we were wasting time. "Avian's taking care of him. We've got to go check for more of them though."

Bill nodded and the three of us ran back into the trees without another word to Gabriel or anyone else.

"How much ammo do you have?" I asked Bill as we jogged through the trees.

"Two mags and a pocketful," Bill answered as his eyes scanned the trees.

"West?" I asked as I checked the chamber of my own handgun, replacing the bullet I had used on the Bane.

"Full mag," he replied as he checked it. "Nothing extra though."

"Here." I shoved a handful of bullets into his hand, pulling them out of my pocket.

I pressed faster back to where I had found Graye and the Bane, West and Bill quickly falling behind me. I smelled at the air. The scent of the Bane I had killed wafted through the air, undetectable to anyone but me, I was sure. I quickly passed its

129

body, following the path it had created through the grass and undergrowth.

I ran another half mile before I saw it.

I froze beneath a low tree, jumping behind it as it came into view. My ears searched for any hints of an attack. When I found none, I turned my eyes back to the mechanical beast before me.

I'd never seen a helicopter so close before. It looked like an oversized mechanical bug, its blades still and less threatening looking. It was hard to believe the machine could be so silent. It was a piece of raw, powerful destruction when it was flying.

But if there was a helicopter here, that meant there was more than one Bane. They always flew in pairs.

Bill and West finally caught up to me, huffing as they came to my side.

"A chopper?" Bill said as he crouched, a gun in one hand, his finger on the trigger. "Then there's another one out there."

We scanned the trees, our senses strained and ready to spring.

"Stay close," I said as I started west, heading in the opposite direction we had just come from. "If you can't shoot it, run. Let me take care of it."

They followed silently as we came to the other side of the helicopter. A clear trail led in the exact opposite direction the other had gone. They had split up to cover more ground. The Bane didn't bother to cover up their trails. They had nothing to be afraid of, no one to hide from.

We followed the trail for two miles, seeing no traces of the Bane other than his footsteps.

"You think it doubled back?" Bill whispered, his gun still raised, finger on the trigger, the same as West and I.

"We would have seen it by now," I said quietly in response. And just as soon as I said it the trail ended. The small patches of grass and moss that had been smashed by its weight suddenly disappeared. I glanced up, my eyes searching.

"It went up," I said, my eyes tracing the path it had taken through the trees. There wasn't much to see but there was broken branches and a handprint on a mossy branch. "It could be anywhere now."

"Maybe we should split up," West said, his breathing betraying his nerves.

"Bad idea," I said quietly. "You wander on your own and what's going to be your barrier?"

"I'd prefer it not have to be you," he murmured.

As I registered West's words I heard the snap behind us. "Get down!" I screamed as I whipped around, pushing both Bill and West to the ground. Half a second later the Bane fired, the bullet grazing the side of my thigh. I stumbled, half falling on top of Bill.

I had just gotten back to my feet when it started sprinting towards us. Every muscle in my body flexed as I hurtled myself at the Bane.

We crashed to the ground, a mere ten feet from Bill and West. I clung to its shoulder with one hand, beating at the back of its head with the butt of my gun with the other. With one hand, it reached back, grabbed me by the back of my neck, and slammed me to the ground.

My hands flung out, grabbing its ankle as it started toward the others, and dropped it to the ground. It turned its empty eyes on me, coiling its leg for a crushing kick to my face that I barely managed to avoid. Two shots were suddenly fired, both barely missing the Bane and myself.

Undeterred by my efforts, the Bane turned its focus back to West and Bill.

131

"No!" I screamed as I leapt back up and jumped onto its back. "Get away from them!"

Something I couldn't explain happened. The Bane froze, me still clinging to its frame, and took two steps back. And then it stood there, staring out at nothing. Before it could do anything else, I scrambled off its back, drew my gun again and blasted a hole in the back of its head. It collapsed to the ground in a heap.

And then I buckled, caving in on my right leg. It didn't hurt, but apparently it wasn't going to hold my weight anymore.

West and Bill were instantly at my side. "How'd you do that?" Bill demanded. "It listened to you."

"What are you talking about?" I huffed as they each grabbed one of my arms and helped me to my feet, supporting my weight for me. "And since when do the Bane carry guns?"

"You told it to get away from us," West filled in for Bill. "And then it stopped and backed away."

Adrenaline was still pumping through my system, making everything seem like a blur in my head. "Why would it listen to me?"

"Maybe because you're partly like them," West said as we scrambled through the trees.

"Whatever just happened, let's just get out of here," Bill said as his eyes stared intently at the path we had just come down. "We've got to get you to Avian."

SIXTEEN

I limped out of the medical tent, cursing under my breath.

There wasn't much Avian could do for my leg. I had tried to tell Bill and West that. He had simply wrapped the wound and sent me out, turning his attention back to Graye. He was still unconscious and Avian was having to pound on his chest every so often to keep his heart beating normally.

"Eve," West called as I headed in the direction of my tent. "Are you alright?"

"Leave me alone, West," I said as I shook my head. I refused to look at him, keeping on my path.

"What?" he asked, his voice sounding taken aback. "What did I do?"

I just shook my head, my jaw clenching together. Something boiled under my skin. He'd better do as I said or he was going to be the victim of an explosion.

"Eve," he said as he followed me, his voice becoming more insistent. "Eve! Look at me!"

"Seriously, West, leave me alone."

His hand grabbed my wrist, pulling me to a stop. I whipped around to face him, my hand rising. I barely registered the shock in West's face before I stopped myself. I'd been about to connect my fist with his jaw.

"What's going on, Eve?" he asked, his brow furrowing, his eyes searching mine. "What did I do?"

133

I finally erupted.

"I can't be around you like this!" I shouted, not even looking around to make sure no one else was listening. "Yes, you make me feel things, but you also distract me so much I can't even do my job! It was my fault Graye got hurt. He was looking for me and where was I? Up a tree with you! He could have been killed! If I had been five seconds later getting to him, he would have been infected!

"I can't do this, West. I can't keep getting distracted. I can't feel things that the rest of you feel. People will get killed if I do."

He stared at me, hurt and anger creeping into his eyes. When he didn't say anything, I looked away. A few people had stopped what they were doing to watch us. "What are you all looking at?" I snapped. Before anyone could say anything, I took off in the direction of my tent.

I shut it all off and kept away from everyone.

After talking to Gabriel, I got myself on scouting duty every day, trading out my gardening hours. He didn't fight me like I had expected, but then again, he had heard my outburst and he knew what I had said was true. I couldn't afford to be distracted.

I also took over all of Graye's night watch duties. Without Gabriel's knowledge, I took over everyone else's as well.

Between scouting duty in the morning and watch at night, I simply slept the rest of the time. I blocked out the noise and light around me and shut myself down. It wasn't hard, with everything I was doing I was actually feeling exhausted. I was finally finding my limits.

Gabriel had thought about moving Eden again after what had happened with Graye but Avian and I had talked him out of it. It was obvious the Bane were getting more persistent.

There wasn't far for us to go without getting too far away from water and the gardens. We were just going to have to fight them off if they continued to come. Even if they were going to start coming with weapons. Plus, we were never going to find a better location than the one we were already at.

Everyone short of two people on scouting duty was gathered together for a light dinner. We had been trying to be careful lately with our provisions. We were in the lull of time between the leftovers of last year's harvest and this year's pickings.

Some of us peeled off, settling into our nightly activities. I found myself with my eyes glued to the fire, watching as the flames danced in the night air. Gabriel, Bill, Graye, Avian, and a mix of others stayed as well. We were all quiet, lost in thoughts of mixed memories and fears, the flow of our lives. The same thing ran through our minds though. Life, our world, what was going to happen to it.

"I can't believe how fast it happened," Gabriel said suddenly as he stared into the flames, seated only a few feet away from me. "Civilization took thousands of years to build up to where we were. And it was destroyed in just four months."

None of us said anything for a while, each reminiscing on how we had gotten here.

"My aunt was one of the first to get the technology," Bill surprised me when he spoke up. Bill usually wasn't one for many words. "She'd been waiting for four years for a new heart. All the money in the world at her disposal and it couldn't buy her a new organ. Until NovaTor's infection was created. The week after TorBane was approved, her husband had her transported to the facility and she was fine the next month. Cured. Until she choked the life out of Uncle Rich twelve weeks after the operation."

135

A log popped in the fire, sending a billow of red-hot ash into the darkening sky.

"Fifteen hundred had the implants. Fifteen hundred was all it took to wipe out six billion and a half," Avian said. I glanced up at him, watching as the flames danced in his eyes. They were always so serious. I wondered how they would look if none of this had ever happened.

"Everything collapsed so quickly," Gabriel said quietly. "The Army, the Navy, the Marines couldn't fight it off. All the weapons and technology we did have and they couldn't destroy this."

I glanced around at all of them. Gabriel looked so sad and I felt a twinge of pain for him. He'd been in the normal world the longest. How things used to be had been so engrained in him. The world was nothing like how it used to be.

My eyes moved to Bill. He was another one of those people who you just looked at and knew there was a story to them. But I didn't know much of anything about Bill's past. He had very little family as far as I knew. He'd never been married, never had any children even though he had to be in his early forties. I didn't think he had even had any parents left before the world evolved. I sensed that in a way, he almost liked this way of living. Because even though everything was so complicated, life was simpler now. You didn't have to worry about having a nice car, a job, or whatever else people used to worry about. You just had to survive. Bill was good at that.

Graye sat silent, staring into the fire, just like the rest of us. He was a person I could never fully figure out. There was a history to him that he never talked about, that he kept locked up and buried in a deep place. I knew he had been married before, had a daughter. How had he escaped the infection when they didn't? Had he had to leave them and get to a safe place? Somehow I didn't think he could just up and walk away from them. Out of everyone in our circle, he was the angriest at our destroyed world.

"Did you ever run into any marauders?" Gabriel asked Bill, nothing more than a small glance in his direction.

"Just once," he answered as he cleared his throat. "I walked a long ways. There were two of them in a truck, scavenging for food. They had guns but they were desperate."

"What happened?" I asked through the dark.

"I walked away with what I walked into there with." He left it at that. Bill would fight until he had no fight left in him.

"They killed each other off pretty quick," Gabriel said, not directing his recollections at anyone. "They fought over food, open territory. Eventually there was no one left who would fight with them over it."

The stars winked into view overhead, burning with intensity. I was going to have to head up to my post soon.

"How did any of us survive it?" Avian said as he rubbed two fingers over his lips.

No one answered for a while. The sky was now almost pitch dark as I stood, pulling my pack tight around my shoulders. "You were smart. That's how."

I walked away from them, feeling one pair of eyes watching me as I left.

The trees chirped with life as the sun started spreading its rays. I stretched my legs, shaking my body awake. It was harder than I expected to switch my internal clock to a nocturnal sleeping pattern.

I heard boots on the ladder and poked my head over the ledge of the watchtower. Sarah looked up at me with dark circled eyes. I gave her a hand and pulled her up over the edge.

137

She half tripped as she got to the top. I caught her and helped ease her down to the rough bench.

"You alright?" I asked.

"Yes," she said with a small chuckle. "I just didn't sleep well last night." She took a deep breath, closing her eyes for a moment.

I looked at her closely, taking in every detail of her. Her eyes were dark. I guessed she hadn't been sleeping well for a while now. She looked like she had lost a little weight as well.

"Are you feeling okay? You don't look so good."

She gave a laugh, her eyes opening again. They looked tired. "You could try being a little more tactful."

"Blame it on the robot in me," I said with a little bite in my voice. She just smiled up at me and patted the space next to her. I sat and watched as the sun continued to creep up into the sky.

"So *are* you?" I asked. "Feeling okay?"

"I'm fine," she said quietly. It didn't fully feel like the truth. "I just had a seizure this morning. Woke me up."

I didn't feel scared often, but this shook me. There was nothing I could do about the seizures, there was no battle I could fight. I could never be strong enough to fix her. "How many a day?"

"It depends. Some days it's only one. Others it's five or six."

I just shook my head as I looked down into my lap.

"I'm fine." It felt like she was saying it more to herself than to me. "So how are things going with West? Better than with Avian?"

I shook my head, my eyes falling to the boards at my feet. "Feelings are too complicated. How is anyone supposed to deal with it? They just make you crazy."

"Crazy sounds like a good description," she laughed. But it sent her into a coughing fit.

"How ironic is it, that whatever is killing me would have been fixed by what TorBane was supposed to be?" Her voice was shaky as she spoke.

"That's pretty messed up," I said, my eyes scanning the trees before us.

"It could probably still fix me," she said, her voice growing quiet. "The tech. It could probably still heal whatever is broken inside of me."

"Don't say that," I said, my voice sharp as I met her eyes. "Those people who all got infected, they aren't people anymore. They're dead. Don't wish to be one of them."

"I didn't say that, Eve," she said, taking my hand in hers. She felt so fragile. "I'm sorry I upset you."

"Sarah?" I heard the call from the ground beneath us. Avian.

She sighed. "He will hardly let me out of his sight these days."

I didn't blame him. He was scared.

"Coming!" she yelled and headed down the ladder. "Hang in there, Eve. You'll figure out what your heart wants eventually."

I looked over the edge as she went down. Avian's eyes met mine and he gave me a sad half smile. I wasn't sure if I managed to return it.

I waited a few minutes before I climbed down, Tuck, the day watchman, coming to replace me. As I walked toward the kitchen area, I realized I was being followed. I turned to see the child shadowing me.

"Can I help you?" I said awkwardly. I had never been around a child before. How did you talk to one?

He just stared at me with his big green eyes.

"Where's your mother?" I asked as I stopped walking and turned toward him. He halted suddenly, nearly tripping over himself. It only now struck me how odd it was that Victoria was actually his mother. She was so young.

"She's working," he said.

I nodded, still unsure how to interact with Brady. I remembered Victoria had been assigned as seamstress.

"Does she know you're wandering around?" I asked.

He shook his head.

"Maybe you should go back to her." I was squirming by now, itching to get away from a situation I didn't know how to handle.

"Can you teach me how to use this?" I hadn't realized he was holding anything until he held up the slingshot. "He told me you could teach me." I looked as he pointed, my eyes catching West's. He gave me a coy smile. I just shook my head at him and turned back to Brady.

"You think you're big enough to handle that thing?"

He gave a very enthusiastic nod.

"Come on," I said as I glanced back at West, giving him the smug look this time. "I'll give you a few pointers."

I thought the smile was going to crack Brady's face as we moved away from the growing crowd.

We walked down to the lake's edge and stopped at a spot with round stones large enough to use.

"Here," I said as I picked up a medium-sized one and handed it to him. "Show me what you've got."

Brady pursed his lips together and placed the stone in the sling. He closed one eye and pulled it back. Just before he released it, he squeezed both eyes closed. It flew about five feet before it splashed in the water.

"Hmm," I said as I looked everything over. "Try this and keep your eyes open this time."

I adjusted his hands, showing how to properly hold the sling. I showed him how to aim it, told him all the tricks I could think of for better accuracy. He was making every target I gave him within an hour.

"How old are you Brady?" I asked as I watched him hit a tree fifteen feet away.

"Four and a half," he answered as he bent and picked up another stone.

"Brady!" Victoria's frantic voice floated over the tents at our backs. "I've been looking all over for you!"

She rushed over and grabbed onto one of his arms. "I'm sorry if he's been bothering you, Eve. I thought he was with Leah. I've been working all morning."

"No, he's been fine. I've just been teaching him how to use the slingshot. He's pretty good actually," I said. That brought the smile back to Brady's face.

"Well, thank you," she said as she looked down at him.

"Actually, do you have some time? I could really use a few new shirts. Mine are getting a little threadbare."

"Yeah, sure," she said with a grin and a nod. "Come on. I'll measure you right now."

I returned her smile and followed her.

Why did my face feel so hollow lately?

SEVENTEEN

Sleep came all too easily when I finally managed to get into bed. When I woke up that evening though, I was ready to explode.

"What do you mean they went without me?!" I demanded of Gabriel. "Bill and Graye *don't go* on raids without me!"

"They left just before mid-day. We weren't sure where you were. Supplies are low. They had to go." Gabriel wouldn't meet my eyes as he spoke to me.

"You're lying to me," I said as I crossed my arms over my chest. "Of course you knew where to find me. I was the same place I always am this time of day. They don't just go on spur of the moment raids. How could you let them go on a raid without me?"

"Calm down, Eve," Gabriel said in a low voice. He glanced around to make sure no one was listening to our argument. Or rather, my explosion.

"Clam down?! They could get killed out there without me! Worse, infected! How could you let them go without me?"

Gabriel sighed, looking around again. "Avian asked that they go without you."

"What?!" I bellowed. "Avian…and you listened to him? You know I'm the best soldier on raids!"

"Of course, Eve. But, he…" Gabriel struggled for words.

"I'm going now. It's only been six hours, I can still catch up with them."

"Eve, we need you here. The three of you are our best scouts and guards. It's best you stay put."

I wanted to hit Gabriel. I wanted to punch Avian so hard it made his head spin. How could he do this to me? "Is Graye even healed yet?"

"Avian cleared him this morning," Gabriel said quietly.

I clenched my jaw and just shook my head. I couldn't believe this. I had gone on every raid in the last three years. I didn't like being left out.

"I'm going hunting," I said through clenched teeth. I didn't wait for a response as I headed toward the armory.

The door banged against the wall as I shoved it open. I jumped as West whipped around to look at me.

"What are you doing in here?" I nearly shouted.

"I just got off scouting duty," he said defensively. "Just putting my stuff away."

I shook my head and squeezed my eyes closed for a moment. "Sorry I snapped at you. Grab your bow, we're going hunting."

"Really?" he said, his voice hitching up a notch with excitement.

"Yeah, come on," I said, irritated again as I grabbed my bow.

We headed out east, towards the higher mountains. We'd been on enough scouting and hunting trips together now to know how each other moved. We listened and watched as a team.

What I didn't expect was West's cool and easy silence. He never once asked me what was the matter, why I was so angry, or even about how I had been avoiding him again. We were just two soldiers, two hunters.

143

We paused as we came to the edge of the trees. A rock cliff jutted out in front of us, dropping down far enough we couldn't see the bottom. Perched on the edge was the fattest wild turkey I had ever seen.

I gave West one glare, which he returned with a smile that said, *Fine, this one's yours.*

I drew an arrow and sent it slicing through the air. It embedded itself in the turkey's fat neck.

"Well, that couldn't have been easier," West said as he stood from our hiding spot.

"Hey, you won't be complaining when your stomach is full tonight," I shot back as I walked forward and pulled the arrow out of the bird. I wiped it clean on a mossy tree trunk.

"Well, it isn't a bear," he joked as he handed me a length of rope.

I just rolled my eyes at him as we tied it by its legs to the back of my pack. We set out again on a trail heading south without another word.

Being so far away from Eden, we didn't try for anything bigger than birds and rabbits. As we felt the temperature drop slightly as the sun started to think about going down, we took a break on a rock outcropping that overlooked a valley.

I closed my eyes and breathed the summer-scented air in. "I almost wish I could just stay out here for a few nights, away from everything."

"Why don't you?" West asked as he leaned back, propping himself up on his elbows.

"You know why. I have jobs, duties." I took a sigh. "I just wish…"

"That you could have a break," he said. It wasn't a question. He knew he'd filled in the blank.

"Yeah," I said as I let my breath out, opening my eyes to the view before me. "It's all just so…"

"Exhausting?" This time he didn't seem so sure.

"I guess," I said as I looked down at my hands in my lap. The hand that had been eaten away from the barbs was covered in more rippled scar tissue. "It's a lot of pressure I suppose. Not that I've really known any different."

"You're pretty amazing," he said after a few moments of quiet. "You know that?"

"Just 'cause your grandfather made me that way."

"No, *you're* amazing. Eve. The human part of you. You'll never stop fighting for them. You always put them before yourself."

And he was right. As much as I liked being with West, as good and alive as he made me feel, I would keep him pushed away so something like the incident with Graye would never happen again.

"They may be all that's left," I said quietly. "I've got to keep them alive. We're already an endangered species."

"Just don't forget who you are in the process," he said as he looked out over the trees.

"This *is* who I am. I've never been anyone else."

"Well, maybe you need to find something that's just for you."

I considered this. What else was there to do besides what I already was doing?

"Maybe," was all I could say. "Hey, how did you get that scar on your neck? I've always meant to ask you."

"Mountain lion," he said, his eyes going back out over the trees.

We sat there for a moment longer, the sky growing darker. "We'd better get going. I've got night watch tonight."

"You mean every night?" he said as we stood and started down a deer trail.

"Every night," I agreed with him.

145

"No one will do a better job."

"Exactly."

I couldn't look at Avian for the next five days. I knew if I did I would explode on him, and there was a part of me that was human enough to not want to do that.

Eden got a big surprise that fifth day though. Graye and Bill returned. In a truck with a flatbed trailer. Full of non-perishables, clothing, shoes, tents, and other supplies.

We came running out of our tents in the early hours of the morning, alarmed by the noise the truck created. It was a sound a lot of people hadn't heard in years and for some of us, a sound we had never heard outside of the city. Half of us came running out with guns, ready to mow down a Bane on an ATV. Graye had jumped out, arms waving.

We all pitched in, helping to unload the supplies, shipping off the clothing and shoes to Victoria, sending the food to the kitchen help, and sorting everything else out where it needed to go. Once all the work was done, the two of them pulled Gabriel, Avian, and I into a tent.

"Something is happening out there," Graye said. It was only then that I noticed the slightly panicked look in his eyes. "We went in during the night but Bane were coming out of everywhere. It wasn't like before when just a few of them came after us. I don't know, I mean, maybe they were just being more aggressive. We had to take the truck, just to help keep them off of us!"

"Slow down, Graye," Gabriel said, holding a hand up to him. "Were there actually more Bane?"

"I don't know. Maybe. They were just everywhere. We couldn't seem to hide from them."

"They're getting more aggressive," Bill said, his voice low. "We used most of our ammo keeping them off of us."

"We have four bullets left!" Graye said with a fearful sounding chuckle. "It's a good thing we got the truck to start or we wouldn't have gotten out of there."

"If they're getting so much more aggressive, is it going to be possible to go back again?" Avian asked, keeping his voice down. "Especially if they're becoming more active at night?"

Neither of them said anything for a moment. They exchanged looks and I knew their answer before either spoke.

"If it keeps going like this, there's no way," Bill answered.

"I don't know how we made it out of there, much less with all the supplies we got," Graye said as he rubbed his hands together.

"Do we move again?" I asked as I looked at Gabriel.

"It's likely they're getting more aggressive everywhere," Avian said when Gabriel seemed at a loss for an answer. "West said it's designed to spread. There isn't much of any one left to spread it to. It's desperate. Any other cities will probably be the same way. And besides, we have the gardens here. We'd be smarter to stay put."

I swallowed hard as another thought occurred to me. If the Bane were getting so desperate, they were likely to keep pressing further and further into the country and outskirts looking for what was left of the human race.

Something within told me our dangerous world would soon become much more dangerous.

Gabriel pursed his lips and gave a small nod. "That's it then. No more going back into the city. We can't afford to lose anyone else."

I felt an itch inside of me as we disbanded. We needed to do something. I didn't like the feeling that we were just sitting and waiting around to be attacked. But what were we supposed to do? There were billions of Bane out there. How were we supposed to take a stand against them?

EIGHTEEN

I woke up the next afternoon with a plan.

They were going for an all or nothing assimilation. We had to fight back. We were going to have to use the same approach they were using themselves.

We had to get rid of them all.

"Avian?" I called before I even entered the medical tent. I found him washing out a handful of bloody rags in a basin of sharp smelling water. I swallowed hard, knowing we wouldn't be able to go after more bleach. Just one more thing that had become so precious. "What happened?" I asked.

"Brady," he said with a sigh. "He fell out of a tree and split his forehead open. I stitched it up."

"Is he okay?"

"He'll have a nice scar all his life, but he'll be fine." Avian wrung out a rag and set it out to dry on the table. He looked up at me expectantly, waiting for me to say whatever I found important enough to say to break my silent treatment toward him.

I paced around the tent, trying to gather my thoughts into a question, or just a statement, or something.

"The CDU, it shorts out anything cybernetic," I said as I continued to pace.

Avian paused, as if questioning what was going through my mind. "Yes."

"There's got to be designs for it somewhere," I said as I rubbed my cheek, continuing to pace. "If we could get those designs we could figure out a way to make it bigger. There's got to be a way to make a pulse that would destroy anything cybernetic within a certain range. Someone has to have designed something like this when everything started."

Avian turned to face me, his face suddenly tired looking. "It's not that simple, Eve. For starters, where would we even look for plans like that? They'd be in a city. We wouldn't even know where to start. And then there's the matter of getting into the city. It might be possible if we could have free reign of the *right* city for about a week, but that's not going to happen.

"And then there's the materials to even build it. And none of us here would know *how* to build it."

I stopped my pacing and stared at Avian, feeling hollow again. "What are we supposed to do then? Just wait here for them to come get us? They're getting more aggressive, more dangerous than ever. What happens when a dozen Bane come? Thirty, forty, or fifty of them? A thousand? I can't fight them all off. We can't fight them forever!"

Avian took a step toward me and placed his hands on my arms. "Calm down, Eve. Take a deep breath."

I realized my breaths had been coming in short, shallow gasps. My head was spinning and my heart was pounding. "What's wrong with me?" Black spots were forming on the edges of my vision.

"Breathe, Eve," Avian said as he placed his hands on my cheeks, looking into my eyes. I forced myself to focus on the intense blueness of his as I took deep breaths in and out. Slowly, the dizziness in my head ebbed away. "Better?"

I bit my lower lip, closed my eyes, and nodded my head. "Something's wrong with me. Maybe I'm sick."

Avian chuckled. "You're not sick. It's just emotion. It's normal."

"I don't like it," I said. Not even realizing what I was doing, I leaned into Avian's chest and wrapped my arms around his waist. His arms came around my shoulders, his chin resting on the top of my head. It didn't take long for my heartbeat to match the rhythm of Avian's. I wanted to stay there forever and just forget everything that felt so out of control. Everything was safe here.

"Why did you tell Gabriel to send the raid without me?" And just like that, I had broken the peace I had found.

He didn't say anything for a minute. "Because I didn't think I'd survive the few days of not knowing what was happening to you."

Part of me wanted to yell at Avian and tell him he should know I could take care of myself. Another part of me felt...open. Vulnerable.

"We won't ever give up, Eve," he said quietly in my ear.

We stood like that for another long moment. I didn't want to leave. It felt like something inside of me finally relaxed, maybe something that had never relaxed before.

"I need to talk to you sometime. I read the notebook," I said. "Later?"

He nodded.

"First I need to go talk to West," I said, taking a step away, breaking the bubble of comfort. "I have to look through that notebook. There were all kinds of notes in it. Maybe there will be something that will help us figure out a way to win this."

Avian's face fell at the mention of West, but he made a good effort to cover it. "It couldn't hurt."

My eyes met his again and not thinking about what I was doing, I placed my hand on his cheek, feeling stubble forming there. My eyes searched his, wanting to give him promises, not even knowing what they meant. Wanting to give promises I knew I would never be able to keep.

And so I didn't say anything. I simply stepped outside of the tent into the blinding light.

Summer had a way of bringing the people of Eden to life. Everyone bustled around, going about their duties with a smile on their face. In the summer people seemed to feel safer, knowing there was plenty of food and that we wouldn't freeze to death.

I understood then why people kept secrets so often. What if I were to suddenly announce to everyone that we could no longer go on raids? That we could expect at any time to have the Bane come down on us?

Sometimes it was better not to know.

I'd still rather know though.

West was by the lake. He stood in only a pair of pants, washing out his clothes. He looked up at me, his shaggy hair flopping across his forehead as he did.

"I want to look at that notebook again," I said, coming to a stop ten feet away from him, stuffing my hands in my pockets.

"Well, hi, Eve. I'm doing great this beautiful afternoon. How are you?" he said, his eyes slightly annoyed but playful looking.

"Great," I said shortly. "I'd like to look at the notebook again."

His expression stiffened. "Why?"

"Does it matter?"

"Kinda."

"I think I have a right to look at it as much as I like, considering most of it is about me," I said, feeling an itch of annoyance start in my chest.

"Only about a third of it," he said sarcastically as he stepped out of the water, wringing a shirt out.

151

"Why does everything have to turn into a joke with you?" I asked, my tone sharp.

"Geez, Eve," he said as he narrowed his eyes at me. "Wake up on the wrong side of the bed today?"

I clenched my teeth together. My eyes dropped from his, to the pile of his things at the base of a tree. I saw the notebook there, lying next to his pack. Without hesitating, I walked over to it and grabbed it. I started heading back in the direction of my tent.

"Hey! Eve!" he yelled as he started after me. "What do you think you are doing?"

He grabbed my arm, pulling me around to face him.

Before I even realized what I was doing my left hand wrapped around his throat. For half a second, everything flickered black.

"Eve! Stop it! What are you doing?" I heard Sarah's screams from behind me. I dropped my hand. West started coughing violently and fell to his hands and knees. Sarah dropped next to him, her hand on his back.

I took two steps away from him. My mouth opened and closed a few times before I found any words to form. "I'm...I'm sorry. I..." I couldn't seem to find anything else to say so I turned and jogged toward my tent, notebook in hand.

I sank onto my cot, breathing hard. What had I just done? I didn't even remember making the decision to do what I did. I didn't think I was even that worked up over his reluctance.

I pressed my hands over my eyes, trying to calm myself. My chest was hammering again.

Two minutes later the flap of my tent was pushed aside.

"You attacked West?" Avian asked, his voice stiff.

"I'm sorry, Avian! I don't know what happened! It's almost like I blacked out." I couldn't even look up into his face. My eyes remained fixed on the floor.

He didn't say anything, just stood in front of me.

Why wouldn't he say anything?

"Let's take a look at that notebook," he finally said quietly as he sat beside me. I closed my eyes again and leaned into him. He wrapped an arm around my shoulders and gave me a tight squeeze. I took several deep, long breaths.

I sat back up, feeling slightly better, and opened the notebook.

"All this is about you?" Avian asked as we started flipping through tattered pages.

"Just the middle ones," I said.

"That's so bizarre," he mused. "I can't even imagine what it was like for you to read it all."

"Bizarre," I breathed. Avian chuckled.

We turned to the pages that came after all the entries about me. I didn't understand what most of it meant, just that it was the notes about the evolution of the technology that was a part of me and how it changed into the infection.

My eyes were glued to the page as we came upon one entry.

It is spreading. Lab assistant Kelly Strong, who received a hearing implant, has been complaining about uncontrollable movement in her left leg. Other reports have been coming in from other patients as well.

We all assumed project Eve's technology started to evolve because of the chip. How terribly wrong we were. We made TorBane work faster, made it stronger. But we just made it mutate into something that is uncontrollable.

We've made a terrible mistake.

"They should have stopped it right then," I said as we turned the page.

"They thought they could control it," Avian said quietly.

He thumbed through the pages for a moment, hesitating when he started seeing my name pop up, like he didn't want to invade on my privacy.

"It started with me," I said quietly. "I was the first one they tested TorBane on. West said I would have died without it."

And I recounted everything I'd read. How the technology had fixed me and saved my life. How the military blackmailed NovaTor into doing their experiment. How they shut my emotions off.

"They made it so I can't feel anything," I said, my eyes falling from his.

"Do you really believe that?" he asked, lifting my chin so I had to look at him.

I didn't respond.

"Because I don't believe it for one second," he continued. "You might be different. You don't always understand what you're feeling. But you feel. I know you do. You wouldn't keep doing what you do for Eden every day if you didn't."

I could only give him a small smile. I'd never be able to put into words the relief I felt with Avian's assurance that I wasn't empty.

We continued to flip through pages, reading hurried, scribbled notes about what could have been done differently to

154

prevent all of this. If they had been just a little more patient with the technology, they could have saved the world.

"Hang on a second," Avian said, turning a page back.

"What?"

He didn't say anything as he brought the notebook up closer to his face. There was a drawing on the page, an octagonal shaped thing, with other crazy drawings inside of it. Hurried notes were scribbled all around it. None of it made sense to me.

Avian flipped to another page. This one had more drawings. These looked more detailed, like maybe they were the things inside the octagon. Tiny writing was crammed inside of the drawings, so small I had to look very closely to read it.

"What is it?" I asked, looking at Avian.

His nose was only about an inch away from the pages, his eyes squinting. "I don't even know what half of this stuff is. They're materials. Reactive elements. I think this is it."

"What we need to destroy it?"

"I guess," he said as he shook his head. "I didn't think it was this complicated. I had always assumed it was just some kind of electrical pulse but this is far more complex. I never studied engineering or that kind of thing much so I don't really understand it all. But this is more involved than I had thought it would be."

"The infection must be harder to kill off then we realized," I said quietly.

Avian turned the page, finding the next one to be full of notes. I didn't even bother reading it. I wasn't going to understand what it was talking about.

He read through four more pages of notes. After a few minutes he kept flipping back and forth between a few of the last ones.

"It's not finished," he said as he looked up at me. "It's here, I think. But it's not complete. The notes on how to create the core, the thing that makes the whole thing work, they're not here."

"He got infected before he could complete it," I said quietly. West had told me how his grandfather and his father had evolved fairly early on. How could they not, being so involved in everything?

"Why didn't West tell us he had this?" I asked as I narrowed my eyes on the pages. "We could figure it out. West had the instructions on how to save us hidden away in his jacket the whole time. Why has he been hiding it?"

"Hang on, Eve," Avian said with a little sigh. "I'm not positive that is what this even is. We don't know the scale of this thing. For all we know it's for nothing more than our very own CDU."

"Still," I said, the pitch of my voice rising. "Why didn't he tell us? Why has he been hiding it?"

Avian didn't have anything to say to that.

It started building up inside of me. An unfamiliar sensation. It took me a while to recognize it.

It was distrust.

Every moment I had spent too close to West flashed through my head. All the times I had let him kiss me, touch me in any excessive way, filled me with regret. I had been so stupid. I hadn't trusted him in the beginning. I had let my guard down too quickly. He was human, he knew the peril we were all in. So why would he hide something like this?

"He's not getting this back," I said as I stood and started pacing my tent. "How can he even call it his? This kind of information belongs to us all."

"It doesn't do us a lot of good," Avian said as he stood. "If we can't understand what any of it means. How to use it."

"We'll figure it out," I said through clenched teeth.

"You know where an electro-physics engineer is?" I was surprised at the tone Avian used. It wasn't harsh, but it was still unexpected. It felt like he was taking West's side.

"No, but I'll find one," I said as I glared at him.

"Good luck," he said as he stepped toward the door. "I'll see you at dinner."

I headed to the gardens after that. I needed something to distract myself. I was afraid what I might do with all this angry energy built up inside of me. Ripping weeds out of the ground seemed to help a little.

West wasn't at dinner that night. I felt like I should feel guilty or something for what I'd done. I wanted to throttle him though. Why did West have to keep so many secrets?

Avian kept ahold of the notebook, which was fine with me. None of it made sense to me and I had no desire to look over the parts about me again. I remembered every word like they had been branded into my partially cybernetic brain.

Alone on the watch tower that night, I paced from one end to the other. The night was passing slowly, as they had been for the past few. I kept thinking about the notes, wondering how we could use them, *if* we could even use them. My brain hurt from thinking about all the things I could do nothing about.

My eyes scanned the trees.

Something felt off. I couldn't explain it, but I could feel something.

I shifted the rifle in my hand, too on edge to sling it back over my shoulder. My pack was cinched tight to my back. In my agitation, I had sorted through it all twice. Food, water, ammunition. Everything I needed to survive on my own out in the wild. For as long as it would take me to reach a city and take what I needed.

But Bill and Graye claimed it wasn't safe to go into the cities anymore. I didn't think I could fully believe that though until I'd witnessed it myself. Maybe it wasn't safe for them, but it might be for me. I was at least not in danger of getting infected.

They could still blow me apart though.

This dangerous world was becoming impossible.

NINETEEN

My breathing came in steady rhythm as my bare feet beat against the gravel. I checked my surroundings as I ran. The houses were starting to fall away and trees rose up around me. The sound of another set of feet was catching up to me.

I brushed leaves out of my tangled hair as I ducked into the bushes. It felt unnatural for it to be so long.

My feet were agile as I leapt over a fallen tree and crashed through the undergrowth. My pursuer continued to chase after me.

I analyzed the terrain before me, picking out the best path. My hesitation was too long though. The next second I was tackled to the ground.

All I saw after that was red and gleaming metal parts.

The dream haunted me as I joined the others in the gardens the next afternoon. I'd never had that one before.

Red.

There had been so much red.

"Set this in there, will you?" Sarah said as she extended a cucumber toward me. I grabbed it from her and set it in the basket at my feet.

The heat was getting intense, made all the worse by the clouds that were coming in. The air was heavy with humidity. Several people begged for it to rain.

159

With summer midway over, the garden was producing well. This was our second round of early harvesting. There was an abundance of squash, peas, beans, cucumbers, and other delicious vegetables. The kitchen crew had been busy canning the last week or so. Our new cellar was getting its shelves filled quickly.

"Do you know what it is Avian's been working on lately?" Sarah asked as she handed me another cucumber. "He's been obsessed, but he won't tell me what it is he's doing."

Avian and I had both agreed to keep our discoveries quiet. Until we understood what it was we were looking at, we didn't want to give anyone false hope. I was ignoring the fact that maybe that was the same reason West had never told any of us about the notes.

"Why does this project seem so strange?" I diverted. "He gets into different projects sometimes."

"I don't know. He's just being so secretive. And he's been weird lately. I don't know how to describe it."

I did. Desperate hope filled with total inept ability.

"I wouldn't worry about him," I said as I reached for the next vegetable she handed me. It slipped through Sarah's fingers before I grabbed it.

Sarah cursed under her breath, shaking her hand.

"You alright?" I asked as I bent and picked it up off the ground.

"Yeah," she said as she shook her head and went back to work.

"You sure?"

"I'm fine!" she snapped at me.

I watched her closely after that. I didn't understand what the fact that Sarah seemed to be having a hard time keeping her grip on things meant.

But I was sure it wasn't good.

That evening, I watched as one of the afternoon scouting groups arrived back at camp. Among them was West, who wouldn't even look me in the eye as he grabbed a bowl of soup and headed straight for his tent.

Good. I didn't want to talk to him either.

I didn't know if I would ever be able to trust him again.

That night as I went up the tower for watch duty, Avian followed me, West's notebook in hand.

"I recognize these things here," Avian said as he sat on the bench. "These things here could be found at any hardware store. Most of these," he said, pointing to something else. "Could be found in just about any lab. But these," he said, indicating another few things. "I'm not even sure what they are."

My eyes scanned the trees. I had that feeling again.

"There's got to be someone out there who knows what it is," I said distractedly.

"Have you talked to West about this yet?"

I shook my head. "I don't think I can face him without doing something stupid again."

"He may know what we're looking at," Avian said quietly. "We should talk to him."

"Feel free," I said as I paced.

"I'm serious, Eve. He might know something. I think he's a lot smarter than any of us realize. What he said about the infection having been designed to spread. It makes sense. He's bound to have picked up on a lot of things from his family."

"He was thirteen when everything happened. I doubt he learned too much about electro physics, or whatever."

"Don't underestimate inherited intelligence. I think we should talk to him."

"Fine," I sighed. I fought back the urge to send Avian back to his tent. It was setting me on edge to have him talking at me. I needed to be on full alert.

As darkness overtook the light Avian fell asleep on the bench, the notebook balanced on his chest. I sighed in relief when I heard his heavy breathing. Finally, silence.

The air felt thick as the clouds kept building. There was a charge running through the atmosphere, like the sky was ready to split apart at any moment.

Two hours before dawn would have broken, the thing I had been waiting for finally happened.

The sound of a chopper buzzed through the air. A few moments later I picked up on the sound of another. I barely made out the tiny black dots in the sky to the west of Eden.

I cursed under my breath. They were slowing down in their approach.

Twenty seconds later, the glow of a stream of fire blazed through the pre-dawn sky.

"NO!" I screamed, true horror filling me for the first time.

Avian jerked awake as the scream ripped from my throat. His eyes followed my line of sight.

Both helicopters had fire billowing out from them.

They were burning the gardens.

"Gabriel!" Avian bellowed as he leapt down the ladder and started sprinting through Eden. I flew down after him, heading directly to the tree line.

I had to be careful not to crash into any trees in the nearly nonexistent light as I plowed through the woods. I pulled my pack in front of me, digging though it for more ammunition, putting it into a side pocket.

The glow of the flames told me I was getting close. It took me a while to realize the sound of the helicopters had disappeared.

162

I was about fifty yards away when it came running at me. A nearly all metal Bane leapt at me from the trees. I pulled my gun and blasted its head open before it got within ten feet of me.

I had just gotten to the fence line when another tackled me, its hands closing around my throat. My gun flew clean from my hands. I rolled, coming on top of it. Getting my hands free, I attacked its head with my clenched fists. As soon as the outer metal was broken I started pulling at wires and gears. Its form grew still a few seconds later. I pried its dead hands away from my throat, picked my handgun up from the dirt, and fired.

Finally, I turned back to the fence, my fingers linking in the chinks. I could only stand there and watch as the rows of peas, spinach, tomatoes, and pretty much everything else, burned. The fruit trees were totally engulfed, the flames reaching up into the night from the branches.

Shouts started racing toward me in the chaos the early morning had become. There was nothing we could do but stand at the fence and watch everything we had built the last five years burn.

Maybe there was a God out there. The sky finally couldn't hold any more pressure and the rain started to fall. As I watched the fires sizzle out, a hand slipped into mine. I didn't even have the will to turn and see who it was. It felt like nothing mattered anymore.

We were finally done for.

TWENTY

Even though no one had died, the feeling of death and despair hung in the air like a ghost.

We salvaged what we could out of the garden. Two tomato plants, half a row of squash, a small patch of potatoes, and one broccoli plant was all that had survived. The amount of food it would eventually produce would feed everyone in Eden for less than a week.

Inventory of our stores was immediately taken. We had enough to last about four months if we all went on starvation diets.

Two days after the burn, I had taken Bill with me on scouting duty. He got the truck that I had found at the cabin to start and together we filled the back with everything that had been in the storage room beneath the house. That would buy us another month or so if we were careful. Nearly everyone cried when we drove the truck back through the forest and showed them the supplies.

Three weeks after the burn, I came back from my morning scouting duty, joining the others for dinner. We were each given a roll and half a scoop of canned corn. After receiving my plate, I sat next to Sarah. My skin was turning a light shade of pink under my normally tanned tone. The sun had been brutal the last few days.

"You should go see Avian about that," Sarah said as she looked at my arm that rested next to her pale white one. "He has some aloe he could put on it."

"I'm fine," I said as I tore a small piece off of my roll. "I'm sure someone will need it more than me. It's not like it hurts."

Sarah nodded her head, not wanting to argue with me. She scooped her corn into her spoon and raised it to her lips with a shaking hand. I looked at her closely as she chewed the bite carefully.

Sarah looked like a skeleton. She had started dropping weight even before the burn happened, and then when we all went on starvation rations, she started declining even more rapidly. She was frightening to look at now; I didn't want to know how she would look in a few more weeks, let alone a few months when the food ran out.

"I'm not very hungry," I said as I picked my plate up and scooped my corn onto her hers. I broke half of my roll off and set it there as well. "Why don't you have mine?"

"Eve," she said as she looked at me with tired eyes. "You have to eat too."

"I'm not hungry," I said again as I stuffed what was left of my roll into my mouth. As I stood, my stomach growled. Before Sarah could protest further, I walked toward the medical tent. Just as I was about to step inside, West stepped out, nearly crashing into me. My eyes dropped to the tear in his shirt. His sleeve was soaked in blood and there were fresh stitches in his arm.

"You alright?" I asked stiffly.

"Fine," he said shortly. "I just fell." He walked away without saying anything else.

A strange rock seemed to form in the pit of my stomach as I swallowed hard and stepped inside.

"Hi," Avian said as he looked up at me with a small smile. He pulled off a pair of bloodied latex gloves.

"I have an hour or so," I said as I sat on a stump, pulling my knees to my chest and resting my arms on them.

"You should be sleeping," he said as he busied himself with cleaning up. "You're going to over work yourself."

"I'm not sure that's possible."

"Of course it is," he said as he finished up and sat across his examination table from me. "You're still human. Look how much weight you've dropped already."

I didn't look, but I knew Sarah wasn't the only one who had dropped a few pounds. We all had.

"Are you still eating your rations?" he asked me.

"Yes," I lied. But I sensed Avian knew I wasn't telling the truth.

He knew better than to argue with me though, so he just turned and pulled the notebook off of a shelf.

Over the past few weeks, we had been studying the last pages of the notebook. Avian had been trying to match its parts to those of our own CDU, but he wasn't making much headway. It all just ended up leaving him frustrated.

I watched him as he studied the illustrations.

How was it possible for someone to be so good? We'd been so fortunate to have Avian in Eden. He'd given up his life in a way to keep us alive, tying himself to this one place, a constant prisoner. How had I been so lucky to have him come into my life? It could have been anyone who found me, some twisted man who could have taken advantage of a young girl who didn't know who she was, didn't know anything.

My chest felt tight when he looked up at me. I realized he had asked me a question and I mumbled something I hoped would serve as an answer. A weird feeling formed in my stomach. I didn't know how to identify it. I had that hollow feeling but also had a burning desire to fill it back in with something. And I couldn't seem to look away from Avian as he continued studying. I found my eyes studying his hands as he flipped through pages of the notebook. I recalled the day he had held my hand. The oxygen seemed to freeze in my lungs.

"I have to go," I suddenly said. I stood and walked out of the tent before he even said anything.

The hollow feeling continued to get worse as I walked toward my own tent. I soon felt sick from it.

What was wrong with me? Where was this coming from?

I lay on my bed and squeezed my eyes closed, forcing myself not to think about anything as the back of my eyes burned.

The glass felt smooth under my fingers, flowing perfectly, one molecule into another. How was it possible to make something so perfect and even? It warmed under my hand, a ghost of my flesh forming in fog as the heat of my body met the cool of its surface.

I realized then that the air around me was freezing.

Turning, my body chilled as my eyes scanned the cinder block walls. No outside light tricked in, only a single light bulb hanging from the ceiling cast a cold shadow on everything. My chest tightened as I searched for an escape. There wasn't even a single door, just the window. A bed was pushed into one corner of the room. This was as good as a prison cell.

As I turned back to the window, a pair of earthy eyes stared back at me.

"West!" I screamed as I put my hands against the glass. "Get me out of here!"

He stared at me, his lips set in a firm line. A single tear slipped down his cheek.

"West, please," I said, slapping my palm against the cool surface. "Please let me out!"

"Please, grandpa," he said, turning away from me. "Can we please let her out?"

There was suddenly a shadowy figure behind West, standing in a doorway.

"She may attack you again. You know she doesn't trust you," a gravelly voice said.

West turned back to me. Another tear rolled down his face. Slowly he raised a hand to the glass, our palms and fingers separated only by the window. "I know," he whispered.

My eyes widened in the window's reflection as his expression harden, betraying the hurt I had caused him. I shook my head, taking a step away from the glass. I crawled up into the bed, tucking my knees under my chin, my eyes never leaving West's.

"She's not really human anymore," the shadowed voice said again. "If she were she would see what she is doing to you."

West continued to stare at me with mixed emotions on his face. He brought both his hands up, pressing them to the glass as if he wished he could slip through it, and push me further away, all at the same time.

I saw him mouth my name, but the rumble of a noise I couldn't identify was rising quickly in my ears. For a moment I was panicked the building might be collapsing on us, one floor crashing down on the next. But the walls weren't shaking, dust wasn't falling from the ceiling. The noise continued to grow to a deafening point. It saturated every corner of my body.

"Eve!" I saw him scream though the glass. And then everything was silent.

The next second the window exploded into a billion stars of red death.

I jerked upright with a gasp. My hands wiped at my face, trying to brush away the shards of glass that weren't really there. I felt momentarily panicked when I realized everything was totally black. Had I not just been dreaming? Had I been blinded by something while I slept?

The panic ebbed away as I realized it was simply dark because of the muggy night. I leapt out of my bed as I realized that meant I was beyond late for my night watch. I pulled my pack on and jogged out of my tent.

Most all the fires had completely died out and there wasn't a soul around as I crossed camp. Gripping the rungs, I scaled the ladder to the watchtower. I jumped violently when I was about to climb over the ledge and a head popped over. West looked at me with a smirk.

"Hope you enjoyed your beauty sleep," he said as he extended a hand and pulled me up and over the edge.

"I don't usually oversleep," I said as I pulled the straps of my pack tighter, my eyes scanning the trees.

"You've been working yourself to death for the last month. And running on no food. If you were human you'd be collapsing from exhaustion more often."

My stomach turned to stone as I recalled what the man from the dream had said. *She's not really human anymore.* West chuckled, but I couldn't seem to force even a crack of a smile.

West sat on the bench, patting the empty space next to him. I eyed him for a moment. I hadn't been close to him for a while now. The last time we had touched I could have easily killed him. He must have known his life was in danger.

I sat.

West turned his gaze to the dark night. I followed, looking into the endless star-peppered sky.

"Do you ever wonder if there is anyone else out there?" he asked quietly, his eyes never leaving the stars.

"No," I answered honestly.

"I can't imagine there isn't," he said. "All that space. We can't be the only living things out there.

"Makes you feel kind of important though, if we are the only ones. All that beauty and it's there for only our eyes."

I looked over at West, watching him as he observed the heavens. His hair fell across his brown eyes, in need of a haircut. His shoulders were shrugged up to his ears as he leaned back. In that moment I saw something in West. Not the boy who always turned everything into a joke, always got to me in a bad way. But the boy who had to live with the knowledge that it was his family who had destroyed the world.

"I want to hate you, you know," he said, though he still didn't look at me. "For the way things have been between us these last few weeks. I want to hate you for attacking me like that, for taking the notebook. For all the ways I see you look at Avian. I want to hate you for the ways you make me feel. For the way I feel every time I think about the times we kissed."

"I don't want you to hate me," was all I could say.

"That's the thing. I can't. I don't think I could ever hate you Eve."

"I'm still just not sure I can trust you."

West finally looked at me, his eyes almost empty looking. "That I can hate."

TWENTY-ONE

Bill and Graye headed off to the south while West and I headed east. Now that I had figured out I could be around West again without attacking him, I had agreed to let Gabriel put him back in our scouting group.

The sun beat down on us with an intensity that was beyond miserable. Had I felt pain like the rest of everyone I was sure my sunburned skin would make it beyond uncomfortable to move, much less go on an entire scouting operation.

West and I walked silently through the woods, eyes searching the tree line. Birds chirped in an annoying afternoon chat. Insects hummed. But there were no other sounds. No traces of any Bane.

"Clear?" West whispered, clutching his rifle tightly in his hands.

"Clear," I said as we finished sweeping around the perimeter of the gardens. West waited at the bottom while I scaled the biggest nearby tree. When I reached the top, I shook its branches with as much force as I possessed. The entire top half of the tree swayed.

One hundred yards away I saw a figure wave at me. They knew it was safe to come work.

I dropped down to the ground and straightened my pack. We had to be more careful than ever these days. The Bane obviously knew where the gardens where and must know we

would be nearby. It wouldn't be too difficult for them to track us down now, using the gardens as a trap. That was why we scouted the area every morning first, before a small crew came to tend.

Not that there was much to tend anymore. The heat wave wasn't letting up and everything was withering away. Soon there would be nothing left.

West and I set out to the north again.

"What do you think is going to happen to us now?" West said quietly as we walked.

I didn't answer for a moment, trying to collect my thoughts. "Eventually we're going to have to move. Sooner than later."

"Why do you say that?"

"It's obvious. We have supplies for a while but winter is coming. We don't have enough to last that long. We're going to have to move where it's warmer or we're going to starve to death," I said as I stepped over a log. "We have natural resources here, animals to hunt, but it's not going to be enough to sustain everyone through the entire winter."

West was quiet for a while. "Have you talked to Gabriel about this? You're right, but he's going to have to be the one to initiate it."

"I will," I said as I readjusted my grip on the shotgun in my hands. "The problem is, how do we move that many people without being spotted by Bane? How do we move that many supplies at once?"

"That's a good question," he said quietly as his eyes jerked to the right. A squirrel scampered down a tree.

I briefly considered shooting the animal. I decided against it. With as little meat it would provide it wouldn't be worth the ammunition. As if on cue, West's stomach let out a rumbling growl. I chuckled.

172

"Okay, we've seriously got to bring back some food. I can't take the starvation rations anymore," West said in exasperation.

"When we're ready to head back we'll look," I said as I started the climb up the low hills that looked over Eden.

I was grateful we didn't see anything the entire day. While it was boring to be walking endlessly through the woods, it was better than running into something we didn't want to. As we started back in the direction of Eden, we kept our eyes peeled for anything to eat. I sensed there was something West wanted to talk to me about, but had been putting it off the entire day. And now he had to be quiet if he wanted to eat.

The woods were silent as we moved, as if sensing we were on the lookout to take something home to Eden's bellies. Something to the left caught West's eye and he drew his bow and an arrow before I even caught sight of what he had seen. The arrow sliced through the air and the next second we heard a scream.

A human one.

We were both bolting through the trees without a second's hesitation, my mind running through the possibilities of what we might find. Surely not Bane. They didn't feel pain and therefore would never scream. Could it be Bill? Graye? Everyone else knew better than to wander this far from Eden on their own.

He was slumped against a tree, clutching at his left shoulder. He had already broken off the shaft of the arrow. His eyes were squeezed shut in agony. He bit his lower lip to hold back the scream.

"Holy…" West breathed as the man came into view. I didn't recognize him. "I thought it was a deer or something. What is he doing out here?"

We both dropped to the man's side, his eyes flying open in delirious confusion.

"You've been shot with an arrow," I said, my voice calm and even. "We have a doctor at our camp. I am going to have to pull the arrow out or it will cause more damage as I move you."

The man's green eyes opened wide, searching the sky for things only he could see now.

"West, help me," I said as I placed my hands on the base of the arrow that was still embedded into his chest. "This is going to hurt him."

West shifted forward, placing his hands on the man's shoulders, being careful to stay clear of the wound. In one swift movement, I yanked the rest of the arrow out. The man screamed in agony.

"We need something to stop the bleeding," I said as I tried to recall what Avian would do in a situation like this. West slid off his pack and pulled his shirt off. It was damp with sweat but it would work. I pressed it into the wound and together we secured it with a length of rope from my pack. Another scream leapt from his throat as I picked him up, gathering him securely in my arms.

"What was he doing out here?" West asked as we jogged through the trees. We were still far from Eden. So much for getting food for tonight.

"On the run maybe?" I said as I glanced down at him. He'd had only the clothing on his back. I hadn't seen any provisions with him, no tent, no food.

It took us nearly an hour to get back to Eden. Even my arms weren't strong enough to carry him by myself the entire trip and West had taken half the load. The man had turned a pasty white and he shivered violently, despite the blazing sun above us. He bled through West's shirt. My left arm was covered in his blood.

Avian was in the medical tent when we stumbled into it. He set the notebook down and jumped to his feet.

"Who is he?" Avian asked as he pulled on a pair of gloves and removed West's bloodied shirt. He started cutting away the man's own t-shirt. He barely even whimpered as his wound was jostled. Until Avian began cleaning it. Then he screamed.

"He was just in the woods. We didn't realize it was a person," I said as I moved out of Avian's way.

"I thought he was a deer," West said, his eyes looking tortured. "I couldn't really see anything. Something moved in the trees and I just shot."

"Where'd he come from?" Avian asked. He threaded a needle. I watched with wide eyes as he started sewing the man back up.

"We don't know," West said quietly. "Is he going to be okay?"

"A chest wound like this is serious. It's close to his heart and his lungs. There are a lot of major blood vessels in that area. I can't repair the internal damage so there's a risk that even if the bleeding stops on the outside, it may not stop on the inside."

West's face blanched white.

The man opened his eyes, which rolled around in his head. "My wife," he said. His voice was rough sounding and then I noticed the tears rolling back toward his ears. "My son. They found us. I...was out. They got them...had to run."

We all looked up at each other. Avian dropped what he was doing and opened the box that contained the CDU. Less than thirty seconds later he had it charged up and calibrated.

175

The man jerked away as it was pressed to his bare arm. His eyes continued to roll around in his head.

Organic, but dying quickly.

"Where did you come from?" I asked, leaning over him. His eyes remained unfocused.

"He may not be able to speak right now," Avian said as he cut the threads of the stitches. "His body is going into shock."

"Where did you come from?" I asked again.

"E… east," he barely managed to whisper. "Been running since… day before yesterday." He then started coughing violently. Red splatters coated his lips.

"His lung has been punctured," Avian said in despair as he took half a step back and rubbed his hand over his hair.

"He's not going to make it," I said quietly, looking back down at the man. Avian shook his head.

"I killed him," West whispered, backing up to sit on a stump.

"You didn't know," I said, glancing at him. "You were trying to feed us, keep us alive."

"He's obviously not food," West's voice was hoarse.

Two hours later, the man whose name we didn't even know, took his last shallow breath. Avian checked his pulse and pronounced him dead. Gabriel instructed Bill and Graye to bury him on the outskirts of camp. After it was done, Gabriel, Avian, West and I gathered back in the medical tent.

"They're getting close again," I said as I paced the length of the tent. "Attacks don't usually come from the east. It's just mountains for miles and miles."

"Graye was right," Avian spoke. "They're getting more and more aggressive. This man probably lived in a cabin somewhere with his family. They tracked him down. We all know what they did to the gardens a few weeks ago."

Gabriel rubbed at his beard, deep in thought. I wanted him to say something, to tell us what to do. But he didn't seem to know what to say.

"We're going to have to leave," I spoke when he didn't. "We have a few months of food left but it won't be enough to last us through the winter."

"Where would we go?" Gabriel asked. I saw something frightening in his eyes that I had never seen there before. A loss of hope.

"It would have to be south," Avian spoke up, his eyes coming to my face.

"Exactly," I said. "If we can get somewhere warm enough we should be able to scavenge for food until we can figure something else out. I think it would also be wise to go southwest. Heading east first will take too much time. The trucks we have might not make it very far and it could take months just to hike over the mountains with all of our supplies, if or when they break down. By then winter will claim the rest of us."

Gabriel nodded his head, his brain seeming to start to work again. "I agree but going west won't be easy either. We leave now and we'll be crossing nothing but desert in the heat of summer."

"Do we wait?" West asked, the first he had spoken since the meeting began.

"We risk the Bane pressing further in on us if we wait," I pointed out.

"We risk the desert heat claiming us if we go now," Avian said, sitting forward, resting his elbows on his knees. "Temperatures can get close to 120 degrees out that direction. Without massive amounts of water, no one would last long."

We seemed to be at a standstill. What was the right thing to do? The safest thing?

"I say we take it to everyone in Eden," West said. "We have to let everyone know what is happening. They have to be figuring it out for themselves anyway. Let's let everyone decide what to do."

"I agree," Avian said as he sat back again.

Gabriel nodded, his eyes thoughtful. "Fine. We'll call a meeting tonight after dinner."

West and Gabriel exited the tent to spread the word. I stood rooted and closed my eyes. I counted backward from ten to help push out the feelings of loss and despair I didn't know how to deal with. A warm hand slipped into mine, immediately enhancing the calm I was looking for. Without opening my eyes, I raised our hands to my face and rubbed the back of Avian's hand against my cheek. I could sense Avian's eyes on my face and could feel the worry rolling off of him.

I wanted to reassure him that everything was going to be okay. I wanted to tell him that we were all going to make it out of this. I wanted to tell him that I knew exactly what to do.

But I couldn't do any of those things. I didn't have any answers.

I finally opened my eyes and looked into Avian's. His eyes burned as he looked down at me.

It took everything I had in me to let go of Avian's hand and stepped outside into the dying light.

You can't have both.

Avian was right. Even though I didn't know how to handle feelings like this, I knew what I had been doing was wrong. I couldn't have both. It was unfair to them. And it was tearing me apart.

Someone had to sit out and keep watch during the meeting so West volunteered. The rest of us gathered in the center of camp. I watched them as they assembled, saw the way the lines around their eyes were tighter, the way their breathing was just slightly shallower. Everyone was on edge.

Our already slight frames were all the more thin.

"Thank you for coming tonight," I was surprised when it was Avian who took control of the meeting. I glanced over at Gabriel. He sat to the side of Avian, his eyes on his hands in his lap. His face looked empty. "You are all aware of what happened a few weeks ago. I know everyone has been thinking about it but it is time we actually talked about things and what this means for our future.

"We will run out of food in the middle of the winter. We have enough for everyone for a few more months but with most all this year's harvest gone to ash we will not make it to next spring.

"Add to that fact that the Bane have become more aggressive. They're using weapons now. We can't go into the cities anymore. They have been pushing further and further into the country. Just today a man passed away who was on the run after his family was attacked. He came from the east. We've never heard of them pressing in from the mountains like that."

Avian cleared his throat, his eyes dropping to the ground. I realized how hard this must be on him, having to be the one to finally bring this to everyone's attention. He was strong in a way I had never realized before. He may not have been as physically tough like Bill and Graye were but he was a rock, a foundation for the rest of us.

"It has been proposed that we need to move," his voice broke, just a tiny bit." "I don't think there is any other choice. The natural resources we have will not carry us to spring. We're going to have to go someplace warmer. Southwest.

"The question is when and how to move," Avian said as he looked around at our fellow men and women. "If we leave right now we would be crossing the deserts in the hottest time of the year. And yet if we don't leave now our supplies will become all the more depleted. And we risk being found.

"It would be incredibly dangerous to move any way we do it. If we leave all at once it will be easier for Bane to spot us. At the same time, there is safety in numbers. We can have our best scouts with us all at once. If we move in smaller groups it will be easier to stay hidden, to keep a low profile. But each group could have no more than one or two of our most skilled scouts. It also splits all of us. There's the risk that we might not all ever be reunited. Without electronic devices it will be difficult to stay in contact and reconvene.

"It is up to you. We won't force any decisions on you. This affects all of us. The choice is yours."

Everyone was silent for a long while. How was anyone supposed to make this decision? There were pros and cons to each choice. There was no clear decision to make. Each carried the possibility of destruction, with being wiped out in one big cluster or the chance we would never be a group again, a family.

"We could go in two sets," Graye spoke up. "If we split right down the middle, one group could go in a few weeks or so when things will start to cool slightly. We could leave messages for the group to follow, traces the Bane won't pick up on. Leave a trail for each other to the new location. The last group will bring the rest of the food. We have the two trucks, if we camouflage them well enough, we should be able to bring enough supplies. At least until we run out of fuel."

The group was quiet for a bit, mulling over Graye's idea.

"That seems reasonable to me," Avian finally said. "Eve? Gabriel?"

"It seems a viable option," I answered.

Gabriel simply nodded his head.   His behavior was disturbing.

"All those in favor of Graye's plan?" Avian asked, turning his eyes over the group.

The majority of hands, including mine, went up. After a few hesitant and thoughtful seconds, the rest of them went up as well.

"It is agreed then," Avian said with a nod. "We will make preparations. I think until then our priority should be to hunt as much as possible and gather as many other resources as we can find. Traveling would be hard under normal circumstances, but considering the conditions we have been under these last few weeks, it will be even more difficult. We will need food to keep up our strength. Our survival has become all the more challenging."

A flurry of mixed emotions was tangible as everyone left. I watched their faces as they did, Wix, Victoria, Morgan. Each of them had different thoughts behind their eyes, but there was one unifying one: we had to survive.

TWENTY-TWO

The beast hit the ground with a loud cry. A circle of red started forming on his neck before he was even fully down. He twitched for a few moments before the fight seeped out of him.

I slung my bow back across my shoulders and leapt down the small cliff I had been hiding on. I crouched beside the animal, checking to make sure it was fully dead. I saw my own reflection in the buck's eye as he took his last strangled breath.

I pulled my arrow out of his neck and wiped it clean on the grass at my feet. I placed two fingers under my tongue and gave a loud whistle. Two minutes later Bill and Graye joined me. Together we started the mile journey back to Eden with the animal.

We had been hunting nonstop for the last three days. While scouting duty was as important as ever, it was now just as important to find food. We had brought back three does, a few foxes and rabbits, and now this buck. The kitchen had been busy cooking, bottling, and drying the meat, others tanning the hides.

Not only would our food supplies have to last us the few weeks until the first group left, and then another month after the second group left, it would also have to last the week, maybe two, journey into the unknown. And who knew what immediate food sources would be like once we reached where we were going.

It had been brilliant on Avian's part to put everyone to work on making preparations to leave. With everyone so busy, there was no time for anyone to sit and worry too much about the fact that we were moving, that we would be traveling so far. Everyone had a role to play. Hands were needed to forage the woods nearby, searching for berries and edible mushrooms. Others were needed to collect water in any containers we could spare.

As I walked through Eden, after I had dropped off the buck, I caught a glimpse of Gabriel. He sat at the entrance of his tent, staring out over the rest of us. He watched as the rest of us worked. He wasn't supervising, checking to make sure everything was done right. He was just gone. He'd checked out.

Checking to make sure no one was watching me, I poked my head inside Avian's tent.

Sarah had not come out of the tent since before the meeting. When I pressed Avian about it he simply told me that she was not feeling well. I didn't think he was intentionally lying to me. He was lying to himself.

"Sarah?" I said quietly through the dim light. "Sarah?"

Only silence greeted me. I stepped inside, closing the flap behind me. It felt muggy inside and it was suffocatingly hot as the sun beat down above. "Sarah?" I said again as I knelt next to her cot.

A thin sheet was gathered up around her neck, damp and clinging to her skin where it touched her. Her brown curls were matted and stuck to her face. Her skin clung to her cheekbones. Her eyes were closed. They looked like they were sinking into her head.

"Sarah," I called again, my voice insistent. I felt the urgent need to wake her up. Now. "Sarah," I said again as I placed my hands on her and shook her slightly.

"Eve." The tent was suddenly flooded with light as Avian opened the flap. "Leave her alone." He waved me out.

"She looks like death," I whispered as I followed him out into the light. "What is happening to her?"

Avian pursed his lips together, his eyes dropped to the ground. His hand rubbed over his short hair. He did this when he felt stressed or worried.

"She's getting worse, isn't she?" I asked.

It took a moment before Avian nodded his head. "She's not having as many seizures but she's sleeping the majority of the time. She's woken up a total of maybe two hours in the last twenty-four. She can't keep much of anything down.

"I think she might have cancer," he said. He sounded totally defeated. "It explains the respiratory failure, the seizures, the overall declining health. And once symptoms like this show up... It's advanced. I don't know what else to do for her," he said in a hoarse whisper. "Maybe if I were an actual doctor..."

"Hey," I cut him off, giving him a sharp look. "Don't talk like that. You're an amazing doctor. Sometimes nature just can't be fought."

He nodded his head, his eyes still on the ground.

"There's West," I said as I looked back toward the center of camp. "Come on. We're supposed to meet again."

Avian, West, Bill, and I all sat around the long dining table and smoothed the plans we had written out over its rough surface.

"If the scouts continue at the rate you have been going, we should gain at least a few more weeks worth of food supplies, maybe even another month," Avian took control of the meeting again. It bothered me that he had not even asked Gabriel to join us. He knew as well as I did though that it was pointless. Gabriel was gone for the time being. "We need a few more things that we're going to have to go look for. We need more water containers. We'll go through what we have quickly.

"We're also going to need a way to transport a large amount of people. The supplies we will have to haul will fill the beds of the trucks. Bill, the trailer you and Graye brought back from the city will work. I'm hoping we can fix up the old one that was rusting away by the lake. I've already got a few people working it. This trip will go much faster if we can ride instead of walk.

"We need a way to communicate with the second group. A way to leave signs the Bane won't notice. Any ideas?"

No one jumped right away. "Think about it for a while, let us know if you come up with anything," Avian said.

"The other issue. It will be invaluable if we can take the trucks with us the entire way. We're going to have to look for gas stations, as far on the outskirts of towns we can find. We also run the risk that any fuel that will be left will have gone bad. It's been nearly six years since any new fuel was brought in. It may very well destroy the engines."

"We don't exactly have any other choice though, do we," West piped in.

"Exactly," Avian said as he looked up at West. "Bill has maps, we'll carefully plan our route, try to avoid any Bane, any big city areas."

With this, Bill reached into his pack and pulled out a book that must have weighed a good ten pounds. He flipped it open somewhere near the middle and started scanning through pages.

"Where did you get that?" I asked, my eyes growing wide. Maps weren't common.

"Got it from a man who didn't need it anymore," he said, not looking up from the map.

"This is where we're at," Bill said as he pointed to a place on the map. I recognized the shape of the lake, the terrain of the mountains. "This is the closest city," he dragged his finger over the page. "We should find somewhere to get fuel on the outskirts here. It's a small city so there is a chance there won't even be any Bane. They tend to flock to the larger ones. We could get out of there scot-free."

"What about the groups?" I asked as I looked up at the faces around me. "Who is going to go when?"

Avian didn't answer right away as he took all of us in, gauging the abilities of each individual. "Obviously you have to go in the first group, just in case we run into any problems with Bane." I nodded in agreement. "I'm also going with the first group."

"What about the rest of them?" I immediately protested. "What if they need you?"

"And what if the first group needs me?" he said as he looked at me sharply. "I can't clone myself, Eve. I can't be in both places. I'll ask for a volunteer and train them in every way I can before we go. There's no other choice. I think it's clear that the first group will be in the most danger. That's where I feel I need to be."

"If Eve is going with the first group, it would probably be best if Graye and I went with the second group, to even things out," Bill said. "Gabriel can also go with us, since you two are going with the first group."

"That's a good idea," Avian nodded in agreement. "I suppose you can pick which group you want to go with," he said to West, his jaw suddenly tightening up.

"I'm going in the first group," he said without any hesitation. His eyes flicked up to mine.

"Fine," Avian said. "We'll let the rest of Eden decide when they want to go, with some monitoring to make sure things are even."

We disbanded with plans to scout for water containers and a time later that evening to meet with everyone in Eden to layout the plans. Then it occurred to me: if Avian was going with the first group, Sarah would have to come with us as well. From what I had just seen, I couldn't imagine any way she would be able to move. I didn't think she would even be able to walk out of her own tent, much less survive the thousand miles or more that were ahead of us.

Groups were chosen. Avian and Bill had monitored and made sure things would be even, that there was no one group that would be bigger than the other, that one group would not be left without someone to make sure everyone stayed fed or protected.

Something settled over Eden as our futures were laid out before us. Things were becoming more real every day. We were going to have to leave the place we had all called home. This had been our safe haven, the place we had fled the world to. And now we were leaving it behind.

The next morning, birds chirped annoyingly loud as I padded silently through the undergrowth. They were complaining about the heat as well. My eyes watched the lay of the land, recalling certain trees and rocks.

I stepped away from the trees toward the cabin. After watching the area for a moment to make sure it was clear, I walked inside.

The groan of floorboards sounded from one of the back rooms and I quickly crouched behind the dusty couch, my handgun held firmly in my clammy hands. As I heard steps approaching, I poked my head out. My eyes met a pair of worn brown boots.

"What are you doing here?" I said as I stood. The barrel of West's shotgun was immediately pointed at my chest.

"Geez, Eve!" he snapped as he jumped. He immediately lowered the gun. "I could have shot you! I don't think even you could recover from a blow like that."

"Probably not," I mused, my eyes scanning my surroundings again. "How do you know about this place?"

"I scouted it out, same as you," he said as he headed back to the other room. "I'm assuming this is the house where you found all the food?"

"Um hum," I mumbled as I followed him. The room held two large white boxes that were hard sided and nearly as large as me. It also contained a sink, a few cupboards, and a small counter space. West opened the cupboards and my eyes grew wide as I recognized the round white bottles he started pulling out.

"Bleach." I breathed. "I didn't see it when I was here last. And look at those, they'll be perfect for storing water," I said as I spotted some empty plastic containers on the top shelf.

"Here," West said as he pulled a length of rope out of his pack. "Tie them on for me."

The containers secured to West's pack, we searched the rest of the house for more but didn't find anything useful. We headed outside and started pacing the perimeter.

"Look at these," I said as four blue barrels that were nearly the same size as me came into view.

"Catchment containers," West said, his voice hitching up a notch in excitement. "See that pipe that leads into the top of this one?" he said as his finger traced the line that ran along the roof line and dropped into the first barrel. "These connect them. It's set up as a big containment unit but they would work individually. They'd hold probably 200 gallons between all of them."

"They're nearly empty," I said as I knocked on the side of one. "We could each take one back with us tonight, bring the rest tomorrow. It's nearly time to head back anyway."

We got the catchment system unhooked and drained the rest of the water out of them.

Maneuvering the barrels through the woods wasn't easy but it was worth every push. This was exactly what we needed to survive the heat of the desert.

The silence hung heavy over us as we moved, discomfort growing by the minute. I felt like I had two people inside regarding West. One part of me was constantly infuriated at the way he reacted to everything, the things he said, the way he looked at me. The other half wanted me to constantly move closer, to let him wake up the all too human side of me. Right then I wasn't sure which Eve I was.

West finally broke the silence. "Did you really mean it when you said that you couldn't be around me?"

I instantly wished for the silence back.

"Yes," I answered simply as I maneuvered my barrel around a boulder.

West stopped short in front of me, making me stop as well. He looked back at me, his eyes hard to read. He stuffed his hands in his pockets. "You have no idea what you want, do you?"

"What are you talking about?" I demanded. "The only thing I want is to survive, to have Eden survive."

"No, Eve," he said as his eyes hardened as he shook his head once. "That's not the only thing you want and you don't even know it. You don't think that I don't see what is happening to you? I know you feel something when we're together, that you crave more of it. If you didn't it wouldn't

189

keep happening. But then there's Avian. When you are around him, you're different. You're…yourself. You can't stay away from him, unlike me, even when you're furious with him.

"You want us both," he said more quietly. "But you also need to realize that you *can't have both*."

"I know that," I whispered as I looked away from West and started pushing my barrel again.

TWENTY-THREE

Everyone was ecstatic when we brought the barrels back and I sensed a small feeling of pride that I was part of the team that had located them. I found myself seeking Avian out to report the good news.

I heard his voice floating out from the open aired medical tent. Another voice joined his and they burst into a chorus of laughter. I slowed my approach, stepping behind a tent to conceal myself.

Avian stood next to Victoria, pointing to something in a book. He looked up at her and I watched as his eyes trailed over her red curls. I saw the light that danced in his eyes. His shoulder brushed against hers as he reached across the table for a gauze wrap. She held out her hand as he demonstrated his technique for stopping blood flow.

Victoria had volunteered to be Avian's apprentice. It made sense considering she had been our seamstress. They had been spending a lot of time together the last few days.

I swallowed hard as I turned and walked the other way.

I had to consider then the fact that had never seemed important until now. Avian was older than me. Had the world not fallen apart, we would be in different places in our lives. There was a good chance Avian might be married, might even have a son like Brady.

Maybe he should be with someone like Victoria. Maybe he should have a family. Maybe he should be with someone who could give him a life I never could.

But could I handle seeing him with someone else? I'd never had to face that thought before.

The light burned away with the blazing heat of the day, a violent colored sky painted above our heads. Dinner was quiet as we quickly ate our small portions and set about our evening activities. Fires were built as the last of the day's light faded away. I stood on the edge of the lake against the tree line, just watching.

Morgan, the woman who took care of our horse, walked to her husband Eli, placed a kiss on his forehead as she sat beside him. Gabriel wandered out of his tent, joining his wife Leah at the dining table where she talked to a few other women. Under the table he rested his hand on her knee, a brief moment of affection flashing in their eyes as they looked at each other.

Was that what love was? Brief touches and physical assurances of another's presence? Or was it what that touch made you feel inside? Was it the impression that it left inside of you and stayed with you for as long as you would remember?

Would I ever understand what that word meant?

I was too aware of the lack of Avian's presence. He and Victoria made a brief appearance at dinner before disappearing back into the lamp-lit medical tent. Brady scampered around with Wix, laughing at the jokes his babysitter made. The two of them had been spending a lot of time together with Victoria being so preoccupied with medical training.

My eyes found a lone figure, sitting hunched against the light of a small fire. My feet were moving toward it without my head thinking about it.

I sat on the log next to West, close enough my shoulder brushed his as I settled. He glanced over at me briefly. He held a long stick in his hands, stirring the coals that fell of the larger logs.

"Tell me about where you came from, West," I said as my eyes fixed on the flames. Something inside of me felt hollow again and I craved *something* to fill it back in. "What happened after the evolution? How did you come back into my life after I left yours?"

He stared into the coals and I could envision the images that flashed before his eyes. But what things had he seen that I couldn't imagine?

"My father evolved first," he said, his voice low and rough. "It wasn't any surprise I guess, working and operating on them like he did. He changed the second week of the spread. I was kept in solitary when my grandfather realized what has happening. He locked me away in our apartment. I was there by myself for two whole weeks.

"A few men broke in through the locked door," West said as he shifted positions, resting his forearms on his knees. "They were wearing biohazard suits. As if that would have stopped TorBane. They said that my grandfather had been infected but that he had told them to come and get me and transport me away. I grabbed my grandfather's notebook before I was shoved out the door. They took me and a few others to a van and then we just drove. For days."

I tried to bring up the images that I knew must be in my brain. Somewhere inside there must have been a record of NovaTor, of the scientists' faces, of West's. But there was nothing.

"I slept most of the drive but I could tell we were a long way from home. Finally, we were let out at a camp. It was very different than this one," he said with his jaw suddenly

193

stiff. "That camp was filled mostly with military personnel and government officials. I was the only teenager there.

"Everyone had a duty to perform. I suppose like here, but there it was your only reason for existing. They all knew who I was, who my family was. They never said it but they hated me for it. People didn't talk to me and I spent a lot of time alone. I scrubbed the dishes three times a day until my hands were raw and bleeding. For three years."

The heat of the day finally gave way to the mercy of the night. A breeze picked up, ruffling my tied-back hair. My eyes ascended to the star dusted sky, resting on the moon as it shone with furious intensity.

"I couldn't take it anymore," West continued. "I gathered provisions and just left. I wasn't really sure where I was going, but I thought that even getting infected was almost better than being treated the way I had been."

I looked over at West with hard eyes. How could real life ever be worse than getting infected? What had they done to him for him to say that?

"I spent probably close to a month traveling on my own. I didn't see another soul, not a single Bane. It nearly drove me mad, being alone like that.

"And then I met two men who had been out hunting. They took what little food I had and brought me back to their camp. There were twenty or so of them. They were survivors but they weren't a family like here. It was every man for himself first, help your fellow man stay alive second.

"But they knew how to survive. They taught me how to hunt, to survive in the woods. I owe them a lot I guess. They could have just killed me on sight out wandering in the woods," he glanced over at me with awkward hints of a smile. I saw scars behind that smile. He dodged away from my probing stare, looking back down at the fire.

"Victoria found us there. She was beaten and could barely stand. She had Brady with her, not even able to walk yet. Brady had to grow up in the middle of that group. No child should ever have to learn to live in that setting.

"The group was out on a scouting duty, different from how we do it here. We were sent out in groups, all of us, to collect any food we could find and bring it back. Victoria and Brady were in my group, along with another man. That's when the attack happened. We heard the blast, even from a few miles away. But it wasn't the Bane, it was one of our group. Stupid enough to toss a grenade at one of the Bane. Our camp was gone. Soon we heard the helicopters and we knew the others were gone too.

"The man who was with us, he heard something coming up on us. He told me to take Victoria and Brady and run. He went back to keep them off our trail."

West was quiet after that, his eyes resting in the dirt at our feet. I knew the fate of the man who had saved them.

Life had never been easy for West. In a way he had been shunned his entire life. When he was a child, he had been shut out because of the fact that he was one. And then because everyone had known who he was. I couldn't blame him for keeping his knowledge and information to himself anymore.

The next night I stayed silent as I crept to the medical tent. Its flaps were tied back again even though today had been much cooler. Avian and Victoria were inside, slowly eating as they sat side by side. They talked quietly in easy conversation, no awkward or tense silences between them.

They looked…happy.

I walked away, an uncomfortable feeling in the pit of my stomach.

I didn't even realize where I was going until I was at Sarah and Avian's tent. A lamp softly glowed from within and I pushed aside the flap.

To my amazement, Sarah was propped up slightly, a plate of food in her lap. It was double portions to what the rest of us had been getting.

"You're alive," I said. I had had doubts if I would find her to be so.

She gave me a weak smile and a glare as she forked some canned carrots into her mouth.

"I've been worried," I said as I sat down on Avian's cot across from her. "How are you feeling?"

"I've been better," she said. Her voice sounded terrible.

I stared at Sarah while she ate. She was nothing more than a skeleton now, her skin too loose on her frame. Her hair was a matted mess and truthfully, she smelled off.

"What is the matter, Eve?" Sarah said as she finished the last of her dinner and set her plate aside. "Something is bothering you."

My eyes stared at nothing as I tried to collect my thoughts. She was right, something was wrong, but I didn't know where to start. It felt like *everything* was wrong.

"Is Avian in love with Victoria?" I suddenly blurted.

"Victoria?" Sarah sounded startled. "Have they been spending time together?"

"Quite a bit," I said quietly. "He has been training her."

Sarah watched my face for a moment. "You're jealous."

"Jealous?"

"You don't like him spending time with her, do you?" she said with the tiniest hint of a smile.

"No," I said with a relieved sigh before I could think to be more tactful. It was freeing in a way, to finally be able to vocalize what I felt.

"Do you know what you feel for Avian?" she asked, her voice soft and kind.

I bit my lower lip and shook my head. "I wish I did."

"*How* does Avian make you feel?" she asked.

I looked up into Sarah's eyes. How *did* Avian make me feel?

"Avian makes me feel safe, even though I can keep myself safe," I finally said, feeling like my chest was swelling. "He makes me feel normal, like I'm me. He knows me. He *matters*, far more than he should, to me."

"And how does West make you feel?"

"Alive, I guess," I said, an almost frustrated sigh escaping my chest. "I feel like I grow when I'm with him but not always in a good way. He pushes me to be more human but then he also brings out the Bane in me."

Sarah looked at me, silent with contemplation. I hoped almost violently that she was thinking of the answers to give me. If only she could lay things out clearly, tell me exactly what I needed to hear.

"I don't know which one is going to be right for you. You are going to have to learn that for yourself. But I think there is going to be a time that eventually comes when you're going to realize it in an instant and there's going to be no question in your mind."

"Can't that be right now?" I said wistfully.

She chuckled, shaking her head slightly. That brought on a round of coughing. I helped her lay down and tucked her blankets up under her chin.

"I'd better go. Got to keep prepping for the trek," I said as I moved to the flap of the tent.

"Trek?" she questioned, her brow furrowing.

I was about to explain when I suddenly stopped myself. "Never mind," I said. "Just get some rest."

Sarah only nodded, too tired to question me further. She rolled to her side and was almost immediately asleep.

I stepped out of the tent and started for my own. I wasn't even halfway there when a figure moved toward me in the darkness. I was familiar enough with his gait to know it was Avian.

"Hi," I said, my voice rising in pitch a bit and I stopped a little too suddenly.

"Hi." He stopped just a few feet from me. We stood there in momentary awkward silence. I wanted to walk away because just then I didn't want to be around Avian for a reason I didn't understand. But at the same time I didn't think I could walk away. I was so relieved to see him, to have him notice me again.

"How is the training going?" I asked, taking a hard swallow.

"Very well," he said, a smile instantly filling his face. "Victoria catches on quickly."

I took another swallow, only able to nod my head.

"You haven't told Sarah we're leaving," I said.

"No," he said simply, his voice catching in his throat.

It felt as if my insides had hardened and I could only nod my head again. My eyes dropped to the dirt at our feet and my arms wrapped around my midsection.

Avian closed the distance between us and placed his warm hand on my cheek. I squeezed my eyes closed as relief flooded my system. I craved more.

"Things are going to be okay," he whispered.

My eyes rose to meet his. "I don't see how," I said.

"Somehow they will be." His eyes burned as he stared back at me.

There were a million things I wanted to say to Avian in that moment. I wanted to tell him that I wanted to know it was

198

him that I wanted. I wanted to tell him that I didn't want to be alone tonight. I wanted to tell him that in a way I wished it was just him and I that were leaving to go into the unknown.

But how could I say those things when I didn't even know if he felt the same way anymore?

"Goodnight, Avian," I said quietly as I took a step away from him.

"Goodnight, Eve," he whispered back, his burning eyes following me as I walked away into the dark.

TWENTY-FOUR

Two days later, the flap of my tent was opened in the dead of night. Avian stepped inside, his face grave and sharply illuminated by the lantern in his hand.

"Can you come with me?" he asked. I had never heard his voice sound so rough. There were red rims around his eyes. I nodded once and followed him through the dark without a word.

Somehow I knew before we even left my tent that we were going to his. The darkness felt heavy and cold, despite the summer heat. My hands were clammy and my insides hollow.

We stepped inside and I felt myself freeze up in despair.

Sarah lay on her cot, her eyes closed, lined with a frightening shade of red. Her face was covered with a sheen of sweat and her entire frame trembled slightly. Her breathing came in terrifying gasps.

"She's been unconscious for more than twenty-four hours," Avian said, his voice sounding as if it were being dragged over rocks. "I can't wake her up."

I knelt at her side, pushing the hair back from her face. Her torso twitched violently as her body fought for air.

"Sarah?" I said quietly, taking one of her bony hands in mine. "Sarah?" I said again, my lips pressed into her clammy skin.

Avian sank to his cot, resting his face in his hands. In a few moments his shoulders started to shake as the tears consumed him.

I knew then why Avian had asked me to come. He had wanted me to be able to say good-bye.

I closed my eyes as I pressed my lips to her hand again. Every time Sarah had gathered me up in her arms, every encouraging word she had spoken to me as a young teenager reverberated in my mind. Flashes of her smiling face swam through my head. I recalled all the squabbles she and Avian had gotten into, remembered all the days they wouldn't talk to each other afterwards, and then the awkward apologies that followed.

West, Bill, or even Gabriel might say that I had never had a mother, never known a sister. But they were wrong. I'd had Sarah.

"I will always miss you," I whispered, surprised at how rough my own voice sounded. Avian's sobs became all the louder. "I will always remember you. I don't know that I would have turned out as human if it wasn't for you. You gave me a family when I didn't have one.

"Thank you for everything, Sarah."

Avian gave a heart-wrenching cry, his shoulders shaking violently.

The sound of Sarah's labored breathing became all the more terrifying over the next hour. Her skin started turning a grey-purple and her hands grew cold. I squeezed her hand all the tighter.

Just before dawn, Sarah's body was finally still.

We buried her by the lake. Bill and Graye had found a perfectly smooth salmon colored rock and had somehow managed to carve her name into its surface. Gabriel snapped out of his stupor just enough to speak, to give honor and remembrance to her name. Avian hadn't said a word since he had come to get me the night Sarah died. I held his trembling frame the rest of that day and all through the night.

TWENTY-FIVE

I rolled the blue barrel up the ramp and it settled at the front of the truck bed with a small sloshing sound. I hopped down and West helped me roll the next one in. The rest of the first group started packing in the remaining water, then loaded the supplies and our food stores.

The boxes I grabbed rattled as I picked them up and I suddenly realized just how valuable all of our ammunition had become. We couldn't grow ammunition; we couldn't scavenge it out of the woods. Ammunition had to be found in civilization and it had become nearly impossible to go into the cities. We were going to have to be more careful than ever.

Sarah's death seemed to have woken something back up in Gabriel. I had talked to Avian about it. He'd explained that more than likely, Gabriel had just snapped. He'd been trying to keep everyone alive for so long and finally, after recent events, he just couldn't take anymore. But he was back to his old self, taking charge and making sure things were taken care of. It was he that had come up with our future means of leaving messages, just twelve hours before we were to leave.

"What are the Bane?" Gabriel asked.

"The Bane?" I asked, confused at his question.

Gabriel nodded. "The Bane. What are they?"

"Robots," West said. I hadn't heard him approach us and jumped at his voice.

Gabriel nodded again, bending down to pick up a rock. "And what are they made of? What makes them tick?"

"Metal," I said, watching him pass the rock from hand to hand. "Nanites. Pulses and currents. I don't get what you are…"

"Exactly." Gabriel interrupted. "They aren't organic. Not anymore. They don't see the world. The Bane don't notice nature, not in the way we do. We'll use nature to hide our messages." He crouched to the ground, gathering stones that had any size to them. Carefully, he started stacking them, one on top of the other. "The Bane won't notice them. They will just see the rocks. But we, Eden, we will see the messages. They're called cairns."

"We could leave notes at the bases of them," West said, his voice excited as he observed Gabriel's work. "The things we've found, any warnings. If we place them under the stones the Bane will never see them."

"Exactly," Gabriel said, his smile disappearing into his beard. "My wife Leah has been copying the maps as exactly as she can for the last few weeks so we can leave locations. We run a smaller risk that we will be permanently separated that way. Pick a destination in the direction we are headed and let us know where to go. We have our general direction but there is going to have to be room for change. Who knows what we're walking into."

The work on the trailers was completed that night. The one that had been rusting away for years, left abandoned, was the one that the first group would take. The second one that Bill and Graye had brought back from the city would transport the second group. And if either of them failed to function, we always had our legs.

On our last night in Eden we feasted, at least as best we could on our starvation rations. Food never tasted so wonderful as I helped myself to two rolls, a heaping scoop of canned corn, a baked potato, and rabbit. For a moment I thought about seeking out Sarah so I could share my portions. Then I remembered.

I glanced down the table at Avian who sat talking hurriedly with Victoria, pointing at something in the book that was laid on the table before them. Not that it truly mattered, but her status and usability in Eden would be greatly increased if we ever all actually made it south. She was going from seamstress to back up doctor.

The thought that that would free up Avian crossed my mind and the smallest hint of a smile tugged at my lips.

West sat next to me, wolfing down his food faster than he could chew it. I laughed, shaking my head at him.

"What?" he said around a mouthful of bread. "I'm starving!"

"I know," I said with a smile.

"You going to finish yours?" he said, eying the remains on my plate.

"Yes," I said as I raised my eyebrows at him. "I intend to finish every bite."

He chuckled then. Underneath the table he gave my knee a small squeeze.

We finished packing most everything that night. The members of the second group had to open their tents up to those in the first since everything had been loaded into the truck. I was glad I had watch duty that night; I wouldn't have known how to handle that awkward situation.

I looked out over the tents that night. I was starting to realize that this place we were staying at wasn't Eden. Eden was wherever these people were, Eden was them.

I wondered if there were any other places like this. It didn't sound like it from what I had heard others say. How had I been so lucky to have come here?

Sarah wouldn't have called it luck. To her it would have been fate. Maybe it was.

But Eden would be breaking up in the morning. Would it ever be fully put back together again? What were our numbers going to be like if it did? Who would be lost along the way?

By dawn, Eden was teeming with life. Nerves were running high.

People said hurried goodbyes with hurried hugs, tears pooling in their eyes. They knew this could be a permanent good-bye. My chest hardened as I watched Avian talking to Victoria again. He gave her a slightly longer than necessary hug good-bye.

Bill and Graye walked up to me and to my surprise, a pang formed in my chest. These two had been my team. We were part of the elite, the best. In a way they were my brothers.

Bill wrapped his arms around me and pulled me into a hug. "Be careful out there," he said quietly before he released me.

I gave him a small smile. I looked over at Graye and he could only give me a tight-lipped smile and a nod of agreement. "Just remember that they can still blow you up," he said with a smirk.

"Thanks," I said with a chuckle as I shook my head. "You two be careful. You're smart, you know how to survive. Just keep doing what you've been doing."

"Promise," Bill said, his cool gray eyes on me.

I walked back to the truck, joining Avian and West. "Everything ready?" I asked, feeling both anxious and reluctant to leave.

"I believe so," Avian said as he hoisted his bag of half the medical supplies into the back of the truck. We couldn't fit much more in it.

Gabriel walked up to us, his hands stuffed into his pockets. His lips were invisible in his beard as he pressed them tightly together.

"We'll reach the first destination this evening," Avian said as he turned to Gabriel. "We'll leave the marker with any notes on what we encounter today."

Gabriel nodded. "I wanted to thank you," he said, his voice suddenly rough sounding. "For keeping things going when I snapped. It was selfish of me."

Avian pressed his lips together and nodded. "No one can really blame you."

Gabriel extended his hand and Avian gave it a tight shake. He then shook West and I's hands as well. "Be safe," he said. "We have to keep Eden alive. We may be all that's left out there."

All the members of our first group loaded onto the trailer and into the truck. The day watchman, Tuck, volunteered to drive. Morgan climbed into the front cab with him and so did another woman by the name of Bea. The other fourteen of us got to ride the bumpy thousand miles on the flat-bed trailer.

The members of the second group gathered around as Tuck started the truck to life. As he pulled away they waved, tears falling down half their faces.

The first hour was slow going as we made our way through the forest over uneven ground. We had worked hard to keep ourselves hidden so that we couldn't be found by any still-remaining marauders or Bane. We each had to hold onto the short railing that lined the edge of the trailer to keep from being bucked off.

No one said anything for the first few hours but we all knew what the other was thinking. There was uncertainty and fear about traveling into the unknown. There was the very real possibility that this truck wouldn't continue to run for more than another mile. Or it could break down in the middle of the desert. Helicopters could buzz over our heads at any time, reign down on us with dozens of Bane and infect us all.

There were endless horrible ways for us to die on this journey.

But it was sure death by starvation or infection if we stayed.

We jarred over a rough patch, everyone jerking violently to the right. "Careful!" I was surprised when Avian shouted at Tuck.

"I'm sorry," he called. "I don't see a clearer path."

Avian said something under his breath as he turned his eyes forward.

"You okay?" I asked quietly. I suddenly felt all too open to everyone. There wouldn't be much privacy for the next week or so.

Avian shook his head, his eyes darting to the cab of the truck. "Morgan's pregnant," he whispered.

"Pregnant?" I repeated. I glanced at the back of her head through the window. It explained why she was sitting up there.

Avian nodded. "Sharp, rough movement like that isn't very good for the baby."

"Should she be coming with us if she is carrying a child?" I asked. Suddenly this journey seemed all the more perilous.

"I thought it would be safer. Victoria would be able to stitch a wound or anything basic but her training is limited. Not that I know that much about taking care of a pregnant woman but I thought it would be better. She's not that far along anyway. She should be just fine."

I glanced at Morgan's husband, Eli, saw that he was watching us. I thought I was supposed to say congratulations or something but it didn't seem like something to celebrate anymore. Our world wasn't a safe place for children.

After two hours the truck pulled to a stop and Tuck poked his head out the window to look back at us. "This is going to get really rough and I'm going to have to go really slow. I think it would be best if everyone got off and walked for a bit."

Without another word, everyone hopped off and we started the slow journey down the rocky face of the mountain on foot.

As we moved I watched Avian. He walked at the front of us all. He held a rifle tight in his hands, his eyes scanning the trees and sky before us. I couldn't recall ever seeing Avian with a gun. But his hands were perfectly positioned, his frame aware of everything around him. His shoulders were set tight, his knees bent slightly, ready to fight or run at any second.

I had never seen the soldier side of Avian before. Avian was probably better trained than I was to survive in our new world.

Curious, how a person's value is placed. We needed soldiers. We needed people who could protect us, who knew what they were doing when it came to weapons. But we had also needed someone who could take care of us, stitch us back together. Even with the limited amount of training Avian had, he was more valuable to us as a make-do doctor than as the best trained soldier we had.

"So what do you think it will be like?" West's voice jarred me back to my senses. "When we get to our new location?"

"Uh," I stuttered, trying to refocus my attention from Avian to West. "Warm? I don't know."

He laughed, adjusting his grip on his rifle. "I hope, wherever we end up, it's near the ocean. I remember going to the beach as a kid with my father a few times."

"What was it like?" I asked.

"Big." He breathed. "It never ends. It's really beautiful. And scary."

"How could a body of water be scary?" I asked.

"That much water is a lot bigger than you," he said as he glanced over at me. "You think you could control the violence of the ocean?"

I was quiet after that, trying to imagine what the ocean would look like. It was hard to envision it as a threat. "I'd like to see the ocean someday."

West looked over at me with another smile, bumping his shoulder against mine.

For the briefest moment, it felt like my heart jumped into my throat. But the strange part was that for just a second, my vision went completely black.

I tripped over the stones under my feet, throwing my hands out to catch myself before I fell.

"Whoa!" West said, obvious concern in his voice. "You okay?"

"Of course," I tried to recover, brushing the dirt off my knees. Avian glanced back at me, a probing look in his eyes. I shook my head and after a lingering hard look, he turned his attention back upfront.

I didn't think I had ever tripped before.

"And I hope it never snows," West continued, brushing my incident off. "After last winter I wouldn't mind if I never saw snow again."

"Agreed," I said distractedly.

We were both quiet for a few minutes as we kept pace with the rest of the group. "Do you think we'll ever be able to stop running from them?" West asked.

I thought about my response before I spoke. "I guess if we could hide ourselves well enough. Push far enough into the country. If they can't find us, they can't infect us."

West kept his eyes glued to the rocks at our feet. "I'm so sick of running," he said quietly.

"Me too."

We finally got to the base of the mountain and out of the canyon. We would be stopping here until dark, when it would be safer to travel. We had only traveled the last few hours in daylight because it was too dangerous to come down the mountain in the dark. We all would have killed ourselves on the rocks and cliffs. For now we would take shifts, some would sleep while others would keep watch.

I'd be staying up all night, as usual.

"Avian," I said as I walked to his side. "I'm going to get a few minutes of sleep before nightfall."

"I think I'd better do that too," he said as he looked around at those who were traveling with us. "I think it would be best if I stayed up at night since my rifle has a night vision scope. Coby," he said to a man walking past us. "I'm checking out for a while. Keep an eye on things, will you?"

He nodded, securing his handgun.

"West," I called as I spotted him. "Keep watch for a while?"

"Sure," he said with a nod and automatically turned his eyes to our perimeters.

Avian and I walked towards a tree, each greedy for the shade it would provide. We settled on the wild grass that grew at its base, side-by-side in the coolness.

"I've never seen the soldier side of you before," I said as my eyes slid closed.

"There hasn't been much opportunity," he said as he gave a sigh and relaxed. "It feels weird being back in that mode. It was drilled into me constantly for over two years and it kept me alive for another four months. Then it got pushed to the back of my mind."

"Eden has been lucky to have you," I said quietly as I shifted around to get more comfortable, sleep already creeping in to take me over.

"I could say the same about you," he said, his voice drifting away.

A few moments later I joined him.

TWENTY-SIX

I tried to press my back further into the corner. My vision blurred and the dark shadows before me blended together.

"She's never been this aggressive before," a voice said. It felt like someone was screaming into my ear. Everything was too loud. I pressed my hands over the sides of my head, trying to block it all out.

"She's afraid," a lighter voice said.

I couldn't make out anything anymore as I opened and closed my eyes, trying to clear my vision. My head felt fuzzy and clouded.

The next second all I could make out was the scent of steel under me. And that my head felt cold.

Then there was the sound of a drill.

My eyes slid open, blinking immediately closed against the dimming but still bright light of the evening sun. I turned my head to the side, raising my hand to block it from my face. At the same moment my pillow moved and I opened my eyes to find myself nose to nose with Avian.

"You were having a nightmare," he said quietly as he pushed a few stray hairs out of my face. I realized then that I was lying on his arm as a pillow, still under the same tree. After I glanced around at our caravan and knew things were still safe, I relaxed again, resting my head back on his arm.

"Yeah," I said quietly. "Did you sleep much?"

"For a while."

I lay there for a little longer, listening as Avian breathed, the sound of everything that was still okay in the world. A part of me wanted to never have to move again, to lay here until the sun died and time ceased to exist or matter anymore.

"We should probably get going," Avian said, always right about everything. I nodded, pulling myself up to my feet, then helping Avian to his own. He went to take a step back toward the group but before he could, I slipped my hand into his. I had been wanting to do that for so long, but starving myself of it.

Avian looked down at me, his eyes open and intense at the same time. I brought our hands up to my cheek and just held it there for a moment. I took a deep breath, very aware of the steady rhythm of my heart. Then I let go and walked back to the group.

The sun slid below the horizon in the west, the temperature immediately dropping. I watched as Avian stacked some rocks at the base of another tree where it would be obvious to see, the note he had written tucked securely under the largest stone inside a waterproof bag. We all loaded onto the trailer and for the first time, Tuck set out on level ground.

"It won't go any faster than about forty miles-per-hour," Tuck called out the window.

"It's a miracle that it still runs at all," Avian called back to him. "Let's just pray that it will keep that pace."

Tuck nodded, turning his attention back to the level ground before him. Those who traveled with us had grabbed their blankets out of the back of the truck and started arranging themselves to get more comfortable. It was cramped quarters but they used each other as pillows, everyone suddenly getting much closer to one another than they ever had before.

Avian sat at the front passenger side of the trailer, rifle ready at any moment. I sat in the opposite corner in the back, watching the landscape as it fell behind us. West lay at my left, his head resting against my thigh as he drifted off to sleep. As far as I could tell, all the others were asleep before we even got to the road. It had been a long, hard hike down the mountain.

The pavement of the road wasn't perfectly smooth. After not being taken care of for so many years it had cracked and started to break down. The only sound that met my ears was the wind around us, the grumble of the truck, and its tires rubbing the road. The truck's one working headlight created a tunnel of light before us that made me slightly uneasy. It felt like a beacon jumping up into the sky, alerting our position.

I reminded myself that the Bane weren't supposed to come out during the night.

Except for when they burned gardens. And infected fallen soldiers.

It wasn't long before we reached the outskirts of a small city. My nerves pitched as houses came into view. Tuck pulled off the road and continued through the fields. I saw the shadow of buildings that created the small city.

As we got to the outskirts, we reconnected with the road and pulled into a gas station.

Tuck pulled up to one of the pumps and Avian jumped off the trailer, grabbing a hose and started punching a few buttons. Nothing happened. Avian started walking toward the back of the store, waving Tuck forward with the truck. I hopped off, jogging ahead to catch up with Avian. I kept my shotgun level to my eye, my finger on the trigger. I wasn't going to be caught off guard if anything woke up.

"Here we go," Avian whispered, a bit of a smile forming on his lips. He waved Tuck over to a pipe that rose up out of the ground. At the top it had some sort of hand pump and a hose that ran off the side of it.

I watched in fascination as Avian opened a small round cover on the side of the truck. Tuck shut it off and stepped out, walking the length of the truck back and forth to stretch his legs. Avian put one end of the hose in the hole in the side of the truck and started pumping.

"This is going to take a while," Avian huffed as he worked the stiff joints. "Watch the perimeter."

I nodded once and walked to the side of the store, checking to make sure it was clear. I snuck back around to the front of the store, still clear. My nerves tight, I crept up to the glass front door and peaked inside. It had been raided and the shelves were mostly barren.

I continued to pace the perimeter of the building the entire ten minutes or so that it took Avian to pump the truck full of gas. When he finished he asked me to wait with the truck while he ran inside to look for something.

Less than two minutes later Avian jogged back towards us, five blue bottles in his hands.

"What's that?" I asked, eyeing it warily.

"It cleans the fuel," he whispered as he set three of them in the back of the truck and set to pouring the other two of the bottles in with the gas. "I don't know if any of it is still good, the fuel or the cleaner, but I figure if it has a chance of helping we've got to try it."

I nodded. When Avian was finished, he set the empty bottles on the ground. He motioned for the three of us to get back inside. A few people stirred as the truck was started back up but they were asleep by the time we pulled back on the road and continued down it.

"We should be good for another three hundred miles or so," Avian said quietly. "Depending on what kind of mileage this thing still gets. And if it keeps running."

I nodded again, watching the darkness around us. It was frustrating that I couldn't see anything. I took a little comfort in the fact that Avian could though. He kept looking through his night vision scope every few minutes.

West eased his head back up onto my thigh, a soft snore letting me know just how asleep he really was. I tried to ignore him, remembering what had happened earlier when we had just brushed shoulders. My vision was already black, I didn't need my brain going black as well.

"Is it harder now?" I asked Avian quietly. My fingers felt for the wings around my throat. "To keep going now that they're all gone? Now that you've lost all your family?"

"I still have you," he said very quietly. "As long as you're still around I've got something to keep fighting for. And them as well," he said as he observed those sleeping around us. "They're my family too."

That swelling in my chest started up again. I both craved it and didn't want it. It made me say stupid things.

"Are you in love with Victoria?"

Avian's eyebrows knitted together. "What?"

"Are you?" My face suddenly felt hot.

"Victoria is a smart woman and she is beautiful, but... Why would you think that?" I was surprised to see that Avian's face looked almost hurt.

I suddenly wished I had never said anything. What had been the point of this conversation? "I just... I didn't..." I couldn't find words that wouldn't make me want to jump off this trailer and hide myself in a hole in the ground from humiliation.

"You're jealous," Avian said with dawning in his voice. A bit of a smile tugged on his lips.

"Jealous," I said, meaning to form it as a question. That was what Sarah had said I was feeling.

"It's not a fun emotion, is it?" he said as his face grew more serious, though a tight lipped smile formed. As he said it, he glanced down at West.

"No, it's not," I said quietly, my eyes falling down to West's sleeping form.

TWENTY-SEVEN

I felt too exposed, too open. I suddenly missed the mountains, the trees. They protected us. Now in the open desert, I wanted to get out from under the wide sky and distant horizons as fast as possible.

The sun was blinding as it gleamed against the sand. Amazing how the Earth could change so fast, in just the eight hours we had driven, going from forest to stark desert. We had pulled off the road for the day into a patch of rocks and a plant Tuck had told me was called cactus. There wasn't anything else to hide us from being seen. It was poor camouflage but it was all we were going to get.

Breakfast was prepared, canned pears and bread left over from the day before. I now understood why Avian had been so insistent on storing so much water. With every bite I took I felt like my tongue was sticking to the top of my mouth. I would have guzzled down an entire gallon if I didn't know how precious our supplies were.

"I kind of like this heat," West said as we scouted the perimeter. It looked like waves were rising off the hot clay. "There's something, I don't know, comforting about it."

"You mean suffocating, right?"

"No," he smiled. "I don't know. I just kind of like it. I wouldn't want to deal with it all the time but it's kind of a nice change. Dry. Not like how it's felt so humid all the time lately."

"I guess," I said as I glanced back at the caravan. Everything looked blurred from this far away, like it was engulfed in water. Maybe we would be better hidden than I had thought. They just looked like an extension of the rock outcropping and cactus.

West sat on a large boulder, patting the space beside him. I took one more look around before I joined him. We sat together in awkward silence for almost a full minute.

There was something on West's mind, I could feel it.

"What?" I simply asked.

He took a breath to speak then stopped. His eyes glanced up once before falling back down to his weapon in his hands. "You're going to make a choice someday, aren't you?"

"What do you mean?" I asked, even though I already knew exactly what he was asking.

West didn't say anything for a while. He just held my eyes.

"Never mind," he finally said.

"I don't think so," I said, shaking my head. Heat was rising in my blood. "You don't just get to say something like that and then say 'never mind.' You can't take something like that back."

"I don't want to talk about this, forget I said anything," he said shaking his head and breaking eye contact. "I can't think straight. My head is in all the wrong places these days."

I just watched him for a bit. He looked so sad. "I'm sorry, that's probably my fault." My eyes fell, looking down at our hands where they rested side by side. I slipped my fingers into his.

The world flickered black for a moment. And then suddenly everything went dark.

I opened my eyes to the washed out color of canvas. Two faces leaned over my field of vision, both filled with concern and another emotion that surprised me: fear.

"What happened?" I asked as I pulled myself up into a sitting position, shaking what felt like fog from my brain.

West and Avian glanced at each other. "What happened?" I demanded again.

"You... passed out," West said. I noticed the sweat that suddenly beaded on his forehead. I glanced at Avian who couldn't meet my eyes.

"It's over one-hundred degrees out there," West said as he sat back on his heels. "You're not used to the heat."

"And you are?" I scoffed. I didn't believe West. I hadn't passed out from the heat. He was lying and Avian knew it.

"You're obviously fine now," West said as he pulled himself to his feet and left the tent.

That night, once everyone was asleep on the trailer again, I couldn't hold it back any longer.

"What really happened to me earlier?" I asked quietly. "I didn't really pass out, did I?"

"I didn't see it happen," Avian finally said after a long, thoughtful pause. "West walked you back to the group. You were awake, but you weren't there. Your eyes were totally blank and you wouldn't respond. He said you two had been talking when you suddenly just...froze up."

"Froze up?" I asked. Even as I did, I knew what he was talking about. The way I had blanked and then tripped the day before. The way I had felt like I was suddenly gone when I had nearly choked West.

"You weren't there for a while," Avian said, his voice cool. "It was like you were empty all of the sudden. Hollow."

221

I swallowed hard, not because of the dryness or the heat this time. "Am I going to turn into one of them?" my voice sounded hoarse.

"I think if you were going to you would have already." Avian's voice was tight. "There's been plenty of time for you to change, plenty of opportunity for you to be infected. I think this is something different."

"What then?"

"I don't know."

TWENTY-EIGHT

As pressure built in the air I felt uneasy. It reminded me of the night the Bane burned the gardens. The stars disappeared, plunging the night into a darkness I had never known.

One good thing about traveling through the desert was that there were few towns that we had to skirt around. It slowed us down a great deal having to drive around a city. There was always the risk that we would find Bane on the outskirts.

"Pull over here," Avian said in a harsh whisper as we approached the next gas station. "Kill the lights." Tuck did as he said immediately.

Avian jumped off the trailer, his rifle held at eye level. I jumped off at the same time, my own shotgun held firmly in hand. His eyes never left the glass front of the store as he stalked slowly towards it. I released my safety, gauging how many extra shells I had in my pocket that I could easily grab if needed.

"There's two of them inside," Avian whispered. I saw the gleam of their metallic parts. Their eyes stared back out at us, empty orbs.

"Should we go to a different gas station?" I breathed.

Avian shook his head. "We most likely wouldn't make it to another."

"Together?" I said quietly.

"On my count," Avian breathed. "Three... two... one."

The glass exploded into a billion shards, followed by screams from those who were sleeping unsuspecting on the trailer. The next second, the two Bane leapt through the remains of the glass, barreling straight towards us.

Countless shots were fired but only the one charging at me dropped. By the time I had realized what had happened it was too late to load again.

"No!" I screamed as I sprinted toward the Bane who was barreling straight at Avian. I leapt between the two of them, slamming my body in it.

We hit the ground in a tangled mess of arms, each trying to destroy the other. It's steel cold hand wrapped around my throat, cutting off my air supply.

"Dis... dis..." I gasped for air. "Disengage!" I screamed out. It stopped moving immediately.

I clawed its hand away from my throat, realizing then that as I had jumped to get between the Bane and Avian my handgun had fallen out of its holster. Instead, my hands beat at the frame that covered its neck and lower face, exposing the gears and wires beneath. I lost it, ripping and shredding everything I could get my fingers around. I didn't even care when the volts of electricity the infected body produced shocked me over and over again.

I sat back, straddling the now still body, my breaths coming in shaking, gasping swallows. I glanced back over at Avian only to see him surrounded by the rest of the group. Their faces were a mix of shock, awe, and fear.

They all finally knew my secret.

I looked back down at the Bane, my hand rising to my throat, and took a hard swallow. In its blank eyes, I saw everything I hated about myself. All the things that were wrong with me, all the things I couldn't remember but knew the truth about.

I spit in its face and stood to walk back to the others.

"Let's gas up and get going," I said.

No one said anything as Tuck and Avian pulled the truck around to the hand pump and filled it. They all got back on the trailer but I felt their eyes on me as I stood at one corner of the building, pretending to be watching the perimeter, even though I couldn't see much of anything.

Avian and Gabriel had worked all these years to keep my true nature a secret. It had only taken a few moments to undo all that effort.

"Are you okay?" West asked quietly from behind me.

"I'm fine," I said, my voice rough.

"Are you sure?" he whispered.

"I'm fine!" I said harshly. "You lied to me again."

"Lied?" he asked, his eyebrows furrowing.

"I didn't pass out earlier," I said quietly. "It was like I was suddenly one of them, wasn't it?"

West swallowed hard, his eyes guarded as he looked back at me. "It was the same way you looked when you tried to choke me."

"And why does it only seem to happen when I'm around you?"

West looked back at me, hurt plain on his face.

"You know," he said. "You used to be so much easier to deal with. You didn't used to freak out over every little thing."

He turned and walked back to the group.

Avian left a message and a cairn at the gas station, warning the second group to take extra caution.

The pressure in the sky kept building, turning the air muggy and heavy. We stopped two hours after we had gassed up, hiding ourselves in a cluster of sickly looking trees. Tents were set up, five of them, as a precaution to the saturated sky.

Not five minutes after we had everything staked and secured, the sky finally broke.

I'd never seen rain like that.

I kept the perimeter, Tuck volunteering to keep watch with me. I was soaked through almost instantly and it was difficult to see far. Small wisps of steam rose from the sunbaked ground, heat and cool colliding.

The world was doused in a hazy color of gray as the sun fought to break through the heavy clouds above us. The rain continued to pour, soaking us in more rain than I had ever seen fall at one time. Small streams started tracing lines in the desert, running to unseen rivers. We set out our empty water containers to refill from the heavens.

A few hours into my scouting Avian walked out, using a raincoat that had been smartly packed to keep his head dry. He walked over to me, and covered my head. He handed me two carrots.

"I doubt we're going to see any of them in this," Avian said, having to speak louder than normal to talk over the noise of the rain pounding above our heads. "They don't like the water too much."

"I'm not taking any risks," I said as I bit the end of one of the carrots off. "And what was that back there? At the gas station. You know I can take care of myself."

"I know," he said as his eyes fell to the ground. "Just instinct, I guess."

He stood there with me for a while, our eyes watching the rain as it fell, our feet getting soaked as it did.

"Did you say something to West?" he asked. "He's acting kind of...put out."

I swallowed my bite before answering. "I told him that I knew he had lied to me earlier. I also pointed out the fact that I only have these blackouts when I'm around him."

"Really?"

I nodded. "The first time was when I choked him. It was like I didn't know what I was doing."

"And then when you tripped," Avian said, his eyes staring out over the desert. "You two had been talking. I've never seen you stumble before."

I nodded again. "And then yesterday."

"Why do you think that is?" he asked.

"I don't know," I said as I shook my head.

"If being around him makes you lose control of yourself, it's a danger to us all. We can't afford to have you gone, to have you check-out, even if you don't mean to. And we can't afford to have you turn on us."

"I wouldn't do that," I defended as I glared at him.

"I know you wouldn't," Avian said as he looked at me. "But what if you don't have a choice? I mean, you didn't want to strangle West, did you?"

"Of course not," I said. "I mean I was mad at him but I would never actually do *that*."

"That's what I mean. If you don't have control over this it's dangerous for us all for you to be around him."

I mumbled something, hoping it would pass as acknowledgement.

"I wanted to ask you..." he started.

"Stop right there!" I shouted as I took five steps forward into the rain, my shotgun level to my eyes.

Thirty yards away, two figures stopped in their tracks, their hands held up.

"Please," a female voice called through the torrent. "We just need something to eat. We've been lost in this desert for days."

I walked toward them, gun in hand, Avian following me, his own handgun held steady. As the figures became clearer, I saw it was a man and a woman, looking to be in their late thirties.

"Please," the man said. "We mean you no harm. We just need something to eat. If you can spare anything."

"Where'd you come from?" Avian demanded, his gun pointed right at the man's chest.

"The southeast," the man said. "We've been running for almost a year now."

"Come with us," Avian said.

We walked behind them, their hands held behind their backs where we could see them. I looked down at their feet. Their shoes were held together with strips of material and lengths of rope. Their clothes were torn and ragged looking.

We led them to one of the tents. Morgan and Eli were inside resting and jumped at the sight of the strangers. "Who are they?" Eli demanded as he put himself between the newcomers and his wife.

"We're about to find out," Avian said as he walked back to the truck while I kept an eye on them. A minute later Avian walked back in, the CDU in hand.

"What are you going to do with that?" the woman asked, eyeing it warily.

"Just make sure you're really human," I said.

Avian made one swipe down the woman's bare arm, water rolling off of her to the floor of the tent.

"What are you doing?" she jumped, huddling back into the man.

"This puts out an electrical current. Being this soaked will make it much more intense," Avian explained as he met their eyes. With hesitancy, she let him wipe her arm more. The man tried drying his own arm.

They didn't fight us as Avian touched the device to their still damp skin. Organic.

"What are you doing out here?" Avian asked.

"Things are bad back east," the woman started. "There is hardly anyone left, if anyone. The Bane have gotten so aggressive. It wasn't safe anywhere. We had no choice but to come west."

"It took us a year to figure out what was happening anyway," the man said, his eyes wild with recollection. "It's amazing we stayed alive."

"What do you mean?" I asked.

The two of them exchanged a look, a million memories between them. "We were on a year long sailing study," the man started. "That's how we met. We were both working for the university, doing marine studies. There were six of us on the sailboat. We hadn't been into port in nearly six months, hadn't seen another human being beside the six of us in that long either.

"We came in for supplies only to find the ocean-side town abandoned. Or so we thought."

"We went to look for food," the woman said, her eyes haunted. "That's when we saw them, sleeping in the buildings. It was dark but we saw them, hundreds of them. Just staring out at nothing. We didn't know what had happened."

"We split into groups," the man said. "We hid ourselves as best we could. Got supplies at night because occasionally we saw ones that were awake during the day. We did okay for a few years but they started pushing further and further into the country. They started looking for us. Using weapons to take us down, make us easier to infect. We didn't think it was safe anymore to stay. So we started walking."

"That was a year ago," the woman said hoarsely. "We've been running ever since."

"But you're still alive," Avian said quietly. "That's the part that really matters."

"What are your names?" I asked, finally relaxing my shotgun.

"Tess," the woman said. "And this is Van."

"I'm Avian," he said. "This is Eve, that's Morgan and Eli."

"Thank you for giving us shelter," Van said as he put his arm around Tess. "We will be out of your way soon."

"You're welcome to travel with us," Avian said. I stiffened at his hasty acceptance. "We are headed southwest before the winter comes. We plan to find somewhere safe and set up camp again. Ours was just destroyed. The rest of our group is coming later."

"How many of you are there?" Tess asked.

"Here now, seventeen. There are another seventeen that will follow. With the two of you that will bring us up to thirty-six members of Eden."

"Eden," Tess said, a hint of a smile in the corner of her lips. "We would love to be members of Eden."

Avian nodded, a smile on his own lips, as he placed his hand on her knee for just a moment.

We fed Tess and Van as much as we could. But it wasn't much.

When I woke up that evening the rain had not let up. The clouds were still dumping on us and Tuck told us that unless it stopped soon there was no way we were going to be able to drive that night. The windshield wipers didn't work anymore. He wouldn't be able to see a thing. Avian was also worried everyone would catch sick if they sat out in the rain on the trailer all night.

Everyone settled down in one tent or another that night, each silently grateful to be able to sleep on stationary ground after two nights on the trailer. I watched as West went to one tent, Avian to another. I stationed myself just outside one of the tents they hadn't chosen, volunteering as usual to keep night watch.

TWENTY-NINE

Two days later everyone had just started falling asleep when Avian's attention perked up. He stood in his place on the trailer, his eyes narrowing at something ahead of us.

"What is it?" I asked quietly in an attempt to not wake anyone. I took the safety off my shotgun.

"Stop the truck," Avian told Tuck. As he did, Avian hopped out, myself in close pursuit. He walked up to an old road sign and only then did I notice that there was something different about this one.

"What are those?" I asked as I looked closely at the white dots beneath the words leading to somewhere that now meant nothing.

"Morse code," Avian whispered as he ran his fingers over the dots.

"What does it say?" I asked as my eyes swept the area again. No threats in this desert forsaken place.

Avian shook his head, his eyes frustrated looking. "I don't know."

Without hesitation I walked back over to the trailer. "Wake up!" I said loudly. A few bodies stirred. "Come on. Wake up."

Some of them eyed the gun in my hands warily, others simply rubbed the sleep out of their eyes. "Does anyone know how to read Morse code?"

West yawned as he raised his hand. "Come on," I said, waving him toward the sign. "Sorry to wake everyone. You can go back to sleep now."

I heard a few grumbles as we walked toward the sign. Most of them lay back down but a few of them watched what we were doing with curiosity.

"You know Morse code?" Avian asked as we walked up.

"My grandpa thought it was a fun game when I was little," West said as he rubbed his eyes again. "That's a scientist's version of fun for you."

"What does it say?" Avian asked as he looked back at the sign. "This isn't the regular paint that was used for signs. It's too irregular and the paint doesn't look that worn. This was put there in the last few years. After the Evolution."

West squinted through the dark to read the sign. As he did, he stepped around it, looked at the back, then looked at the edge of it. "It just says 'look beneath'."

Avian furrowed his brow at West, then looked back at the sign. Then we all saw the slightly bent form of the metal sign in the bottom right corner.

With a hefty tug, the three loose screws at the top of the sign were ripped out and I let the metal sign fall to the ground with a thud in the dust.

Our eyes grew wide as we took in what had been hidden under the old road sign. Words were crammed onto the wood board beneath, and a detailed but obviously hand drawn map spread over most of it. There had unquestionably been people here, trying to leave a message for anyone who might find it.

"Holy…" both Avian and West breathed.

"Where is the map leading?" I asked, my eyes following the hand drawn lines.

"Right to the middle of one of the biggest cities there was," Avian said quietly.

If you're reading this, congratulations on surviving. To be brief, there is a group of us, hiding in the city. We have unlimited supplies of food, water, other necessities. We also have electricity and can offer you protection. A life. If you can reach us. This is a map to our location. Travel at night and travel silently. Good luck.

Below that, in another person's handwriting, was written: *May the force be with you.*

"What does that even mean?" I asked. *May the force be with you.* It sounded like gibberish to me.

Avian chuckled again. "It was a line from a very famous movie." When he saw my confusion at the word movie he just shook his head and laughed again. "Never mind. Just know that it is a very human thing to say."

"How is that even possible?" West asked, fully awake now. "For a group of people to be living in a city?"

"I can't imagine anyone is that careful," I said quietly.

"But if they were..." West said wistfully. "Can you even imagine? Having actual electricity, living indoors?"

"No," I said, furrowing my brow at him. "I can't imagine it. It would be too dangerous. Avian said that was one of the biggest cities. It is going to be flooded with Bane. We couldn't even get fifty miles outside the perimeter."

"But they must have a way of getting people in if they've left this message," West continued. "They said to travel at night and to travel silently. Why would they have us walk into a death trap?"

"This could have been left a few years ago," I said, my voice rising. "They could all be infected by now, dead. There could be no one left in the city anymore."

"But if there are *people* there..." Avian said. "They could have access to *anything* if they can get around that city."

"You can't be serious about this," I demanded as I turned my eyes on him. "We can't take this risk. We have a mission to complete. Find a new, *safe* location for Eden and settle. Lead the others to us."

"We could change our course," Avian said as he walked back to the truck. He grabbed Bill's atlas out of the trailer. He opened it up and quickly found our location. "We were going here," he said as he pointed to a place that was due south of our current location. "We could get there by dawn if we can get the truck to drive fast enough. But we could go here," he said as he drug his finger across the page to a place that was west of our location. "Frankly it will be a nicer location. We'll have access to more water, there will be more natural resources. And it is close to the ocean so there might also be more options for fishing. Temperatures shouldn't be any different."

"But it is surrounded by cities," I observed as I read the names around the textured green space Avian had his finger on.

Avian nodded his head. "But it is less than sixty miles from where these other people are supposedly hiding out. We could go to this new location, even if it is only temporary, hide out and send a scouting party to check things out."

"This is suicide, Avian," I said. "A city that size? We don't have a chance of even getting to the outskirts."

"But if there are people there..." Avian said again. "Eve, we've already lost so many people this last year. As far as we knew, we were the only ones left. But if there are more of them out there... We have to stick together, to keep humanity alive."

I looked up at Avian, searching his eyes. There was hope burning there, but I was surprised at another thing I felt coming from him: a total lack of fear. I had underestimated Avian so much.

"This isn't just our decision," I said quietly. "This affects all of them too," I said as I indicated those waiting on the trailer for us. "We have to let them decide as well."

Avian and West looked up to those who were watching us silently. Everyone was awake now. Their faces were anxious looking, mixed with hope and fear. They could read what was written on the sign as well as I could.

"What do all of you think?" Avian said as he took a few steps toward them. "I assume you heard everything we said."

No one spoke up at first and I sensed they were afraid to voice their opinions.

"Tuck," I called on him. He jumped slightly at being directly addressed. "What do you think?"

"I…" he stuttered. "It is dangerous, but if there really are people there I think we have to go."

"No, we don't," Tess, the newcomer, spoke up loudly. "Like Eve said, this is suicide! Have any of you ever been to a city? We have, and it's been years. It's bound to have gotten worse."

"Eli?" I asked when Tess was finished.

He glanced at Morgan where she stood at his side. "I'm not willing to risk putting my family in danger, but if there are some who want to go into the city to scout, I'm okay with changing course. It could only be temporary. I trust the three of you to keep us safe."

The majority of the heads in our group nodded, much to my surprise. Maybe they did still trust me with their lives, even if they now knew what I was.

"Let's put it to a vote then," Avian said, putting his hands on his hips. "All those in favor of changing course and hiding out while some of us scout the area, raise your hand."

Every hand but mine, Tess and Van's went up.

"That's the majority," Avian said with a nod. He turned his intense blue eyes on me, his brow furrowed with mixed emotions. "Are you going to be with us Eve, if we change course? Would you go with the scouting party?"

I glared at him. Where had my cautious Avian gone? Who was this daring risk taker?

"Of course I will go with you," I said, my jaw tight. "If anyone is going into the city I *have* to go with them. I'm the only one that can't get infected."

The smallest hint of a smile formed in the corner of his mouth but I didn't miss it. I almost returned it.

"Alright," Avian said, clapping his hands together. "We'll get our new destination mapped out and get going as soon as we can. We've still got a few hours of darkness left."

"Crazy idiot," I muttered under my breath as we turned back to the map. Avian just gave me a smug smile as he started drawing on the map.

A few minutes later we all loaded up, heading out west on the crumbled highway.

"We'll find somewhere safe to hide everyone for at least a few days," Avian said as he squinted against the wind that blew in his face. "If everything goes smooth, we'll get everyone settled in the morning, get some sleep, and then the three of us will head into the city tomorrow night."

"I'd like to come too, sir, if that's alright with you," Tuck said from the driver's seat.

West chuckled and Avian couldn't seem to help himself as he cracked a smile. I wondered if anyone had ever called Avian "sir." "That's up to you. You seem competent enough with a gun. If you're willing to take the risk you're welcome to come."

Tuck just nodded.

"I'm assuming you will be coming with us?" I asked West, who had been unnaturally quiet the last few hours.

"Of course," he said, his voice almost sounding insulted. "I'm not going to let you and Avian have all the fun."

An hour and a half later, a few looming figures to the south of us drew my attention. They almost looked like...giant birds. "Avian, what are those?"

He squinted in the direction I pointed then he raised his rifle to his eye level to look through the night-vision scope. "They're planes," he said as he glanced down at the map in his lap. "This is an old Air Force base. Tuck, pull over."

"Military?" I asked, my attention perking. "They would have weapons inside somewhere?"

Avian shook his head and shrugged. "Maybe. The base I was stationed at was just abandoned when things started falling apart. Who knows what we'd find in there."

"Would we have time to go take a look around?" West asked.

Avian looked at the map again. "We're making good time. We should have about an hour of wiggle room. You really want to go inside? There could be dozens of them in there."

"It's really secluded out here," West said as he looked around us. There wasn't even sagebrush growing in the cracked earth. "I doubt this small base attracted them."

"I think West is right," I said as I scanned the area. "It doesn't seem like a likely place for Bane."

"Alright," Avian said as he nodded. "Eve, obviously it's best if you go in. We'll stay here and keep an eye out for if anything happens."

"No way," West said as he shook his head. "I'm not letting her go in there by herself."

"I can take care of myself," I said as I rolled my eyes at him. "I think you would know that by now."

"Even so, I'm not going to just sit here," West said as he locked eyes with Avian.

"Get over it you two," I said in an exasperated tone as I jumped out of the trailer and started walking toward the looming buildings. A moment later another set of feet jumped to the ground and jogged to keep up with me.

West and I padded silently across the sand and clay, guns in hand, ready to fire at the slightest movement. As we approached the buildings my eyes grew wide.

"They're huge," I breathed as I took the size of them in. The place just went on and on, a massive landscape of waved metal. I had never seen a building so big.

"You should have seen the NovaTor building we used to live in," West said. I gave him a hard look before he let out an awkward chuckle. "Okay, maybe not."

We found a door in the vastness of the north wall. It was locked. I tapped it, testing its thickness. "It's pretty thin," I said as I squinted through the dark. "Ready to see how enhanced I am?" I said with a coy smile. West just shook his head and laughed.

I punched a hole through the waved aluminum. A thin scratch ran down the length of my hand, a few tiny drops of blood dripping to the ground. Ignoring it, I reached through and opened the door from the inside.

The interior of the building was massive. Everyone in Eden could have set up their tents inside and still had plenty of room to roam. "They must have put those planes in here," West said as he too took our surroundings in. There were no traces of any life around, cybernetic or organic.

"Come on," I said. "Let's get moving."

We jogged along the perimeter of the building, finding a few rooms in one corner. One contained a desk, papers and books scattered around the room. We found a handgun in one of the drawers and a small box of ammunition. The other room was used for storage. We found a few sets of shoes and pairs of pants to bring back with us.

We went back outside and jogged to the next building. It too was locked. Two seconds later it wasn't.

Proof of West's theory was found inside this building. Through the darkness we could make out the figure of one of the massive planes.

"Isn't that amazing?" West mused. "That we used to have control over the sky like that? I would have loved to learn to fly one of those."

"Maybe someday you'll get your chance," I whispered as I started along the perimeter of the building. We found a kitchen but there was no food left in it. It was in the next room we struck gold.

"Here we go," I said with a smirk as I stood in the doorway.

The walls were lined with all kinds of weaponry. Handguns, shotguns, things I had never even seen before but would learn to use shortly. "Grab everything you can," I said, reaching for the nearest menacing looking piece of destruction and salvation.

I filled my pockets with ammunition until my pants threatened not to stay on my hips from the weight. I grabbed three oblong balls with small pins stuck in the top. I wasn't sure what they would do but if they were in this room they must have had destructive force. I shoved them into one of the pockets at the side of my knees.

"What you said before, about only blacking out around me, it's true, isn't it?" West said as he continued to load up.

"Yeah," I grunted as I strapped two guns to the side of my pack.

"I guess I thought you were just mad at me before, as usual, when you said it," he said quietly as he worked. "Why do you think that is?"

"I don't know," I said, feeling a little frustrated. I just wanted to be doing something useful and not have to deal with feelings right now.

"Do you think maybe feeling what you do kind of...overloads you?" he asked quietly.

"Maybe," I said as I felt along an upper shelf. I pulled down another box of bullets.

West was quiet for a while after that and I could sense all the turmoil he was in. "I don't know how to stay away from you, Eve. I don't think I can just shut my feelings for you off."

"Can we not talk about this right now?" I said, my hands faltering in their hurried work.

I heard him walk up behind me. I felt his hand on my arm, slowly turning me around. I met his brown eyes, alive and dancing in the darkness. His hands came to my waist, softly pushing me back against the wall behind me.

"I know how I make you feel, Eve," he whispered, his lips only an inch away from mine.

I was about to push West away, knowing we had a job to do when West pressed his lips to mine.

And then the lights went out.

THIRTY

When I opened my eyes the sky was starting to lighten, a pale shade of blue and pink. The tips of trees surrounded my vision. For half a second I thought we were back in Eden. But the shape of this lake was different, the trees a different species, though similar. And there were only nine tents instead of a few dozen.

The people of our group bustled around, finishing setting up the tents, putting their belongings inside, washing their sweat-crusted clothes out in the small lake.

How long had I been out for? It must have been a few hours if we had finally left the desert behind and found a forest.

I sat up, realizing I was lying on the trailer. I shook my head, trying to clear the fog that was still nesting in my brain. I spotted West at his tent. He glanced over at me and my eyes narrowed at him. His left eye was surrounded with a ring of black.

My eyes then found Avian. His bottom lip was split.

I didn't even have to ask what had happened.

I got up, still feeling a little off, and went to look for my tent in the back of the truck. I realized that it was already being set up. To my surprise it was Tuck who was assembling it.

"Thank you," I said as I grabbed a pole and helped him. "I can take care of it."

"It's no trouble," he said, his lips pulling into a small smile.

I tried to return it, unsure if I had succeeded. It felt strange working next to him, I didn't know him well. Tuck had only been with us for just over a year.

"Was it bad?" I asked him quietly.

"What?" he asked as he started hammering a stake into the ground.

"The fight."

Tuck gave the smallest of chuckles. "A few fists flew but it was over pretty quick. I reminded them that we didn't have time for squabbles."

I just shook my head, letting out a frustrated breath. "I didn't do anything did I? Nothing…I don't know."

"Just zombie walked," he said as he stood and wiped his hands off on his pants. When I gave him a blank stare he continued. "You just walked back to the truck with West, loaded up with weapons. But your eyes were…"

"Blank," I finished for him. "Was that all?"

He nodded. "You just sat on the trailer where we placed you, staring out into nothing."

My insides felt all twisted up as I imagined what I must have looked like. "Was everyone afraid of me?"

He didn't answer right away. "Some of them were a little concerned. Avian kind of chewed them out for it though. He made a good point. You've protected everyone for the last five years, why would you turn on us now?"

"Thank you, Tuck," I said. He just nodded and walked back toward his own tent.

Tess walked up to me, a wary look on her face.

"Why did you just agree to their plan?" she asked, looking uncomfortable to be talking to me. "If you're so afraid to go so close to the city, why would you allow them to come here? You know how dangerous this is."

"I'm not afraid," I said. "It's all of them I'm worried about. I will go wherever they do to keep them from getting infected."

"So it's true?" she half whispered. "That you can't be infected?"

"Yes," I said as I swallowed hard. "I've been touched by Bane, multiple times."

"Why is that?"

I felt uncomfortable. I didn't know this woman, didn't know if I could trust her. "I just can't."

"And that's why you're not afraid," she said, giving me an almost harsh look, and walked back toward Van.

I decided I didn't like Tess very much. But she had been right.

I couldn't avoid them any longer. I finally sought out Avian, finding him keeping watch on our western perimeter, in the direction of the cities. I stood there, ten feet away, not even knowing what to say.

"We should get prepped to leave tonight," Avian mercifully broke the silence. "We need get as familiar with the route as we can."

Even though Avian spoke of plans, he didn't move. I nodded my head, unable to do anything but stare in those infinitely blue eyes.

"I'm sorry," I finally managed.

"I don't blame only you," he said as he slung his gun over his shoulder and started back towards camp.

We found West and Tuck and took the map back to the trailer. Setting it down, we all gathered around it. "We're here," Avian said, pointing to a spot next to an exact replica of the small lake. "I think we can take the truck this far," he said has he pointed to another spot. "From there we're going to have to walk. I'm guessing it's about fifteen miles. Even if everything goes smooth and we don't run into any Bane, it's going to take us nearly all night to get there. If we don't find these people by morning we're going to have to find somewhere to hide for the day."

"This is insane, Avian," I said as I shook my head. "There are going to be so many of them. This is like sticking your hand into the middle of a beehive and expecting not to get stung."

"But if the people that are hiding in the city have put other messages out there, they must watch for others," West said. "Maybe they have some form of transportation they can take to scout."

"An electric vehicle would be virtually silent," Tuck said as he studied the map. "If they have electricity and can power one, they're around. They aren't as fast as a normal car but it should be fast enough to outrun a Bane."

"That may be," Avian said. "But we can't count on that. Everyone we're leaving behind has to know that we may be gone more than just tonight. We may be gone for a while."

"And how long do they wait 'til they have to assume we're dead?" I said harshly. "Then what do they do?"

"Survive," Avian said as he glared at me. "As they've been doing for the last five years."

"Did you want to talk about anything else?" I asked impatiently.

Avian shook his head. "I think we're set, as long as we are all ready to leave tonight."

We each nodded our heads that we were. "Have any of you slept yet?" I asked them. Their pause told me they hadn't. "I'll keep watch since I've been sleeping for the last however many hours. Or whatever it was that I was doing."

245

West gave me a little half smile. Avian glared at him. They finally turned and went to their tents.

The four of us loaded our minimal supplies and the majority of the weaponry into the back of the truck and headed directly south.

I felt unprepared as Avian checked the map and we pulled over less than an hour after we had left the rest of the group. As the houses started to crop up, we parked it next to a few other vehicles that had been long abandoned. We all hunted around for stones of any size and stacked them up directly behind the truck.

Thankful for a nearly full moon to see by, we set out at a jog, each in a hurry to get this suicidal task over with.

The houses seemed so forlorn, their windows empty and hollow. All of the families that had once lived there now didn't care about their upkeep, didn't laugh or tell stories within their walls. The houses were all just overgrown pieces of a dead history now.

When we had looked at the map all I saw was city after city stacked together, crammed into such a small space. As we came into the center of the first one, my blood chilled.

"I don't understand," Avian breathed as he cautiously walked up to a building. Dozens of Bane stared back out at us, their eyes inactive and empty. "Why do some of them attack and some of them just stand there?"

"They look like they're just waiting for something," Tuck said, going nowhere near the building.

"Let's not find out what for," I said as I started back down the cracked road.

I wasn't sure how they defined one city from the next. It all just seemed like one endless city that kept repeating over and over. And empty eyes watched us everywhere.

We jogged for as long as Tuck, Avian, and West could breathe for. Tuck held his side as we slowed, Avian's breathing became heavy, and West struggled to keep up. I had to constantly remind myself to slow down. Not all of us were machines.

Buildings grew taller around us as we approached the middle of our map. If there were people still alive, we should find them soon.

We had just turned a corner when I stopped dead in my tracks, West plowing into me from behind, Avian and Tuck nearly tripping over him.

The barrel of a shotgun pressed tightly to my chest.

THIRTY-ONE

"Who are you?" a thickly built man with graying hair demanded. "How'd you get here?"

"We walked," I started, holding my hands up, despite the weaponry that hung all over my body. "We found your sign. We came looking, to see if there was anyone still alive."

He lowered his gun slightly. Now it was just pointed at my feet. "We haven't seen anyone else in well over a year. We weren't sure there was anyone left."

"There are more of us," Avian started. "We're only part of a fairly large group. Half are still back east. The rest of us are hidden about sixty miles from here."

"You're coming with me," he said.

There was a vehicle parked behind him. It looked like a miniature version of our truck. We climbed into the bed, the other man cautiously sat behind the wheel. He kept glancing back at us every few seconds. As we started down the street I was expecting the normal engine noise I knew a vehicle should make. This one was soundless.

"Electric," West said when he saw my confusion. "Now I believe you owe Avian and I an apology?"

"For what?" I asked.

"For doubting, for telling us we were wrong. There are people here. Apparently more than one considering he said 'we'."

I just shook my head and watched the buildings as they whipped by. Avian, who sat smashed against my side in the tight quarters of the small vehicle, slipped his hand into mine.

Empty eyes of the Bane watched us as we sped down the crumbling streets. I watched for signs of other life, surely this man was not alone out here. But I didn't see any, just the sad reminders of the empire the human race had once had.

"Where do you think he is taking us?" Tuck asked.

"It will be somewhere incredibly secure," I said as I continued to observe. "They probably don't have enough CDUs to give to each of their scouts. I assume they have them. I'm sure he's taking us wherever there is one."

Avian's hand tightened around mine and I noticed how he readjusted his hold on his rifle. Unease washed over me. Not for fear that I might be shorted out in the next hour, but that Avian might do something stupid trying to protect me.

"Don't," I whispered to him.

"I'm not going to let them do anything to you," he said, keeping his eyes forward.

"But I'll never forgive you if you get yourself killed because of me," I said quietly, giving his hand a small squeeze.

"Same goes here," he said as he glanced over at me for just a moment.

We drove for not more than ten minutes when I started seeing them. Humans, standing on top of the towering buildings, watching us from above. Each was heavily armed and looked like they knew how to use their weapons.

We slowed down as we approached a building that had levels upon levels and spanned massively in both directions.

"A real hospital," Avian breathed.

The vehicle we sat in pulled around to the back of the hospital and straight through a huge door. As we stopped inside and the door closed behind us.

249

There were five armed men just inside. They each looked as surprised to see us as the first man had been.

"Where's Royce?" the man who had brought us here asked as he climbed out of the truck. He indicated for us to climb out, his gun pointed at our backs. I wondered if he realized how ridiculous he looked with his one single shotgun when we each had at least three firearms on us.

"He's upstairs," one of the men answered him.

"That way," he said as he prodded West in the back with the barrel.

As we moved I observed rows and rows of vehicles in this concrete expanse of a room. Each of them were shiny and beautiful. They had picked through the best of all the cars, trucks, and vans they could find.

We walked to an elevator and the doors slid closed behind us. When the doors opened again there was a hallway stretched out before us, buzzing with the hum of electric devices behind closed doors.

We walked where the man told us to, stopping at a door midway down the hall. The man knocked, listening.

"Come in," a voice called.

There were four people inside, gathered around a large desk, looking over some papers. A man with well-trimmed gray hair and a beard straightened. I assumed this was Royce.

"I found them on patrol," the man behind us said. "They said they found one of our signs and came to take a look."

"Are there more of you?" the man asked, his gray eyes showing hints of excitement that had given away the rest of them.

Avian nodded his head. "There are sixteen more of us waiting outside the city. The other half of our group is at our old camp. About 800 miles away."

The man's eyes widened. "You've traveled a long ways to reach us. How was the journey?"

"We made it," Avian said simply.

"Forgive our unfriendly welcome," he said as he walked around the table, his arms folded over his chest. "I'm sure you understand the precautions we have to take these days."

"Of course," Avian said. I heard the anxiety that was creeping into his voice.

"Come with me, please," Royce said as he stepped around us and out of the room. We followed silently.

Just looking at Royce, one would think he was a leader. His stature was tall and confident. His shoulders were sure, his gait unfaltering. He looked like a man who knew what he was doing, all the time.

Royce led us down the hall and into a room that had no windows and was totally empty of anything other than a leather case lying on a table. He opened it up as we stepped inside. Other soldiers followed us in. I didn't miss the weapons in their belts, in their pockets, and obviously in their hands. And I was very aware of the fact that they had closed the door behind us.

It looked different than ours but it was unmistakably a CDU. As if on cue, West, Avian, and Tuck adjusted their stances so they were standing just in front of me.

"This shouldn't hurt gentlemen, and lady," Royce said with a tight-lipped smile as he charged it up. The center of it glowed a brilliant blue. "Just a small shock."

Avian stepped up first, pulling the sleeve of his shirt up and offering his arm. It twitched as the device was pressed to his arm. West went next, followed by Tuck.

"Thank you, gentlemen," Royce said, giving them that same tight-lipped, fake looking smile. "My lady."

251

The three of them tightened around me. As they did, Royce's eyes hardened and he stopped in his tracks. "You know all newcomers must be tested. She is no exception."

"She is," West said quietly.

"She's different," Avian said, trying to keep his voice calm.

As if their words had opened up a book on our faces, Royce's eyes widened and he took a step back, drawing a handgun out from the belt of his pants. As he did, the rest of the people in the room drew their weapons as well.

"Hold on!" Avian shouted as he backed further into me, holding his hands up toward our captors. "She's not a Bane! But she has cybernetic parts in her. She's different from them."

"They're all the same!" Royce shouted as he aimed his gun at my head. "She's a danger being here. My scouts should have shot her before she came within a hundred feet of this building."

"She can't be infected!" West shouted at the man. "She was experimented on. My grandfather was Dr. Evans. He worked at NovaTor Biotics. She was his preliminary test before TorBane was fully developed."

"Dr. Evans?" Royce spat out. "That heartless scum bag created the infection. He wouldn't have bothered with a hybrid. In his quest for savior status he destroyed the world."

"Yes he did, but I assure you he was my grandfather. My father evolved early on and someone set Eve free after everything happened. She's human but he did things to her that make her different. You can't test her or it *will* kill her," West's voice sounded pleading.

"They are all the same!" Royce shouted as he thrust his gun in our direction again. "I don't know how she's tricked you into thinking differently but it's a miracle she hasn't infected you yet."

At the same time, both Avian and West turned and each took one of my hands.

"She doesn't carry the infection," Avian said, his voice serious and low. "She's been with me for the last five years and she's never turned against us. She's done nothing but protect us."

The door at our backs suddenly opened and a very tanned looking face with jet-black hair popped in.

"What is all the shouting about?" he asked, his voice sounding slightly alarmed.

"She's one of them," Royce said, his voice cold. "They're claiming she's different."

The new man's eyes jumped to my face and his eyes narrowed at me. "Eve?"

"How do you know my name?" I spoke for the first time since we had been brought in.

"It's really you," he breathed as he stepped inside. "You survived."

"Dr. Beeson?" West asked with uncertainty in his voice.

"West!" The man didn't hide his surprise when his eyes met West's. They paused for a moment when their eyes met, almost as if some sort of unspoken message passed between them in that moment. Dr. Beeson's eyes grew serious, and he gave the smallest of nods.

"You were the one who took over my observation," I said as the name from the notebook echoed in my memory.

He nodded, his eyes still wide.

"So, you're saying they're telling the truth, Erik?" Royce demanded.

"She is different, yes," Dr. Beeson said as he glanced over at Royce. "She had a chip implanted into her brain that

253

enhanced her. She was a preliminary experiment that led up to the infection. Since she was given TorBane at such a young age, and so precisely, it blended with her DNA, stayed under control. If you use that on her, it *will* kill her," he said as he indicated the CDU Royce still had clutched in his hand.

"If I turn on you, you can shoot me yourself," I said to Royce with hard eyes.

He looked at me long and hard, distrust written all over his face.

"Remove her weapons from her," Royce said. "I won't have you walking around here armed like that."

I saw West's eyes flash to my face in momentary panic. I shook my head at him. I didn't like it either but I also didn't see any other way to get through this.

Their men relieved me of my weapons. When one of them reached for my pack, I grabbed his wrist, shaking my head at him. His eyes grew wide and he withdrew his hand, backing away. I almost smiled.

"You're sure she's different, Erik?" Royce asked again, his eyes narrowed.

"Quite," he said as he opened the door and held it open for everyone.

Royce finally lowered his weapon. As he did, the rest of his men followed suit. "Forgive me if I'm not exactly welcoming," he said as his face softened, though his eyes were still cold on me. "I'm not so keen on the reliability of a human-Bane hybrid I've never heard of."

"I wasn't so keen on the idea myself when I first found out what I was," I said back, never loosing eye contact.

Everyone else in the room probably missed it, but my enhanced eyes caught the twitch in his cheek as a smile was fought back.

"Well, gentlemen," Royce said as he started for the door. "And lady. Welcome to Los Angeles. This is our sanctuary in the middle of hell on Earth."

We followed him back out into the hall and Dr. Beeson broke off from the rest of us. He looked nervous and pale as he walked away.

"Our offices are on this level, as well as several of our labs," Royce said as he indicated the doors down this hall. We followed him back where we had come from and reentered the elevator. My stomach felt strange as we started to descend. The door opened to a different level, this one bustling with people, opening up into a big lobby.

"This is our other headquarters," Royce said as we stepped out and into the busy room. "Everything runs from this room. All the scheduling for patrol, shifts in the kitchen, maintenance, it's all managed here. Everything is logged in, tracked. We keep a tight schedule but everything runs smoothly."

I noticed the solid steel shutters that covered the front door, all of the windows, and every other opening.

"Keeps out things we don't want getting in," Royce said when he noticed me observing them.

"You keep them out during the day, even in the middle of all of this," I said, impressed.

Royce nodded as we continued to follow him toward the back of the big front area. We entered another hallway, this one wider and more open than the one upstairs. "Restrooms are right there," he said, pointing to a pair of wooden doors. I wondered what he meant by "restrooms."

We turned a corner and came into another fairly large room with tables and chairs set up everywhere. Along one wall was some sort of glass case and beyond that I could see the strangest looking kitchen I had ever seen. It was all shiny steel and smooth surfaces.

"Back there's the kitchen," Royce said as he pointed in that direction. "Meals are served at nine PM, one AM, and seven AM. Pretty much all of us keep a nocturnal schedule here. Dinner will be served in about two hours," he said as he glanced at his watch. "Most of us wake up around eight PM, just before the sun starts to go down outside. Bed is around ten AM."

"Doesn't this place start to feel like a prison?" I couldn't help but asking. "You never even see the sun."

"Our lifestyle isn't easy," Royce said as he met my eyes. "But it's kept over one hundred people alive all this time."

"There are that many of you?" West asked in amazement.

"For a few years we were gaining five or six new people a year. Then it started becoming fewer and fewer. There's been no one for the last year. We figured there wasn't anyone left."

"We found two more people on our way here," I said as we walked out of the dining room and back out into the hall. "In the middle of the desert."

"We look forward to meeting everyone in your group. I've never heard of such a large group traveling so far. How did you manage it?"

"We drove," Avian answered.

"I'm impressed," he said as he raised his brows. We turned another corner and stopped at a desk where a man in a white jacket sat. He looked up at us with surprise in his eyes as we approached him. "This is Dr. Giles. He's the head physician here. These people here traveled from back east," he explained to Dr. Giles. After the introduction, Royce excused himself for a moment and stepped into a side room.

"Congratulations on surviving," Dr. Giles said. I watched as Avian and Tuck shook his hand, observing closely so I did it

256

just right when it came my turn. The motion felt strange and foreign.

"You're a real doctor?" Avian asked, longing and awe in his voice.

"Board certified," he said with a smile. His teeth were astonishingly white. "Well, used to be before there was no more board to pass. There are three other medical doctors here as well."

The amazement was obvious in Avian's eyes as he shook his head.

"Avian has been our doctor for the last five years," I said, feeling a sense of pride in him.

"Ah, wonderful," Dr. Giles said. "Where was your practice before the Evolution?"

"Uh," Avian stumbled over his words. "I actually never attended medical school. I had two and a half years of medical training when I was in the Army. Since I had the most experience I became the doctor. I learned most of my knowledge through experience."

"Very good," Dr. Giles said, something in his eyes changing. It took me a moment to realize what it was. It was the loss of respect. I suddenly didn't like the doctor half as much. I'd like to see this man treat a bullet wound in the middle of the forest with next to no supplies.

"Do you mind if I take a look around your quarters?" Avian asked, unbothered.

"We have a few open rooms you're welcome to examine," he said, his friendly demeanor back. "And so is our surgery room. We have patients in a few rooms so I'll ask you to keep quiet."

He led us into a room that was so sterile I hesitated in the doorway with my dusty boots and dirty clothes.

Avian walked into the room alone while the rest of us waited in the doorway. His eyes were excited as he observed the strange bed with rails on the side of it. He ran his hands over a piece of equipment that stood as tall as him, all kinds of buttons and screens on it. He opened and closed drawers and I could just imagine what he would have done for all of these supplies.

I realized then what the fact that there were four doctors here meant. If we stayed here, moved the rest of Eden into this city, Avian would never have to be tied down because of his medical knowledge again. He would be free to do whatever he wanted. He could go anywhere.

Dr. Giles took us to the surgery room, but only let us look in through a window. As I observed the steel blades that lay out, gleaming in the light as it shone through the window, my breath caught in my throat. I saw the steel table in the middle of the room and my nightmares came back at me like a punch in the gut.

The sound of the drill and the cool against the back of my shaven head were all I could process.

"Come on," West's voice said from somewhere and I felt him take my hand and lead me back out into the hall.

I stood with my back against the tall desk, holding my arms around me. My eyes were open but I wasn't seeing anything. West stood to the side of me, his arm draped around my shoulders, squeezing me into his side.

Avian finally walked back out into the hall and stopped in his tracks. He looked at me, glanced back in the direction of the surgery room, and his face blanched white. "Eve, I'm so sorry," he said, his eyes looking panicked.

I just shook my head, my eyes glued to the floor. Avian was suddenly standing right in front of me, his hands on either side of my face. As I looked up into his blue eyes, I felt my insides loosen up. I still felt sick though.

"You shouldn't be touching her," Avian said, his voice cold as he looked over at West. "Having her black out here is *not* going to help Eve's case." He spoke quietly enough only the three of us could hear.

West only looked at Avian coldly as he took two steps away from me. All three of us glanced over at Royce who had just stepped out of the room and Dr. Giles who watched us with hesitancy.

"Sorry, gentlemen," Avian said as he stepped away from me slightly. "Just bad memories for some of us."

They both gave slight nods, though they still looked at me warily.

"I'll show you our sleeping quarters," Royce said, dismissing the awkward moment. He walked back out into the main hall and continued down. As we followed, West slipped his hand into mine. I shook it off, remembering what Avian had said to him. It was too great of a risk, having West send me into overload here. West should have understood that.

We entered another hall that was lined with doors. These ones were different however. They had names written on them, some written in clear, precise letters, others painted in colored fonts that I could hardly read.

"These are the living quarters," Royce said as we walked passed personalized doors. "Of course they were once just normal hospital rooms. We've converted them into living space. Each of them has their own restroom. They're not large but they're big enough to keep all of your personal effects in and get some sleep."

"What's a 'restroom'," I whispered to Tuck as we walked.

He gave a slight chuckle and whispered in my ear. My brow furrowed. "If that's what it is why do they call it a *rest*room?"

Tuck just smiled again and shrugged his shoulders.

We came to the end of the hall and opened a door that revealed a set of stairs. As we exited on the next floor up, we discovered another hallway of personalized doors.

"Would you like rooms for this afternoon?" Royce asked as we stopped in the middle of the hallway. "I hope you plan on staying with us. Of course you're free to leave whenever you like but I would encourage you to stay. We can offer you protection, food, comfort."

Comfort. I was pretty sure I would be more comfortable out in the woods than I would be in this boxed-up prison.

"We're not sure what our plans are honestly," Avian said as he glanced at West, Tuck, and I.

"We weren't even sure if we'd find anyone alive, or if we were walking into a death trap," West said.

"I'm sure we could all use some sleep though," Avian continued. "I know at least I would like to stay for another day, explore your facility more. I'm fascinated by how you've managed to thrive in the middle of a city."

Royce nodded. "Of course. This way." He led us further down the hall. "You can use these three rooms."

"Three?" I questioned. "There are four of us."

Royce looked confused for a moment. "I'm sorry, I assumed the two of you would want a room together," he said as he indicated Avian and I. I then remembered how he had watched as Avian had held my face between his hands, how close our faces had been together.

"If you have four rooms," West jumped in, not looking at Avian or I.

260

A small smile crossed Royce's face. "That one is available as well," he said as he pointed at the door across from the other three. "Will you remember how to get back to the dining room in an hour for dinner?"

We each nodded our heads and Royce turned and left.

Before I would have to face any more of the awkwardness between the two of them I let myself into one of the rooms and closed the door behind me.

The room felt so sterile, just like the rest of the hospital. The walls were all white, the bed made up with white sheets, white pillows. Even the wooden drawers and cupboards felt too clean and pristine.

I longed for my tent back in Eden.

I opened a door, finding the restroom. The hint of a smile tugged on my face as I saw the shower, remembering the one real one I had had in the cabin I had found.

A knock on the door startled me. "Who is it?" I called through the thick wood.

"I've brought you some things," a female voice called from behind the door.

Hesitantly, I opened it. The girl behind it looked close to my age. Her eyes were narrow and dark, her hair jet black and perfectly straight.

"My name is Lin," she said, giving me a smile. Her eyes seemed to almost disappear when she did so. "I brought you a few things."

She was standing next to a cart with wheels. She grabbed a gray colored blanket, a few items of clothing, and a few bottles of unknown liquid.

"What are these?" I asked as I opened the lids and took a wiff. They smelled nice.

"To wash your hair?" she said, her face looking slightly confused. The smallest of a laugh escaped her lips but it didn't feel mocking.

"Thank you," I said as I put all my new things under my arm. There was something about this girl I liked. She seemed...warm.

"If you need anything else, any help, I'm just a few doors down," she said as she pointed down the hall. "My door is the one with the white lily painted on it."

"Thank you, Lin," I said again. She gave me another smile and crossed the hall to knock on another door.

I went back into the bathroom and after a few minutes figured out how to get the hot water to flow. My clothes felt crusted as I pealed them off. I quickly washed them in the sink and then hung them to dry.

A sigh escaped my throat as the hot water poured over my beat and scarred body. My muscles relaxed and even my insides felt cleaner as I breathed in the steam. The water ran brown for a while, the desert we had survived going down the polished silver drain.

I used the products Lin had given me on my hair. I ended up lathering it all over my entire body it smelled so nice. My hair felt so smooth after it all washed out.

But the relief the shower and hot water provided didn't last long. The situation waiting outside my door crept back in on me. I stood with my hands braced against the shower wall, the water cascading over my head. I didn't want to go back out there, to where I knew people didn't trust me. Facing Avian and West felt like too much to deal with right now. It was all to exhausting to think about.

After almost an hour, I climbed out of the shower, dried off with the towel Lin had given me, and pulled on the stark green clothes. Grabbing the gray blanket, I curled up in my new bed.

I had finally hit my limit. Just a few seconds later I was out.

THIRTY-TWO

The ceiling above my head confused me when I first woke. Dim lights glowed along the floor as I slid my feet off the edge of the bed. I walked to the now open window and looked out.

How strange, to live in this concrete jungle. Small patches of green cropped up but it was being choked out by the gray cement, steel, and glass. And everywhere I could see eyes. How could they stand it, being in the middle of them all, all the time? How had they kept them out?

The lights glowed brightly overhead as I walked out into the empty hall. My steps echoed as I descended the stairs. I had to take a deep breath as I stood behind the steel door, gathering courage to go out into the unknown. Why was it so simple to go on a raid into the city, knowing I might not come back alive, and yet walking out among those strangers, among other humans, was so hard and terrifying?

I traced my way back to the infirmary, passed the dining hall and kitchen, and out into the bustling lobby. I stood at the entrance of the hall for a while, watching as the people moved around.

In a way, they were all like soldiers. They all had their orders, a task to execute. Some of them entered what I assumed was some kind of information into black boxes, presumably computers, a few cleaned the area, other's brought in sheets of paper. The guard switched as a handful of armed men walked out those glass front doors. I wondered where I would fit into this hive.

I saw no signs of Avian, West, or Tuck and I felt awkward for a while, unsure of what to do with myself. And I didn't like the fact that I didn't know where any of my weapons had gone to.

"Eve," a familiar voice called from behind me. As I turned, I recognized Dr. Beeson. His smile was bright as he approached me. "I was just looking for you. You're companion, Avian, said you were still resting."

"I overslept," I said simply as we stood together.

"Would you mind chatting with me for a while? I'm dying of curiosity as to what has happened to you the past five years."

"I suppose," I agreed. This man didn't seem like a threat, and even without any weapons I was quite confident I could overpower him if I had to.

We walked to the elevator, a dozen pairs of eyes watching us as we did. He pushed the number seven button and slowly we began to rise again. When it slid open I was almost startled at all the brilliant blue lights that ran through the walls, along the floor, on the ceiling.

"We use a lot of power on this floor. This level has been specially wired to keep up," he explained.

We walked down the hall a little bit, stopping at a large solid black door. Dr. Beeson entered a code into a number pad and it clicked open.

The room we entered into glowed with the blue lights, heavily contrasted by the darkness of having no windows into the starlit night. Screens glowed from the walls, flashes of information bursting across them.

"This is my office, my lab," he said as he looked around the room with me. For some reason all the information flashing across his screens seemed familiar, like a language I had forgotten how to speak. "Please, have a seat."

I sat in one of the two overly comfortable black chairs, perched on the edge of it, my hands tucked between my knees.

"So, I assume you know what happened to you?" he asked, his voice losing its cheeriness. He had that slightly uncomfortable look on his face again. "About the things that were done to you?"

I nodded my head. "I know that West's grandfather, NovaTor, experimented on me. The military came in and forced him to place some kind of chip in my brain. I was observed for years and eventually he used the information he gathered from me to create the infection."

I stopped there, swallowing the lump in my throat.

Dr. Beeson nodded. "First, let me say that I never agreed with what they were doing to you. I was a young scientist then, working on my development of the capacity of the human mind to receive wireless signals. I was fascinated with the work he was doing on you. But you were just a girl. What Dr. Evans and NovaTor did was wrong.

"But, if we would have been able to control what happened, we would have saved millions of lives."

"Instead billions were killed," I said coldly.

"Unforgivable," he said as his eyes dropped to the ground. "I first tried to remedy what I did by setting you free. I used the wireless capability of the chip in your brain to wipe your memory clean. No girl should have to remember the things you were put through. I assume it worked?"

"I have dreams sometimes," I said quietly, my eyes falling to my hands. "How much of it is purely nightmare and how much of it is something real, I don't know."

"The brain is a complex thing. I'm sorry I couldn't spare you from everything."

"Will those memories ever be recovered?" I asked.

"I have no reason to think so," he said. "Would you really want to remember the rest of it though?"

I had to think about it for a while. "No."

"There were only five of us that escaped that facility, and yet I'm the only one who made it to Los Angeles. Everyone else evolved so quickly. It's a miracle that I made it out. I tasked one of the other men who made it out to take you out into the country and set you free. I never saw that man again."

"Avian found me," I filled in the empty blanks of the past. "Nearly naked out in the forest, covered in blood, but with not a scratch on me." Dr. Beeson's face faltered at that. Ignoring his confusion, I continued. "They knew something was different about me. They just didn't know what. I only found out a few months ago."

"Tell me what you're able to do," he said, excitement building in his eyes again. "Has the programming evolved more? The cybernetics?"

I sat forward again, rubbing my hand over the thin scar that had already formed on the back of my hand from when I had punched a hole through the metal door at the Air Force base. "I heal quickly," I started. "I don't usually feel pain. Electricity is about the only thing I seem to feel. It's made me pass out before though, pain. My brain still registers it I guess.

"I don't require as much sleep as normal. I don't get tired very easily. I don't need to eat as much as normal people. I'm faster than everyone, stronger than most."

"Have you ever been up against a Bane?"

The smile on my face couldn't be fought back. "More than a few times. I didn't understand what was happening the first time one tackled me. I thought I was going to change. But I didn't."

"Do you understand why?" he asked.

"Not really," I answered.

"Because you were given TorBane at such a young age, and in such a specific, controlled way, your body was able to control the technology. You are able to handle it the way it was supposed to work on everyone. After you were given the chip and we saw that more of your body was turning cybernetic, everyone assumed it was because of the chip. But in reality, it was just a precursor to what the later strains of TorBane would do."

I struggled to keep up with what he was saying. I didn't understand it all, but it made some sense.

"Have you seen any traces of the cybernetic parts that have saturated your system?"

I nodded. "The Bane have these metal barbs that shock you. I grabbed some once and it burned away my skin," I said as I turned my hand over, observing the scars there. "I could see all the gears and wires."

"That must have been frightening for you," he said.

"But you know that I'm not supposed to feel fear," I said quietly as my eyes rose to meet his.

He didn't say anything for a while as he held my stare. I wondered how he lived with himself, knowing he had helped bring about the end of the world and then survived to see the destruction. "You're right. You aren't supposed to feel emotion. But we suspected that eventually you would evolve past the programming. Occasionally there were signs that you were moving past it and we'd have to make adjustments. There were times when you got overwhelmed by your emotions and you just blacked out. Just like those Bane you see outside."

I swallowed hard, my stomach knotting up. "It still happens."

"Really?" he said, his eyebrows knitting together as he sat back in his chair.

"But only when I'm around one certain person."

"And how do you feel about this person?"

"That's the unanswerable question," I said quietly.

"Do you have romantic feelings for him? Or maybe an extreme hatred?"

I gave a hollow chuckle. "I think both."

"It's one of the men you arrived with, isn't it?" he said with a sly smile.

I nodded. "I didn't feel things like this until he showed up at our camp. Something inside of me started waking up. I don't know how to handle it. He makes me feel excited, free, and yet he can anger me so much I almost tried to kill him once. And then I just black out."

"It's probably overloading you, or rather the chip. Your body is telling you to feel things but the chip is trying its hardest to block it all out. Your brain and the chip can't work together and it shuts you down in a way. I don't think you will be a danger to anyone. It's not like you're turning into a Bane. You just kind of...shut down."

It was a relief to have it so plainly explained to me. And to know I wasn't going to try and kill anyone. If only the other parts related to it all could be so easily explained.

"Can we talk about something else?" I asked. My voice sounded smaller than I would have liked it to.

"Of course," he said mercifully. "Would you like to see the woman who was your mother?"

"What?" I said, my voice almost sounding like a hiccup.

Dr. Beeson smiled, small lines forming around his dark eyes. He turned in his swivel chair and pulled a drawer open.

He rooted around in it for a moment and then pulled out a packet of pages.

"Her name was Emma," he said opening the packet. He leafed through the pages for a moment. And then he handed me a photo.

The woman who looked back at me was beautiful. Her hair was tied back, perfectly smooth. Her skin was flawless looking. She had a sophisticated pair of glasses perched on her nose.

If she was about fifteen pounds thinner and her skin a bit more roughed up from the wilderness, she would have looked exactly like me.

"She worked for NovaTor. She was a lab research assistant," Dr. Beeson said, looking through more of the pages. I couldn't look away from the woman's face though. "She was young, just starting her master's degree. But she was brilliant. She was going to go far."

"What happened to her?" I asked.

"What happens to a lot of young, pretty girls," he said with a sigh. "She had this boyfriend. They were on and off every other month. Loved each other like crazy, but also couldn't stand the sight of each other. I don't think Emma ever told him she was pregnant."

He handed me another few pictures. One looked like it was taken at some kind of party. They were all wearing white jackets, holding up a sign that said happy birthday. She stood behind the sign looking rather embarrassed. There was another one behind that picture that was more of a candid shot. She stood next to a table, reading some papers. Her belly was large and rounded.

Dr. Beeson cleared his throat and took the last two pictures back. I thought I saw something flicker in his eyes but couldn't be sure.

"Where is she?" I asked. "Why didn't she take care of me?"

"She died," Dr. Beeson said. "Giving birth to you."

My stomach dropped out. "She died giving birth? That was very uncommon, wasn't it? Women didn't die often during child birth before the Evolution."

Dr. Beeson nodded. "Yes, it was. Tragic. Emma didn't have any family. Both her parents had died years ago, she was an only child. We didn't even know her boyfriend's name. Her work and school were her life.

"We weren't sure what to do with you. There was no family to send you to. You were born more than two months premature. You were underdeveloped. Sick. You were going to die. Dr. Evans senior decided to do the first human test of TorBane on you. He didn't tell anyone he was going to do it. He just did it. He figured you were going to die anyway.

"It might have been wrong, and immoral. But he did save your life with TorBane. And that's the reason you don't infect anyone. You were given the technology before you were even supposed to be born, in such a controlled and precise way. It's a part of your very DNA. It stays contained in you."

I nodded, my brain still trying to process all the information and keep up. "So," I said, having to force my voice to work. "My father, he could still be out there?"

Dr. Beeson's eyes saddened. "I wouldn't count on it, Eve. You know how few are still out there."

I nodded. It was true. There was no way he was still alive.

"You can keep that, if you like," he said, pointing at the picture.

"Thank you."

"Eve," he said in a low voice. He leaned forward, resting his elbows on his knees. "I know how confusing emotions can be, for anyone. It isn't fair that it should be ten times worse for you because of what NovaTor did to you. I think I can help that."

My brows pulled together as my eyes met his. "What do you mean?"

He held my eyes for a long time, like he was analyzing something. He almost looked like maybe he had spoken too soon and now he wondered if he should take it back. But a moment later, he gave the slightest of nods as if he'd made up his mind.

"Your emotional blockers were done with the chip in your head. It was all done wirelessly. And I think I could remove them."

I stared at him blankly for a long moment, not fully comprehending what he was saying.

"I think we would have to do it slowly," he continued. "I'm afraid if I just erased it all at once it would overwhelm you. Your body and your brain couldn't handle it. But I think if we do it bit by bit, over a length of time, you could be brought back to normal.

"You wouldn't have blackouts anymore."

My eyes dropped to the floor, my breathing coming in shallow swallows. I would finally understand what everyone else felt. I could allow myself to feel. There wouldn't be any danger of me attacking anyone any longer.

"Would you like to give it a try, Eve?"

The back of my eyes started to sting just slightly as I nodded my head.

"I can start it right now," he said as he glanced at his computer screens. "It won't take very long. I will however, have to kind of shut you down for a while to do it. It will take a reboot, if you will, for everything to take effect."

Something inside of me swelled as I thought about the possibilities. It was followed by a flood of adrenaline.

"Do it."

THIRTY-THREE

There were only a few people left in the dining hall when I wandered down the next day. I was handed a scoop of pears, a pile of steaming eggs and a glass of ice cold, formerly powdered milk. I sat at a table in the corner of the room, shoveling everything down so fast the real chicken eggs burned my throat.

After Dr. Beeson's reprogram, I expected to feel astronomically different. I'd expected to feel overwhelmed. But I only felt more aware of everything. Like everything looked just a little brighter. But like Dr. Beeson said, we were going to have to do this in baby steps.

I caught sight of Royce approaching from across the room. I observed him as he moved toward me. He was in good shape, especially for being in his later forties I guessed. His nose was straight, his jaw sharp. He looked like a leader you would want to follow.

He sat down at the table across from me. "Erik told me everything that happened," he said directly. There was no dancing around with Royce. I appreciated that about him. "Everything about what was done to you as a child. I also talked with Avian. He told me what you did for the members of Eden. For his sister.

"I'm sorry for my behavior before," he said uncomfortably. I had a feeling Royce wasn't one that apologized often. "What you've been though is unfathomable."

"We could use a soldier like you," he said as he held my eyes steadily. "It's getting harder and harder to keep them out, times are changing. We want to invite you, and the rest of your group to join with us. We would be honored to have all of you here."

I just looked at him, trying to make my brain process everything. I felt sluggish from Dr. Beeson's reboot. "What did Avian say?" I asked.

"He hasn't given me an answer yet. I talked with West and Tuck as well. They both liked the idea but wouldn't give an answer without consulting with the rest of your group."

I nodded. "My answer is the same. It's not just my decision."

Royce nodded. "That's fine. I wouldn't expect anything different. I want to show you something though. All four of you."

I stood, returned my plate and glass for cleaning, and followed Royce out into the main front room. We spotted West reading a book in a corner and Royce indicated for him to come with us. West marked his place, set the book down and joined us.

"There are a few things I want to show you," Royce repeated to West. We spotted Tuck across the room as well, talking to a woman. He joined us.

We entered the medical wing and Avian came walking out of a room with a doctor I had not seen yet.

"That's a wonderful idea," the new doctor said. "I'd love to give it a try sometime."

"When we have more time I'll tell you how I removed a tree branch from a man's chest cavity in the middle of the forest with no medical supplies. *Without* killing him," Avian said with a chuckle.

"Okay," the doctor laughed back. He shook Avian's hand and walked into another room.

"There's something I'd like to show you," Royce said when Avian turned his eyes on us. We all headed for the elevator.

We stepped out into the blue glowing hallway and approached the door to Dr. Beeson's lab. We stopped just outside it.

"I understand your hesitancies in joining us," Royce started. "Living here has its challenges. But I want you to understand the benefits that come with a place like this, besides the obvious of electricity and running water."

He opened the door and we crowded into the room. Dr. Beeson sat inside, staring at the flashing screens before him.

"Erik has developed technology that interfaces with the Bane," Royce started explaining. "Trust me, there are endless Hunters out there who would have ripped this building apart, bit by bit, if not for his research."

"Hunters?" Avian asked, his brow furrowing.

"Hunters, strikers, finishers," Royce said, looking at us. "Call them what you like."

"What do you mean?" West questioned, folding his arms over his chest.

"You know about the three classes of Bane, don't you?" Royce said, his eyes a mix of disbelieving and annoyance.

"No," Avian answered simply.

"May I, Eric?" Royce asked, reaching for a writing instrument that sat on his desk. Dr. Beeson just nodded his head, not even taking his eyes from the screens.

Royce grabbed the marker and turned to a blank space of wall between some of the monitors. He uncapped it and started writing on the wall. His letters glowed brilliant green.

"You have Babies," he said as he wrote the word. "Sleepers…and Hunters. At least that's what we like to call them.

"Babies are the newly infected," Royce said, capping the marker again and handing it back to Dr. Beeson. "This stage doesn't last long. Usually a month, at the most."

"But Babies?" West questioned, his voice hinting at mockery.

"Babies come into this world screaming, kicking, and fighting like you can't believe. But they're also weak, not very smart. They run off of instinct. Just like a newly infected.

"Sleepers are self-explanatory. They're the ones that just stand around, watching us. Are you familiar with how the tech works after you are infected?"

"What is there to understand?" West said. "You get touched, the cybernetics start to take over, and after that all you care about is infecting everyone else. Spreading the cybernetics and creating more Bane."

"It's a lot more complicated than that," Royce said, shaking his head. "Just after you get infected your brain and body go into overdrive. Survival instincts take over. But your brain can't handle the new technology. They conflict. That's why the Babies don't stay Babies for long. Their brains eventually shut down."

"And they become Sleepers," I said.

"Exactly," Royce said. "The Bane basically go into a coma after a few weeks. Their minds just shut down. It takes time for the brain to be rewired. The technology works its way into every part of you quickly, but the brain isn't so simple. Sleepers stay asleep for a long time."

"Like how long?" Avian asked.

"Like a few years usually," Royce answered. "The process is slow. But deadly effective. They wake up and are ready for action. They're ready to complete their task."

"So it is the Hunters that are so aggressive," I said. "They're the ones who are attacking us?"

"The last class of Bane aren't just aggressive," Royce said, his eyes clouding in the way only eyes that had seen too much destruction could. "They're getting smarter."

His words hung in the air for a moment. None of us said anything, unable to accept the truth.

"The Bane, they're starting to think like machines," Royce finally continued. "They're calculating, they analyze. They are starting to think about their actions and they're trying to outsmart us. And it's just going to keep getting worse, the longer they're alive."

"Then how are you all still alive here in the middle of a city?" West questioned.

"Like I said, Erik has developed technology that interfaces with the Bane," Royce continued. "We wouldn't be alive without his research."

That explained how he'd been able to make my adjustments.

"You can control them?" West asked.

"What we can do is very limited," Dr. Beeson said as he tore his eyes away from the screen before him. "It's difficult to transmit information to such a large amount of receptacles. If we could focus only on one Bane we could probably make it do just about anything. But with so many, pretty much all we can do is tell them to keep away from this building."

"So in a way, you make this building invisible, or make them forget that it's here?" West questioned. He eyed the information on the screens closely. I wondered if he understood any of it. "It's kind of like when Eve controls them."

"You can?" both Royce and Dr. Beeson exclaimed at the same time.

I shook my head. "I don't know. I've just made them stop what they were doing before. All I did was tell them to get away. For some reason they listened."

Dr. Beeson's eyes narrowed at me and that look crossed his face again. "The chip in your brain is set up for wireless transmission. As you know, that is how we made adjustments. You were never supposed to be able to *send* signals."

"Evolution, Dr. Beeson," West said as he glanced over at me.

"So, could I be controlled with that?" I asked hesitantly, pointing at the screens. Dr. Beeson looked back at them.

"I don't see why not. The technology is virtually the same. But this computer is password protected, the door constantly locked, so that only myself and my assistant have access to it. No one is going to hijack your brain," he said with the hint of a smile.

"So you see why we are safe here?" Royce said. "In the four years that we have had this set up, we have never had a breach. The Bane are getting smarter, but we're still outsmarting them."

For now, I couldn't help but thinking.

"It's impressive," West said, studying everything before him. "Would you mind if I came back later and talked to you about this some more?" he asked Dr. Beeson.

"Of course," he said with a nod. "Now, I hope you will excuse me. I've got to get back to work."

"Thank you, Erik," Royce said as we walked back out into the glowing hall and closed the door behind us. "This way. There's something else I want you to see."

We walked further down the hall and opened another heavy black door. The room we entered into was largely dominated by a terrifying looking steel chair in the center. Bands for securing a person's hands were welded to the arms of the chair, another set of bands for the ankles. The entire chair was surrounded by five metallic arms that rose from the ground, curving in a bowl shape, giving the slight resemblance to a terrifying bird cage. They shone in a menacing and primal way.

"We've been lucky to have the best scientists and engineers who survived at this facility," Royce said as he approached the contraption. It almost seemed to glow under the blue lights. "We worked on this for four years before they got it right. We started on it before this facility was even fully developed.

"I worked in weapons development and warfare research for the United States government for seventeen years before the Evolution. It was my concept but I couldn't have done it without the entire team here in LA."

"What is it?" Avian asked.

"It's an extractor."

"For what?"

"TorBane."

We all stood in silence for a moment, processing what Royce had just said.

"It extracts the infection?" West said, his voice doubtful. "As in takes the cybernetics *out*?"

Royce nodded and started circling the extractor. "It isn't always successful. The person who has been infected must start treatment within an hour of being touched. After that time frame it seems to always be too late."

"And it's worked?" Avian asked in awe.

"On one man. We've tried it on two others but it was not successful. They had been infected for over two hours though. The process, however," Royce paused, looking us in the eye as he rested his hands on the back of the intimidating chair, "is *very* painful."

"These are magnetic, aren't they?" West asked as he approached the extractor and touched one of the rounded arms. They were taller than he was.

Royce nodded. "Surgery could never find all the tiny parts. And you could never operate fast enough. They'd turn on the table and heal before your eyes. And then they'd infect you. With this method, it gets every little piece. And pulls it right out through your skin."

"But how could anyone survive that?" Avian asked, his brow furrowing. "The process would kill you just from the pain you would experience."

"Anyone going through the treatment is placed in a medically induced coma. It's a slow process. If we pull too fast, all of the person's insides will be shredded to bits. We have to extract everything slowly, allowing the body to heal as everything is being pulled out. And then this," he said as he pointed to a round disk in the ceiling above us, "keeps it from spreading. It's an electrical pulse that contains it. It's not strong enough to wipe everything out. If we crank it up too far, it would kill the person too fast."

"You wanted to see me, Royce?" a voice from behind us said. We all turned at once.

"Yes, please come in, Elijah," Royce said as he stepped forward. "Elijah underwent extraction five months ago. He has fully recovered with no traces of cybernetics left."

Saying this man had fully recovered seemed like a cruel joke. He wore an eye patch; the eyes were usually the first thing to turn. Half of his face looked like it had been dragged over the crumbling road, and not let up for hours. The short sleeved shirt he wore exposed the pocked and scarred skin of his arms. His hands looked similar.

"Elijah had been on scouting duty when a Hunter cornered him. As you know, one touch is all it takes. One of our other scouts killed the Bane and brought Elijah back here. It had only been just over a half an hour when he started the treatment."

"How long did it take?" Avian asked. I saw him swallow hard. I wondered if he was thinking of Tye, like I was.

"Almost three weeks," Elijah said. His voice was as rough sounding as the rest of his body looked.

"This is really amazing," Avian said, shaking his head. He just kept blinking, as if what he was seeing would disappear at any moment.

I didn't blame him. This didn't seem real.

"I have to get back to my duties," Elijah said, looking over at Royce.

"Of course," he said. "Thank you for coming." Elijah stepped out of the room and I heard his footsteps fade down the hall.

"I see no reason for you not to stay," Royce said as he turned and looked at the four of us. "We can keep you fed, keep you safe, comfortable. I think we have an obligation to keep the human race alive. We all do.

"But, I understand that you need everyone to make a decision. We can send vehicles after the rest of your group if you like. We have military tanks that will keep any Bane out and there is room enough for all the members you brought with you."

"If we could have a bit of time alone to discuss this, it would be appreciated," Avian said, glancing at West, Tuck, and I.

"Of course," Royce nodded. "You're welcome to use one of the offices if you'd like. I will be in my own if you need me."

We followed Royce back to the elevator. We entered into an empty room just a few doors down from Royce's office. It was devoid of anything but two wooden chairs.

"This is amazing," West said as he closed the door behind us. "I wondered how they kept them away here but I never would have imagined it was through wireless communication."

"And that extractor is incredible," Avian said, the same excitement in his voice.

"I see no reason we shouldn't go get everyone else," West said as he slowly paced the room.

"If they have military tanks they would probably be safe to even go out during the day," Tuck said quietly. He'd been so quite this whole time that I'd almost forgotten he was with us. "Not that they would, but it would be better than us trying to sneak out and get them ourselves."

"I agree," Avian said. "What do you think Eve?"

I shook my head. Maybe I should have waited until things settled a bit more before I let Dr. Beeson work on my brain. I still felt foggy. "I think we should think about it for a few hours. This all seems very exciting and perfect at the moment, but it might look a little different tomorrow. There's no rush to do it right this second."

None of them said anything for a moment and I could see it in their faces that they wanted to just do this now. But slowly they came down off the high and back into reality.

"You're probably right, "Avian said, rubbing a hand over his head. His hair was getting long from the lack of a shave the last nearly two weeks. He looked over at West and Tuck who both finally gave a nod.

"Let's sleep on it," Avian said with a small nod. "We can go tomorrow night if that's what we decide is best."

They all nodded and headed for the door.

I was the last to exit the room and had gotten just two steps from the door when I felt a hand on my arm. I turned to see Royce standing just to the side of the door, a finger pressed to his lips for me to stay quiet.

I glanced back at the rest of my group, seeing Avian, West, and Tuck retreating back toward the stairs.

"I wanted to speak to you, alone," Royce said in a quiet tone.

I glanced back toward my fellow scouts just once. And then I nodded to Royce.

We returned to the blue floor. I followed Royce down the hall, to the very end. Two armed guards stood to either side of a thick black door. This one was closed, heavier and stronger looking than all the other ones. Royce punched a few numbers into the keypad attached to the handle. It beeped twice and I heard it unlock before he pushed it open.

Almost immediately inside the door was a set of stairs. All three of the men glanced back at me before starting up them, making me feel uneasy.

My eyes grew wide when we got to the top of the stairs. They opened onto the very top floor of the hospital, one big room. But all the walls and the entire ceiling were made of glass. It was almost as if we had just walked out onto the roof.

Dominating the center of the room was a ring. A fifteen-foot wide ring, balanced on five steel legs about four feet off the ground. Inside the ring were more rings, gears, mechanical devices I didn't even have names for. But I knew what it was.

"It's a CDU," I breathed as I took it in.

A small smile crossed Royce's face as he looked at me and nodded. "Yes it is. We call it the Pulse."

"It's massive," I said as I started to circle it.

"It's taken us a long time to build it," Royce said as he crossed his arms over his chest. "We're not sure exactly how far the blast will reach but we are certain it will at least clear the city."

"Why haven't you used it yet?" I asked as I ran my hand along the smooth metal surface. I immediately withdrew my hand though, remembering what it would do when it was live. It would kill me immediately. My thoughts turned briefly to the designs at the end of West's notebook. We hadn't needed them after all.

"It's not quite finished," he answered. "It still needs a power source."

I nodded as I stopped, coming back around the gigantic ring. "I suppose you can't just plug it into any normal outlet."

"The amount of power this thing requires is astronomical," Royce said, his eyes fixed on me. "Even directing all the power that runs to the hospital wouldn't be enough to charge this thing and set it off. We need to tap directly into the power plant that is three blocks from here."

"Why haven't you done it yet?" I asked, my brow knitting together.

He looked at me for a moment before he replied. "Because it is crawling with Bane. Even at night."

The pieces to Royce's puzzle slid into place without much effort. "You need me to go in," I said. "I'm the only one that can't be infected."

He simply nodded, his eyes fixed on me.

I looked back at the Pulse, thinking of what it could mean if it really did work. This entire city, maybe farther, free of any Bane. At least for a while.

"If I help set this off, what's to keep it from shorting me out and killing me?"

Royce adjusted his stance, pushing his hands in his pockets. "We've been working on proofing the entire hospital for the last two years. This room was added a while ago, completely sealed off from the rest of the building. The glass is all going to blow, but the rest of the hospital won't be affected. You'll be perfectly safe inside, along with all of our other electrical equipment."

"And how do I get into the plant without being torn apart, limb from limb?" I asked.

"Heavily armed," he said, a sly smile tugging on his lips.

"No," a voice suddenly said from behind us. Both Avian and West stepped into the room, looks of rage and fury on their faces. "She'll never make it out of the plant alive," West said through clenched teeth.

"You can't ask this of her," Avian said, his eyes dark.

"Apparently Lex forgot to close the door behind us," Royce said as he glared at one of the armed men behind him. The man just gave a shrug.

"You realize what this device will do for us? For humanity?" Royce asked, turning his eyes on Avian and West again.

"But not at the cost of losing Eve," Avian said, his hands forming fists.

"We will not be sending her in there naked," he said with harsh eyes and annoyance. "A tank will drive her as close as possible, our men will take out as many as they can from a distance. She will be armed."

"No," West said, shaking his head. "It's too great of a risk. There will be hundreds of them there, if not thousands."

The three of them stood like that for a long moment, staring at each other with unrelenting eyes.

"I'll do it," I finally spoke. "When will everything be ready?"

"In a few days," Royce said.

"No, Eve!" West hissed at the same time.

"You can't do this!" Avian chimed in.

"Yes, I can and I will!" I nearly shouted back. "Neither of you are in charge of me. I'm the only one that can do this and I am going to do it."

"Wonderful," Royce said as he clapped a hand on my back. "I'll let Dr. Beeson's team know and we will get things prepared."

Avian looked at me with cold eyes and I read a million words of shock, hurt, and betrayal in them. Without another word he turned and walked back down the stairs.

"You can't do this Eve," West said, closing the gap between us. He took my hands in his. "You most likely won't walk out of this. Don't kill yourself to make life a little easier for us."

"Maybe you're underestimating me," I said quietly, slipping my hands out of his. "I *am* doing this."

Before he could say anything else, I stepped around him and walked down the stairs.

I stood a good chance of not making it out of the power plant alive, but I would do it a million times over.

We finally stood a fighting chance.

THIRTY-THREE

West and Avian still wanted to go pick everyone up the next day. And I had to agree, it felt like the right, and safest thing to do. Eden would join the residents of Los Angeles.

We informed Royce of our decision and he set up a team that would go with us and take the tanks to pick everyone else up.

I stood at the back door, the one we had been brought through when we first arrived at the hospital. I looked out into the dark night, keeping guard while others behind me prepped for our departure. I could hear Avian talking to Royce, telling him about Morgan and her pregnancy, making plans for her care. West chatted with one of the other soldiers.

I heard something fifteen yards to my right. Tapping. I peered around the corner, searching for the source of the noise through the dark.

There it was again. A small tapping sound. And once again.

I took two steps out of the door toward the sound, my beautiful, new assault rifle leveled before me.

I heard the sound again. Tapping, followed by the shuffle of feet.

Remaining silent, I crept further into the dark.

The tapping started again, coming quicker and steadier sounding.

I was only ten yards from the entrance to the hospital when I saw it. She looked young, no older than me. But her eyes gleamed as she tapped the spoon against the concrete walls of a building.

My finger was pulling the trigger when I was tackled to the ground. We rolled before it came on top of me, its eyes gleaming in the dark. My firearm was knocked clean from my hands.

Before I could call for help it pressed a hard, cold hand over my mouth, pressing in on me with a crushing force. I plowed a fist into its still human-soft side. It caved around my blow, throwing it off balance enough for me to knock it to the side.

"Close the doors!" I screamed as I got to my feet and scrambled for my firearm. It caught my ankle, taking me to the ground just as I wrapped my fingers around the rifle's barrel. I turned and fired a shot at the mechanical girl who approached behind the one holding on to me. She dropped to the ground in a heap.

Before I could fire again, the machine gripping me squeezed my ankle as it drew me to it. I felt something inside of me crunch and crumple. There was shouting behind me but I couldn't turn to look and see if they were in fact closing the doors.

The thing had just broken my ankle.

And I could actually feel it.

The pain raced up my leg before exploding into the rest of my body. An enraged scream ripped from my throat as I finally righted the rifle in my hands and fired two shots into his chest. But he reached for the barrel of the rifle. He squeezed, crunching it, and bent it back until it pointed at me. He then gave a good hard yank, and flung it off into the distance.

My blood burned hot as my eyes narrowed. I coiled my good let and landed a crushing blow to its face. Its left cheek and eye socket caved in.

But it gripped the front of my jacket in one fist, lifting me a good foot off the ground. I heard shots being fired from behind me and the concrete of the building just behind us exploded as it was hit.

Quick as it had picked me up, it threw me like a rag doll across the street. I hit the concrete outside of the hospital like a rag doll.

And everything was dark.

My eyes focused on the dimmed lights above my head. My hair stuck to my forehead and neck as I turned my head to see where I was. I laid on one of the strange skeletal looking beds and there were tubes and wires sticking to and in my body. They led to a machine with a screen that beeped and flashed things I didn't understand.

I looked the other way, my cheek brushing the top of Avian's recently shaven head. His head rested right next to my shoulder, my left hand held loosely in his. As I brushed against him, his head jerked up. The whites of his eyes were red. He looked like he hadn't slept for a while.

"Hey," he said, a small smile forming on his lips. He squeezed my hand tighter. "How do you feel?"

"What happened?" I questioned, immediately sitting up in panic. My hands were encumbered by multiple tubes that were sticking out of my skin. I ripped them out in one quick move. "Did you get them? Did they get inside?"

"Whoa," Avian said, grabbing my arm before I could jump out of bed. "Everything is okay, Eve. We got them. They're dead."

"You sure?" I asked, my body unsure of what to do now that it had so much adrenaline surging through it.

"Yes," he reassured me, easing me back into the bed. "We got them."

He stood and stepped around the bed and pulled something out of a drawer. Raising my hand, he wiped the drops of blood that were forming where I had ripped out the tubes and placed a small bandage over it.

"How long have I been out?" I asked as I rubbed my eyes. The room came into sharper focus.

"About six hours," Avian said quietly as he sat on the edge of my bed and took my hand in his again. His eyes were serious as he looked into mine.

"Royce was right," I said. "They're getting smarter. They lured me out of the hospital and ambushed me."

Avian clenched his teeth together, making the muscles in his jaw stand out. He gave a frustrated sigh. "We were afraid of that."

"We can't wait to set that Pulse off," I said, shaking my head as I held his eyes. "Even with Dr. Beeson's wireless transmission system they're going to figure out a way to get to us. I have to go into that plant."

Avian was quiet for a moment and I knew he couldn't argue against it anymore.

"West and Tuck?"

"They set out with Royce's team an hour after you were brought to the infirmary. We didn't dare wait to go get everyone, not after what just happened to you. They should be back before dawn."

I nodded my head that I heard him. Grabbing the rail with my other hand, I pulled myself forward with Avian's reluctant assistance. My head swam and throbbed. My ankle screamed as it moved.

I groaned.

"What's wrong?" Avian asked with concern.

"Why do I hurt?" I asked, cradling my hands on either side of my head.

"You're feeling pain?" he said, disbelief in his voice.

I just nodded.

"No idea," he said, easing me back down to lie on the bed. "You sustained a pretty serious concussion and a crushed ankle. It's already healing. But honestly I didn't really worry about the pain. It's never bothered you before."

I squeezed my eyes closed.

It had to have something to do with Dr. Beeson lessening my emotional blockers. He must have removed some of my pain blockers as well.

But why would he do that? Why would I need to feel pain?

"Eve?" Avian asked, his voice quiet. "Who is this?"

I opened my eyes to see that he was holding the picture that Dr. Beeson had given me.

"I found it on the ground next to where the Bane threw you against the hospital," he explained as I took it between my fingers.

"She's my mother," I said, meeting his eyes. I saw in them that I had confirmed what he had suspected. "Her name was Emma."

He asked questions and I relayed everything Dr. Beeson had revealed. About my premature birth, about her death, about why I was given TorBane.

"You look just like her," he said with a smile as he looked at the picture again.

I watched his face, thinking then about how much he and Sarah looked alike when they smiled.

"I wish I could tell Sarah about her," I said, my eyes falling to the picture again.

He met my eyes, his instantly becoming sad.

"I was going to show you something," he said. To my surprise, his hands went to the hem of his shirt and he pulled the fabric over his head.

My eyes instantly went to his chest. There was a third bird tattooed on his chest. The skin around it was red and swollen, freshly inked.

"There's a lady here who has a machine that does the inking," he said as he watched my face. My fingers rose to gingerly touch the third bird. There was a subtle S in the way the wing blended in with the body. "She did this two days ago."

"It's beautiful," I said.

Avian took my hand in his and pressed a kiss to my fingers. He held them there against his lips for a long moment. He squeezed his eyes closed and a moment later a single tear slipped down his cheek.

THIRTY-FOUR

The rest of our group arrived safely at the hospital and two days later I was healed and cleared to go to the power plant.

I shifted the weapons that were secured to me, counting again how many grenades I had attached to my belt. I pulled the vest, feeling uncomfortable. It might have been bulletproof but it was torture to wear.

I glanced around at the four men that sat nestled in the tank with me. Their faces were set hard, no emotions present.

The noise from the track wheels died away and I knew we had arrived.

One of the men opened the top hatch and we all climbed out. We were only about seventy-five yards away from the plant. I could see them even from here, rows and rows of Bane, standing on and around it.

"We'll take out as many of them as we can with this," one of the men said as he patted the firing turret. "We have to be careful not to damage the plant though. The rest of us will pick them off one by one, as quickly as we can."

I nodded, my eyes never leaving the gleaming bodies ahead of me.

Two of the men unhooked the mile long power supply line from the back of the tank. One end of it trailed behind us, going directly back to the Pulse. We unwound the rest of it, attaching the end of it to a hook on the back of my vest that I could easily release once I got inside. I shrugged my shoulders, testing its weight. It would have been too heavy for me to carry if I had been a normal girl. It had taken two of them to carry the entire line.

As one of Royce's soldiers handed me my weapon, I couldn't help but smile. I had to admit, the M4 assault rifle was beautiful.

"You ready?" one of the men asked, gripping the firing turret.

"Fire away," I said as I turned my eyes ahead of me.

The blast from the tank shook the ground and nearly knocked me off my feet. Gleaming metal eyes jumped to life as they turned in our direction. I took off running toward them as the second blast was fired.

Gleaming parts exploded and flew through the air as dozens of them leapt at me. I fired, flashes of light illuminating the streets. Bodies dropped, metal frames shattered, wires sparked. Shots fired from behind me and more bodies hit the ground. Still more and more of them woke to life, leaping to attack.

The line attached to me slowed my progress more than I anticipated. I put all of my weight into it, dragging it behind me as I fired. The plant suddenly seemed miles away, even though I was closing in on only a few dozen yards.

I pulled the pin of one of the grenades and tossed it at the chain-link fence that surrounded the plant. I almost couldn't see it through all the Bane that surrounded it. A few seconds later, metal flew through the air, raining down on me with deadly force.

A hand grabbed at my right arm, closing in with crushing force. I jammed the butt of my firearm in its face, knocking it away for just long enough to blow its head off. Another leapt at me, its eyes gleaming through the dark. It was riddled with bullet holes before it even hit the ground.

I remembered the advice Dr. Beeson had given me and focused all my thoughts on pushing the Bane away as my feet pounded the pavement. A few Bane hesitated as they ran at me, their movements becoming jerky as they fought my wireless commands. I couldn't transmit to them all and keep a very strong connection.

The plant was a mere twenty feet away. While plenty of them had woken, most of them stood motionless, their eyes fixed on the source of electricity ahead of them. Sleepers, I assumed. I had to push my way through mechanical bodies, firing as I went to take out as many of them as I could.

I was plowed into from the side, knocking me to my back. I rolled as I went down, the line wrapping around my midsection. A body leapt on top of me, its hands closing around my throat. Before it could even squeeze, its head exploded from a shot coming from the tank. I jumped to my feet again, untangling myself as I sprinted.

Just as the transformer came in sight, I heard the additional gun shots. But this time they were being fired in my direction. I didn't look back as I pushed myself faster.

Bodies started dropping ahead of me as both me and Royce's men fired. I mowed down the last row of Bane who stood at the edge of the plant, clearing my way to the ladder that rose fifteen feet up to the transformer. The metal sang as I ascended, my boots striking each rung. The ladder vibrated as another body joined me in the climb.

The Bane climbed faster than I had and grabbed my barely healed ankle, threatening to pull me back over the edge. The sound of another shot filled my head and a fraction of a second later blood sprayed from my left arm as my flesh was torn open.　Another shot was fired and the Bane grabbing me dropped to the ground with the hiss of electric death.

Blood started to spill from my arm as I heaved myself onto the platform and pulled the line to give me some slack.　I hadn't noticed the two Bane who were surrounding the transformer until they tackled me to the cement.

One of them closed its hands around my throat and it held me pinned to the ground.　The other pulled a hand gun, releasing the safety.

I narrowed my eyes at the armed one, focusing every thought I had towards it.　The next second, the Bane choking the life out of me dropped to the ground, killed by its fellow kind.　It turned the gun on itself the next second.

I scrambled to my feet again, finally reaching the transformer.　I could feel the currents of electricity emanating from it as I finally connected the line.　It hummed to life instantly.

The sound of metal scraping concrete sounded as I turned to make my escape.　Dozens of Bane climbed onto the platform, their dead eyes fixed on me.　Light flashed through the sky as shots were fired from both directions.

I sprinted forward without thinking, barreling through the bodies in front of me before they could react.　I leapt off the platform, flying through the night sky for one freeing second before I slammed to the ground.

Stay away, stay away, stay away, I thought as my boots slapped the pavement back toward the tank.

Just as I was clear of the ring of Bane that surrounded the plant, I heard an explosion.　The buildings and streets before me were illuminated as the fire billowed out, racing towards me with unstoppable force.　I screamed as the flames ate away the fabric of my pants, melted the rubber of my boots to my feet.　I felt every cell of my skin as it singed and was burned up. I hit the ground just fifteen yards away from the tank as the flames of the Bane's explosive died away.

I couldn't distinguish one scream from the next as I heard feet meeting the concrete and felt hands close around my arms and start pulling me back toward the tank. Every movement felt like tortured death as they hauled me up and inside. The tank roared to life as we crawled back to the hospital.

"Are they following us?" a voice asked.

A few moments later a voice responded. "No, they're flocking around the plant again. That's incredible! The Sleepers don't even seem to care."

I clenched my teeth together as I tried to force my vision to focus on the roof of the tank. My breathing came in labored gasps and I felt lightheaded. I'd made it out of the plant alive but would I make it back to the hospital?

"Hang on!" a voice called to me. A face floated across my vision.

Black spots swam in my vision as I was jostled again a few minutes later. One of my legs scraped against the lip of the hatch of the tank, sending a blood curdling scream ripping from my chest.

I didn't question it anymore. It had been more than my emotional blockers that Dr. Beeson had removed.

Between each gasping breath, I couldn't help but let out another agonizing scream.

Men in white jackets surrounded me and I was blinded by the lights on the ceiling of the white hallways. The only thing I could see was the pair of blue eyes above me, trying to speak words that I couldn't hear.

My body exploded in blossoms of pain as I was moved again, a hard board suddenly beneath my body.

I heard only jumbles of words. My brain tried to sort everything out, trying to grasp onto something that made sense.

"...transfusions..."

"...skin grafts..."

"...cybernetic parts..."

"...accelerated regeneration..."

A strange thumping in my chest startled me. It didn't come in even beats, it was erratic, painful. My breaths came in quick gasps. Even that hurt. It hurt to scream. It hurt to lie still, it hurt to move. It hurt to be.

Finally I slipped under.

THIRTY-FIVE

Beeping noises surrounded me as my eyes slid open. The ceiling tiles slowly came into focus, the sound of air blowing through a vent above me pulling me to wakefulness as I blinked.

I carefully sat up, my head feeling like it was spinning. I was back in a hospital room, surrounded by the now familiar flashing screens, dripping bags, and tubes sticking out of my arms. The room was completely devoid of life other than myself.

I ripped the lines out of my arm, a small bubble of blood immediately forming on my skin. Shifting my weight, I slipped my legs out from under the heavy quilt and off the side of the bed.

I barely suppressed the scream when I saw my legs coming out from under my hospital gown.

My right leg was a mass of crusted and wavy looking skin, small pieces of black rubber melted into the heel of my foot. Despite the intensity of the burn, it looked like it was already healing.

But my left leg was worse. So much worse.

The skin twisted and deformed in disgusting ways, hardly identifiable as human flesh. But from mid-calf down, there was nothing left but a gleaming metal skeleton.

I crashed to the floor, my hands barely reaching out to catch myself before the ground came rushing up at me. I scrambled to my feet, not even noticing how I once again felt no pain from my injuries. The back of my eyes burned as I heard the sound of my metal foot clanking against the tile of the floor.

The hall was devoid of any life as I stumbled out. I blinked hard several times, making my vision refocus as it tried to fail me. I held to the rail along the wall as I dragged myself down the hall. I didn't make it more than ten feet before I collapsed to the ground, a mix of terror, unregistered pain, and shock bringing me down.

As my head fell back against the tile, a pair of boots came into view.

"Eve!" someone shouted. The next moment I felt a pair of arms underneath me and the ceiling came a little closer. A few seconds later my bed was back underneath me.

Slowly, the sight of West's brown eyes came into focus.

"Can you hear me?" he asked, his voice sounding so far away.

I gave a nod, blinking hard. When I opened my eyes again everything was clearer.

"You really shouldn't be getting up right now," West said, taking one of my hands in his. He sat in a seat next to my bed, pressing my knuckles to his lips.

I looked over at him, my thoughts running a million places all at once. "How long have I been out?" I started. It seemed like I was having to ask that question to often lately.

"Only about a day," he breathed, his eyes intense on mine.

I glanced back down, catching the light as it gleamed off the skeleton of my foot. I lay back down, swallowing hard.

"It's a lot better than it was last night," he said quietly. "There was nothing from your knee down."

"How can you still look at me?" I said quietly, laying my other arm across my eyes. "Seeing what I really am? I'm one of them."

I heard West stand, letting go of my hand, he sat on the edge of the bed. He placed his hands on either side of my face. "You are nothing like the Bane," he said seriously, his eyes burning into mine.

I heard another set of footsteps enter the room and saw Avian enter. His face was hard to read as he took in the sight of West and I, so close together. I felt myself hating everything I was again.

"You're awake," he said simply.

"I'll let him catch you up on everything," West said quietly and to my surprise, left without another word.

As I watched Avian standing there, my eyes stung and my lower lip started to tremble just slightly. I couldn't breathe.

He crossed the room silently and gathered me up into his arms, his face buried in my mass of tangled hair. His entire frame shook as he held me tightly. The sob that escaped my chest surprised me.

"My leg..." I barely managed to get the words out.

Avian sat back a bit, placing one hand on the back of my neck, his forehead resting against mine. His blue eyes looked like there might be flames burning behind them as he stared at me. "You will forever be the most beautiful creature on this planet to me, no matter what. I don't care what you're skeletal frame is made of. You're still Eve."

"Avian, I want..." I dropped off, not even knowing how to finish that sentence. I was tempted to put my head in that gigantic ring on the roof, just to stop all the confusion I felt.

"Don't," he said, pressing a finger to my lips. "You just need to finish healing right now."

I took a deep breath, finding some sense of my normal self, and nodded.

"Someday you're going to realize that you're not indestructible."

"How bad was it?" I asked.

Avian sat back, close to the foot of the bed. "The skin on your left leg was totally burned away up to your knee," he started. "Traces of metal could be seen in your right leg, most of the skin was gone, and a lot of the muscle had been burned away as well. Your lower back had been burned but not too horribly. The bullet proof vest protected you quite a bit. It healed pretty fast. You lost a few inches of hair. You were bleeding profusely from the bullet wound in your arm and all your other injuries. You needed a blood transfusion. But within hours you were already healing. I would expect your left leg will look totally normal again within three days."

I nodded, my eyes drifting to the ceiling. "I don't feel the pain anymore."

"I told Dr. Beeson about that," he said. "He isn't sure why your pain blockers were lessened. I didn't realize you'd asked him to remove some of the emotional blockers." There was a trace of hope in his voice that made me blush. The smallest hint of a smile pulled at the corner of his mouth. "Dr. Beeson said it was an accident, messing with the pain blockers. He seemed pretty concerned about it. But he thinks he got it fixed. It seems like it's working. Right?"

I nodded. "Guess you were right about being wary about letting me go to the plant," I said.

He smiled. "Like I could have stopped you."

"You couldn't have," I said. "Now find me some pants and boots so I don't scare everyone away."

He just chuckled and shook his head.

It took him a few minutes but Avian found me some clothes and we walked down the hall together.

"They haven't set the Pulse off yet, have they?" I asked. My boots were too big without any flesh to fill them and the metal foot slid around inside it. I walked with a major limp.

"No," he answered, his always serious eyes forward. "Royce said it takes about two days to build up enough power to set it off. It's charging now though."

"Two days," I breathed. "Do you really think it will work?"

Avian shrugged. "The technology seems right. They have the brains here to do it."

"I can't even imagine what life is going to be like if it works."

"It will be better," Avian said quietly as we entered the main lobby area. "You'll see how life should have been, in a post-apocalyptic way."

By now the lobby was emptying out, everyone preparing for sleep at mid-day. I suddenly missed my days of scouting, of roaming through the woods, free without any walls barricading me in. Hopefully all that would end in just a few short days.

I followed the others up to the rooms, feeling like everyone could see through my pants to my cybernetic leg as I limped along. No one bothered me though, didn't ask questions or pull my pant leg up to bear witness to the horror. I made it to my room without being exposed for what I was.

The ceiling greeted me as I lay down, knowing I wasn't going to be getting any sleep for the next eight hours of silence. Images started to slide across my mind: the blinding light from the explosion that had tried to take my legs, the blue eyes that had tried to call out to me when my brain couldn't handle it all.

Flickers of row after row of Bane. The flash of light from my firearms.

So much violence.

I turned my head when a crack of light started growing on my wall. The silhouette of a man appeared in the door before he closed it behind him.

"Hi," I breathed as he hesitated next to the door.

"Hi," West said through the dark. I could feel the mixture of feelings that were rolling off of him. I knew what it was like to feel like an emotional wreck.

"I won't bite you," I said as I scooted to one side of my bed.

"You sure?" he said light-heartedly as he crossed the room and lay next to me on the bed. He lay on his side, just looking at me for a long time.

West trailed his fingers softly across my forehead, brushing stray hairs off my face. He didn't look in my eyes as he did so, his gaze lingered on my ears, my shoulder, my neck, as he struggled with how to form the words he had in his head. Hesitantly, he picked up the wings attached to my necklace and held them lightly in his hand. I wondered if he knew Avian had made it for me, and the sacrifice he had given for me to have it.

"I thought you were going to die," he said quietly. "When they brought you in after the explosion, you looked so broken, I wasn't sure they could put you back together. It was so much worse than the other night. Your heart barely kept going. For a while I think I'd fooled myself into believing that you couldn't die."

"Good thing I'm not dead then," I said as I placed my hand over his and he stilled it on my cheek. The coals started to burn as we touched. A sense of anticipation started to ignite in my belly.

"I wanted to give you something," he said quietly as he finally met my eyes. "One last thing before I stop this. It won't happen again until you make your choice."

He leaned forward then, his eyes holding mine all the way until his lips met mine. My own eyes slid closed as I kissed West back, feeling the fire leap to life inside of me. West's lips moved with mine, parting as gasps were inhaled. I blazed to life from the inside out, the flames licking along my veins.

Could I ever give up this heat? Would I ever feel so alive again?

West's hand came to the back of my neck as my hand tangled in his hair. I craved more.

Dr. Beeson had lessened my emotional blockers. How far could I push before I blacked out? Would I ever again?

But in the middle of the burn West pulled away, his earth-colored eyes looking into mine as I wished for more.

"I won't do this again until you've made your choice, Eve," he said quietly. I could feel all the hurt and pain I had caused him in the last few months in his voice then. Hate crept into my stomach again. "This isn't right. I like Avian, respect him, despite everything. It isn't fair to anyone. You have to make a choice. Until then, I'm tired of trying to convince you that it should be me. I'm not even sure it should be me anymore."

I tried to find the words to reassure West, to convince him that he was wrong. I wanted to come up with promises and answers then but I couldn't. He'd been right. About everything.

"I'm sorry," was all I managed.

"Just don't take forever," he said as he stood. "If I've got miles of pain before me I'd rather start walking them sooner than later."

And he walked out of the room.

THIRTY-SIX

Something was going on the next night. I'd seen no sign of Royce, most of his scouts, West, or Avian. Their presence was strangely absent from the lobby area. I couldn't find them in their rooms, or in the dining area.

As I came down from the private rooms, I stopped in the main hall, hiding myself when I saw a few of the missing men trickling out of the stairwell. They were all heavily armed, each dressed in bulletproof vests. They were going out for something serious and dangerous and I had every intention of going with them.

I dashed back toward the stairs that led to the second floor. I barely limped as I ran down the hall, layers of tissue already forming over my metallic bones. I burst into my room, grabbing my familiar firearms, strapping them to my person.

As I turned to walk back out my door, an unexplainable thing happened.

My vision flickered for half a second. And then everything turned off.

THIRTY-SEVEN

I couldn't...
Couldn't...
Move.

A flash of light flickered across my vision and my eyes twitched just once as my brain flipped on and off. Another flash of light and I managed to turn my head to the left just slightly. Another and I was able to twitch the fingers on my left hand.

I took a gasping breath as the lights stayed for longer sparks of time. As my muscles unlocked for half a second, I attempted a step forward, only to crash to the floor as my brain flashed out again for a brief moment.

The lights stayed on finally, only occasionally flickering in the corner of my vision. Slowly, movement by movement, I worked my way to my hands and knees.

Struggling for each breath, my muscles finally released and the flashes stopped.

Looking at the clock on the wall, I saw it was almost four hours later than it should have been.

My movements still stiff and jerky, I closed my hand around the doorknob and pulled. Feeling slightly numb, I started to work my way down the hall.

I'd been alone. I hadn't emotionally overworked myself.

I couldn't think of any other explanation. Someone had shut me down.

"Eve," a voice called to me from behind. I turned to see Dr. Beeson jogging down the hall toward me. "I thought you would have gone out with the others?"

"I tried," I said, my voice bizarre sounding, not quite working right. He slowed to match my still clumsy gait. I narrowed my eyes as I looked over at him. "You didn't shut me down did you?"

"What?" he asked, his brow furrowing. "Of course not."

"I've spent the last four hours, frozen and gone in my room."

Dr. Beeson's step faltered as he looked at me, his face blanching white.

"*Someone* shut me down," I said through clenched teeth.

He cursed under his breath and ran a hand roughly through his hair. "West spent nearly an entire night with me, asking questions about the wireless transmission system."

"He..." I nearly choked on my words. "West shut me down?"

"I'm so sorry," he said quietly. "Come with me. They're having problems with the communication system with those who went out. I'm going to take a look at it and see if I can get it fixed."

Numbly, I followed him down the stairwell and into the frantic lobby.

It seemed that everyone who lived in the hospital that hadn't gone out on the mission was gathered. Tension rippled through everyone, setting my nerves on edge. Seeing Tuck by the front door, I joined him.

"What are you doing here?" he asked, his brow furrowing as he looked at me. "I thought you had gone with them."

"It wasn't for lack of trying," I said as I looked out into the dark and silent night. "What's going on?"

"Something pulled your power line about five hours ago," Tuck explained. "Royce's men and a few others went with him to go fix it."

"West and Avian went out, didn't they?" I felt hollow.

Tuck simply nodded. "We lost communication with everyone though. They called for Dr. Beeson to try and fix it. We have no idea what's going on out there."

I turned to see Dr. Beeson working with a handful of other people, their movements rushed and frantic.

A crackle suddenly sounded from the device Dr. Beeson and the others worked on.

"...anyone there? Please come in..." a voice came through the system.

"Yes, we're here!" a woman said as she took the handheld piece that was attached to the system. "Is everything okay?"

"People shot..." the voice cut out. "...at least four dead..." The sound cut out again for a solid five seconds before finally coming back online. "Get the Extractor powered up!"

Everyone seemed to freeze as those last words filled the room. I felt my blood run cold.

"Who's been infected?" the woman asked, her voice sounding dead.

"...Bane hidden...shots fired everywhere..." the voice continued to crackle in and out. "...Royce and West... Avian... didn't see it..."

"Who was it?" I suddenly said, louder than I should have. "Who got infected?"

Everyone in the room suddenly looked up at me, every single pair of eyes. "I'm not sure," Dr. Beeson finally answered.

I looked at the woman who had been speaking. "I couldn't tell either," she said quietly. No one seemed to notice how the receiver had gone dead again.

It was pure adrenaline that forced my legs to work. I sprinted out the front glass door into the dark night.

In that moment I finally knew.

I knew which one I would grieve over. A piece of me would be missing forever if he was gone. A part of me would break. But I would make it through.

And I knew which one of them I couldn't live without, couldn't take another single breath if he were to be taken away from me.

In that moment I finally understood what love meant.

Sarah had been right all along. A single moment was all it had taken.

The wind whipped through my singed hair, my cybernetic legs pumping me faster than I'd ever moved before.

Shouts and screams of agony rose into the night air. Shots were fired and flashes of light pinpointed their exact location. As I rounded the corner, I raised my rifle, firing two shots at the pair of Bane who rushed the struggling group from behind. They dropped to the ground in a heap. One of Royce's men raised his own gun. For a moment I thought he was pointing at me, until the Hunter I hadn't noticed creeping up on me from behind dropped to the ground.

I didn't even remember feeling my feet slap the pavement as I ran toward him, my eyes never leaving his face. In that moment, every memory I had of him, every second we had spent together, flashed through my mind.

I ran straight into his blood soaked arms. I threw my arms around his shoulders, crushing him into myself, pressing my lips to his with a heat that burned me from the inside out. Avian's assault rifle fell to the ground with a clatter as he wrapped one arm around my waist, bringing his other hand up behind my neck. Everything about his lips, his breathing, the way his body melted into mine left me craving more.

There was no destroyed world around us as I kissed Avian and he took my breath away. There was no infection, there were no cybernetics. There was no running, no fighting, no violence or death. There was only Avian and there was only me.

I'd never felt the heat from Avian that West had given me but I realized then that it had been because I wouldn't allow myself to seek it out until I was sure it was Avian that I wanted and needed.

Now I was sure.

West may have made me feel alive but he didn't have the gravitational pull that Avian did. Avian was my world, my universe. He was everything I had that was worth living, fighting, and dying for.

"I love you," I whispered against his lips as Avian consumed me, body and soul. "It's you. It's always been you." And I realized then that it was true. I had always *loved* Avian, it was always him.

I felt the tears as they rolled down Avian's cheek, his lips still moving with mine. "I love you, Eve. More than anything."

"We've got to get out of here!" a man screamed. I looked back, realizing the majority of the group had continued back to the hospital. I barely caught sight of a body being hauled around the corner.

West.

I raised my rifle and fired at the two Hunters who sprinted down the street after us. They dropped with a clatter.

Taking Avian's hand in mine, I half dragged him back to the hospital with me. I realized then that there was blood oozing out of his left arm in two different places and in one spot in his right thigh.

The lobby was a shifting mess of chaos and blood as everyone got back inside, just as the sky started to lighten. People ran in every direction, more than one life on the edge of being lost. Avian and I spotted a group of men in white coats hauling West's twitching body into the elevator. We dashed for the stairs, taking them two at a time. Avian stumbled behind me, blood dripping onto the steel stairs as we ascended.

We followed the shouting as we got to the blue floor, down to the extraction room. A doctor ran past us, back to the stairs. As we stepped into the room, it all finally hit me.

West was infected.

"How long?" I asked quietly, squeezing Avian's hand all the tighter.

"Just over an hour ago, I think," he forced the words out. "They kept coming at us as we tried to make our way back."

A group of men and women forced West's twitching body into the chair, clamping his wrists and ankles secure. He stilled for just a moment when he caught sight of me. "Eve!" he screamed, his eyes wide, terrified and confused.

Metallic veins were already growing in his left eye.

West gave a blood-curdling scream, squeezing his eyes closed as his chest surged forward, his body held back by the bands around his wrists. A pair of doctors rushed back into the room and I watched, horrified, as they injected something into West's neck. He was instantly still.

I couldn't look anymore as I turned into Avian and buried my face in his chest. I heard the doctors fussing around, bandaging his wounds with gloved hands, trying their best to stop West's bleeding.

The hum of electricity alerted everyone that the Extractor was being powered up. Avian took two steps away from it, pulling me with him.

Avian suddenly stumbled, his skin pale and clammy. There was a pool of blood at his feet. "Eve, I..." he didn't finish as his eyes rolled into the back of his head.

"Avian!" I shouted as I clung to his sagging form. I slung him across my shoulders and dashed back down the hallway. Avian was totally limp as I took the stairs two at a time, too impatient to wait out the slow elevator ride down. The sound of my feet against the tile echoed off the walls as I ran toward the medical wing.

"Help!" I shouted as I neared.

As I stepped into the hall, I stopped, taking in the scene before me.

Avian and West weren't the only ones who had been shot. Most of the floor was covered with a slick sheet of red. People rushed everywhere, panicked.

"Help him!" I shouted to no one in particular. Not a single eye turned in my direction. More blood continued to drip from Avian's wounds. "He needs help!" I shouted at the closest person in white. He paid no attention to me.

"Please," I said to a woman who rushed past me, reaching out for her arm. She barely glanced at me and shook her head.

"I already have four patients."

Anger surged in my system and for the briefest moment, the room shifted with lines of black.

I drew my handgun and fired two shots into the ceiling.

Every eye in the room turned to me and every single body froze.

I lowered the gun and leveled it on a woman in those strange starched green clothes. "If you let him die I will not hesitate to kill you."

She swallowed hard, her eyes twice their normal size. She gave one nod and pointed me towards a room.

There was already a blood-covered man in one of the beds but I didn't really care as I laid Avian's limp form in the empty one. The young woman followed me in, her hands shaking.

"He's been shot," I said, my voice calm and even.

She simply nodded and lifted Avian's bleeding arm. "There's no exit wound. The bullets are still inside. It could be a while before I can get the instruments to get them out."

"It can't wait that long," I said as I shook my head at her. "He's already lost too much blood. Can you sew him up? You're a doctor, right?"

She shook her head. "I'm a nurse but I know how to suture."

I grabbed a pair of gloves out of one of the boxes on the wall and pulled them on. "You're helping me get them out now."

The nurse watched me wide-eyed as I dug my fingers into Avian's flesh and felt for the bullets.

They each gave a small ping as I dropped them in the sink. The nurse set to stitching his skin closed while I fished the bullet out of his thigh. I gave a hard swallow as I dropped the last one in the sink.

Once she was done with the stitches the nurse left the room for a moment and came back with a bag of blood. "He needs a transfusion, he's lost a lot of blood," she said as she punctured Avian's skin and the blood started mixing with his own. I didn't like the idea of some stranger's blood mixing with his.

The soldier in the bed next to us limped out of the room, eyeing me as he walked by. "I would have done the same thing if it had been my wife bleeding to death," he said as he met my eyes. I managed to give him a nod as he walked out the door.

315

"This shouldn't take too long," the nurse said as she peeled off her gloves and threw them in the trash. "He could start coming around any time now. I'll be back to check on him in a while."

"Thank you," I said as she started for the door. I reached out and lightly touched her arm. She flinched. "I'm sorry about earlier." She merely gave a short nod, her eyes betraying her fear, and walked out the door.

Just as I was about to sit on the edge of Avian's bed, three heavily armed men walked into the room.

"You need to come with us," one of them said. His eyes were hard, his brows drawn together.

"I'm not going anywhere," I said as I glared back at him.

"You've been deemed a security threat," he said as he took another step toward me. "You fired two shots in the middle of a crowded room, threatened a nurse. You need to be secured."

"I'm not leaving him," my voice was cold and hard.

The three of them took another step, their hands twitching on their firearms.

"I suggest you don't come any closer if you like your nose the way it looks," I warned, balling my fingers.

He merely gave a cocky little smile and took another step forward.

A scream of pain leapt from his throat as my cybernetic-boned fist met his face. One of the men behind him raised his firearm, leveling it at my head. In the same movement I spun, knocking it out of his hands with my heel. The third man turned and ran out into the hall for backup.

"I told you I'm not leaving," I said calmly as I extended a hand to the man with the now broken nose. He simply glared at me and got to his feet on his own, holding his bleeding nose. "You can take these," I said as I handed over my firearms. "But I'm not leaving."

He took my weapons, surprised at my cooperation. "We'll be keeping watch over you. Isaac, you take the first shift. Watch her like a hawk."

Isaac looked at the first man hard, like he might want to hit him too.

"I won't bite," I said as I turned and walked back to Avian's side. The first man left in a hurry, the second stationed himself outside the door.

Not many things scared me but seeing Avian lying there like that did. Now that I finally understood who it was that I needed, was I going to lose him? Was I to only get a few glorious but horror-filled minutes now that I had finally made my choice? I might be losing both of them at the same time. Maybe this was my punishment for taking so long to figure my feelings out. For doing what I had done to them.

But 2,634 seconds later, Avian's eyes blinked open. I jumped back to his bed, after pacing back and forth for what felt like an eternity. I balanced on the edge of the mattress as I took his hand in mine, pressing my lips to the back of his hand. He blinked several times before he turned his head and his eyes found mine.

"Hi," I said quietly, kissing his still clammy skin.

"Hi," he said back, the life coming back into his eyes.

"For a while there I thought I was going to lose you," I said, closing my eyes. "You lost a lot of blood."

"So I didn't just imagine everything that happened?" he asked. "West being infected? You telling me that you loved me?"

I shook my head as I kept his intense gaze. "Are you sure?" he asked very quietly.

"Without a doubt," I said as I pressed my lips to his again briefly.

"When did you finally decide?"

"When we heard over the radio that someone had been infected," I said. "I realized then that there was only one person I couldn't survive loosing. I've lost Tye, Sarah, everyone in my past that I can't even remember. But I knew then that I couldn't live through losing you."

Avian brought his hand up behind my neck, bringing my lips to his again for just a moment. "I love you, Eve. I promise I always will."

"I love *you*," I breathed, relishing in the warmth that radiated into every corner of my body. I finally understood what it meant.

"Eve," he said as his eyes shifted to the doorway. "Why is there an armed guard standing just outside the door?"

I glanced in that direction, seeing Isaac standing there with his back turned to us but his automatic weapon in obvious sight. "I may have used a little more force than needed to get someone to help you," I said, not quite meeting his eyes.

"You didn't hurt anyone did you?" he said with a hint of a sigh.

"There are just a couple of new bullet holes in their ceiling…"

Avian suddenly laughed. He brought my hand up to his lips, pressing a brief kiss there. "That's my Eve."

I gave him a small smile, everything inside of me loving being called "his."

"Have you heard anything yet?" Avian asked as he lay back on his pillow. "About West?"

I shook my head as I sat back, my hands falling into my lap. "I haven't left you since you collapsed upstairs."

"You should go find out what happened," he said, his eyes sad and serious. "See if we were too late."

"Are you sure?" I asked, my brow furrowing. I didn't like the idea of leaving him here like this alone.

"It's just a couple of bullet holes," he said with a small smile. "I've patched enough of them to know that I'll survive."

I held his eyes for a long moment. I didn't want to lose the peace that we'd formed, even if it was in the middle of all this chaos. But I had to know what was going to happen. "I'll be back as soon as I can," I said as I stood. I glanced back at him one last time before I walked out the door.

THIRTY-EIGHT

My guard wasn't going to let me leave the room. I argued with him for a good five minutes and finally convinced him that he could follow me.

A sense of dread knotted in my stomach as I started up the stairs. The blue floor was abuzz with activity as I entered the hall. People went in and out of the stairwell that led up to the Pulse, Dr. Beeson's door was wide open, people coming and going. But most of the activity was coming from the Extraction room.

I held my arms around my midsection as I stepped into the room. It felt like everything inside of me was about to crack and fall apart, like I'd been filled with too many strong emotions and then someone had taken a sledgehammer to me.

A group of people surrounded West's limp body. Bandages were wrapped around half of him but even I could tell the blood had stopped flowing. His wounds were already healing themselves.

Those who worked on West stilled when they noticed me in the room. I fidgeted under all their eyes, not knowing how to deal with their attention.

"Is it going to work on him?" I asked.

A man with flaming red hair glanced at the others before stepping away from the group towards me.

"The extraction process has begun but we are unsure of the exact time frame of when he was touched and when he was brought in. Some are guessing it was only forty minutes, others thought it was an hour and a half."

"And the magic time frame is an hour or less, right?"

"Exactly," the man said, his eyes regretful looking. "Under such stressful circumstances, no one is sure how long it was. If it really was less than hour, he stands a good chance of recovering. If not..."

I nodded, understanding what his trailing thoughts meant. "How long until we know?"

The man glanced at West. "When it worked before, we didn't see any results for over a week. Within a week and a half we started to see positive signs that he might recover."

"So we just have to wait?"

He simply nodded.

I couldn't take any more then. I turned and walked back down the hall without another look back. My breaths were coming in choked sobs before I reached the end of the hall. It felt like someone was trying to squeeze me from the inside out. As I stepped into the stairwell, I leaned against the cold cinderblock walls and slid to the floor. When the guard saw me, he stepped back out, his discomfort obvious. I heard him walk away.

It took me far too long to get myself back under control. The image of metallic veins sprouting in West's eye kept playing over and over behind my eyelids.

I used every ounce of strength I had to force myself off the floor and go back down the stairs.

As I walked numbly back into the medical wing, I saw a man lying on a hospital bed in another room. In my panic of the previous hours, I hadn't noticed that he was injured.

"Royce?" I said as I stepped into his room a few feet. "Are you alright?"

He just gave a shrug, brushing it off. "I'm fine. Just a few bullet holes. Nothing I haven't lived through before."

I nodded.

"I really am sorry about your friend," Royce said, his eyes studying my face. "He seemed like a good man. We all hope for the very best."

I nodded again, my eyes glued to the floor but not really seeing anything. Even though no one had said it, I heard it in the tone of their voices. They might have been hopeful, but they didn't expect a positive outcome.

"When do you plan on setting off the Pulse?" I changed the subject.

"With the Extractor running a lot of power will be diverted to it. It will be another day before the Pulse has gathered enough power to go off."

I nodded, stuffing my hands into my pockets.

"He tried saving West, you know," Royce said quietly. "Avian. Everyone was firing at the Bane who were flooding the platform. But Avian jumped in front of West while he was helping me repair the line. West probably would have died right then if not for Avian."

I squeezed my eyes closed, imagining the horrific scene behind my eyelids. "If I'd been there they both would have been fine."

"You can't be sure of that."

"He wouldn't have gotten infected."

"Maybe."

I turned to leave when Royce spoke again. "Eve, if I ever hear about you firing a weapon in this hospital again I will have Dr. Beeson make you think you're a three-year-old little girl for the rest of your life."

I glanced back at him, a smile creeping onto my lips. "It won't happen again, promise."

He gave a twitch of a smile. Something started to beep on one of his medical devices and two doctors rushed in from behind me. I took the opportunity to duck out.

Avian was asleep when I returned to his side, much to my disappointment. The doctors said they were giving him antibiotics to keep infection out but other than that there was little more they were going to have to do to him.

As I sat with Avian's hand in mine, I thought about what was to come. If the Pulse really worked and we were able to freely roam, what would that mean for Avian and I, now that I had finally made my decision?

I imagined taking him hunting with me, intrigued by the total mystery of it. I'd never seen him out in the woods like that, free to do and go as he pleased. I had little doubt he would be good at it. Avian seemed to be good at everything.

Where would we live once we were let out of this hospital? What would it be like to live with Avian, the way Gabriel and Leah lived together, Morgan and Eli? The thought was strange yet exciting.

Three years ago I watched with everyone as Morgan and Eli stood before everyone, she dressed in a makeshift wedding dress. They spoke words to each other that I didn't understand then. Now they made perfect sense. Would Avian and I ever speak words like that to each other? Would I ever wear a dress for him?

Finally, after two hours of restless sitting, Royce limped into Avian's room, accompanied by his regular armed men. The man with the broken nose was among them. He glared at me with blackened eyes.

"We're getting everything prepped for tomorrow," Royce said as he leaned on his crutches. "I thought you might want to come see before it goes off."

I glanced from Avian's still form and back to Royce. "We can have the doctors page you when he wakes up," Royce said.

"Alright."

The doctors on duty gave me a small black box to carry around and they informed me that it would beep loudly when Avian woke up. Already feeling slightly more like myself, I followed Royce's group to the blue floor and up the locked stairwell.

I had to blink furiously as we reached the top of the stairs, to the old roof of the building. The sun shone with burning intensity. It felt like forever since I had actually seen the sun. I had missed it.

The Pulse had a blue glow emanating from its core already. The loud hum was a testament to the amount of electricity that was being poured into it.

"Those are energy storage devices," Royce said loudly as he pointed to five hulking, black boxes. They were as tall as I was and wider than four of me. "When it's time, all the power stored in them will surge into the Pulse. They're going to be blown to high-heaven when the thing goes off, but hopefully not before they've been completely drained. With any luck we won't ever need them again."

"And you're sure the hospital will be protected from the blast?" I asked as I looked at the beautiful, yet menacing device before me.

"We've put a lot of effort into making sure it is," Royce said with a half-smile. "Trust me, no one here wants to lose electricity or all of our electrical devices. We all lived in the dark for too long. None of us want to go back."

I nodded that I understood as I paced around the Pulse. The central ring of it was spinning rapidly, each of the outer rings moving steadily as well.

It seemed like there were a million things that could go wrong in the next four or five hours. The device could just not work. Its reach could be no further than the walls of this hospital. The precautions to proof this building could fail. I could be dead in just a few hours.

But if everything went off as planned, life was going to change dramatically. We could go out into the city. We could start to rebuild. I dreamed of the outcome for the simple reason of being able to go back out into the sun freely.

I spent an hour, just looking at the beautiful blue glow of the Pulse, trying to not think of anything, to simply zone it all out. But before long I was advised to leave the Pulse room. As the power it held built, I could feel the sting of electrical output. I didn't argue as I descended the stairs. As I did, my pager started beeping.

The medical wing was quieter by then, all of the damage from the previous day's mission taken care of. When I came back into Avian's room I found him sitting up, tying the shoelaces of his boots.

"How do you feel?" I asked as I leaned against the doorframe, my arms folded over my chest.

"Like I've been shot three times," he said with a chuckle. "But better."

"You sure you want to be getting up now?"

"You sound like me," he teased as he stood slowly.

"Just worried about you."

"Now you know the feeling," he said as he took a few steps toward me, limping as he did, his eyebrow raising. "I see you lost your guard."

"I think he got bored."

"Everything almost ready?"

I nodded as we turned and walked out of the room. Avian put an arm across my shoulder, letting me help with his wounded leg. "I think so. It's a bomb of electricity up there. I had to leave."

"I'd be lying if I said this whole thing didn't scare me."

"Royce assures me the hospital will be protected," I said as we continued down the hall. We walked up the stairs to the second floor and went into Avian's room. He kicked off his boots again and laid gingerly back on the bed. "I just needed out of that stuffy room," he said when he saw the smirk on my face. I just shook my head and lay next to him, nestling in the crook of his good arm.

"I've been thinking about something. If you don't like it, just tell me. I will understand."

"What?" he asked as he pressed his cheek to the top of my head.

"I think I should be in with West when the Pulse goes off. Even if he can't hear me, there are a few things I need to say to him. Something doesn't feel right inside of me and I think it's because West has no idea what is going on. It feels too unfair."

Avian propped himself up just enough to look down into my eyes. "I think you should. We don't know what is in his future and I think you should be there when this happens. I don't like feeling like we've gone behind his back with this."

I brought my hand to the side of Avian's face. "I hoped you would understand."

"Even if you say you don't love him, he means a lot to you. He always will," Avian said as he looked down at me. "I would never expect that to change. People affect you, some stay with you forever. West will be one of those people."

I gave him a small smile, blinking several times before I pressed my lips to his briefly. "Thank you."

"What do you want to do once this is over?" Avian asked, changing the subject, and lying back down. He may have understood but West being in the picture had still caused him pain in the past. I didn't blame him for not wanting to talk about West anymore.

"Get out of this hospital," I said immediately, settling my head back against his shoulder. "I just realized that I hate being here. The people are fine, and I will admit it is nice to feel so protected. But this place feels like a prison. I can't breathe. I need some sun."

"I wondered how you were handling being locked up in here," he said.

"I want to see the ocean," I said as I stared at the white ceiling. "West told me about it once. How big and intimidating it is. We're so close to it I swear I can almost smell it at times.

"What about you?"

Avian was thoughtful for a while. "I just want freedom to go wherever I want. I have no complaints about how things ran in Eden. In a way it was a utopia. But I couldn't ever leave. I was limited to this mile radius of wherever the people of Eden were. After the trip out here, of having the freedom to move around even just the hospital as I wish, it's been freeing. I want to just take off into the mountains if I want, to go, I don't know, explore if I want to, without having to worry about someone dying if I'm unavailable."

"You've been a prisoner in a way for the last five years," I said as I nuzzled closer. I'd reinforced that feeling multiple times, telling Avian that he couldn't leave. Everyone had needed him too much. He'd saved so many lives.

He pressed his lips briefly to my forehead. "And I just want to spend time with you."

THIRTY-NINE

The blue floor was a buzz of activity again, people rushing in and out of every room. Such chaos before the storm. It was easy to feel the excitement that coursed through their veins but you could almost touch their nervousness as if it were a tangible thing. I felt my own heartbeat pick up a few paces.

There was only one doctor in the Extraction room when we walked in. He entered something into a computer as we approached, glancing up at us. "I'm almost done, then you can be alone with him."

"How is he doing?" Avian asked. As he spoke, I remembered what Royce had said about what he had done for West. Despite everything, Avian had risked his life to save West's.

"No change yet," the doctor said as he stepped away from the computer, ready to leave. "It hasn't been very long though. We won't know any different for about a week, probably more."

Avian gave a nod and the doctor stepped out.

We walked up to the Extractor silently, each lost in our thoughts. I knew Avian felt no sense of relief at now having West out of the way, no longer a distraction to me. That was just Avian, always pure-hearted and a good man.

"I hope he responds soon," Avian said quietly as we stopped five feet away from the curved arms that rose around West, circling him in an open bowl. "He is a good soldier."

I simply nodded, unable to say much. My throat was tight.

Avian's hand slipped into mine. "Take as much time as you need."

He pressed a quick kiss to my forehead and left without another word. I glanced at the clock as he closed the door behind him. Fifteen minutes to activation.

Thoughts raced through my head in a mixed up jumble of words and emotions. Where did I start and where did I stop? Was this totally pointless if West couldn't even hear me? I had already been told that West was in a medically induced coma.

I grabbed a chair and sat in front of him.

I hated seeing him so broken. West had always been so strong, he had always survived and could take care of himself. He had proven that over the last five years. And here he was, after such a long battle, right as our enemy was about to be wiped out, his system infected.

A horrifying thought occurred to me then. If the extraction didn't work, if it was too late, West would be the only body left around that was still actively infected if the Pulse worked. They would only try to cure him for so long. They could only keep his body around for so long. As it was now, they could no longer touch his skin with their bare hands without getting infected themselves. Eventually, if he didn't respond, they would have to destroy his body.

"You have to pull out of this," I started. "You're too strong to go down like this. I need to say this to your face, to tell you what has happened these past few days. This is too easy and too hard all at the same time. But in case I don't get that chance, I'm going to tell you now and hope that you can somehow hear me."

I swallowed hard, my eyes falling to my hands, my fingers interlocked. "You woke something up inside of me. I didn't used to care about being with someone. About feeling attachment. About getting close to people. And despite how terrible my past is, I'm glad you had the answers for me, most of them anyway. I don't think you can fully understand who you are until you know where you've come from.

"But something was missing between us, West. Loving someone isn't just about feeling passion, or whatever it is. You got under my skin, you drove me insane. And I could have gotten over those things. You learn to deal with people's faults. But I never felt like I could trust you. You deliberately kept things from me, with no intention to ever tell me the truth. I can't have a relationship built on lies. You carry too many secrets."

I paused, taking a few deep breaths, unsure if I would ever be able to give this speech again if West did wake up. It felt like I was ripping myself to shreds. And yet I felt so relieved, to finally understand how I felt. To be speaking the truth.

"I love Avian," I said quietly, my chest swelling with my words. "I have for a while, I just didn't realize it.

"I've made my choice, West."

As the words escaped my lips the building suddenly shook and I faintly heard glass shatter.

This was it.

The lights flickered as all the electricity was directed to the roof. Another blast could be faintly heard. The building shook again, frightening moans echoing through the walls. A third blast sounded, the air surging. And then all was quiet and still.

I was still alive.

Royce had been right. They'd protected the hospital.

Cheering erupted out in the halls. Feet pounded the floor as people ran toward the stairs and elevator.

"Goodbye, West," I whispered.
I walked out the door.

FOURTY

I took the stairs two at a time to find everyone. As I sprinted into the lobby, I saw everyone standing at the front sliding doors, the protective steel doors retracted, looking through the thin glass out into the sunlight.

I was confused by their hesitancy at first, their silence. But they were afraid. Afraid that it might not have worked. Afraid that it might have.

I worked my way to the front of the crowd, stepping out in front of them. A few hundred eyes settled on my back as I hesitated for a moment. Taking a deep breath, I pried the doors open, letting in a rush of sun filled air. Just before I stepped outside, a familiar hand slid into mine. I glanced over at Avian, his burning blue eyes giving me courage.

We stepped out into the light, the streets perfectly silent. Making sure no Hunters were hiding in the shadows, waiting to leap out at us, the two of us crossed the street to another building. My heart hammering in my chest, we looked through the windows.

They were all there, crumpled in a pile of destroyed metal and flesh.

"It worked," I breathed, opening the door. I slipped inside, my eyes widening as I saw dozens of bodies lying around, empty eyes staring up at us. "It worked."

Avian walked up to a woman with a half-metal face and pushed her shoulder with his booted toe. She didn't move. "They're dead," he whispered.

"They've been dead for a long time," I said as I nudged a body. I couldn't even tell if it was male or female anymore. "They just can't kill us anymore."

Not one of them moved as we continued to check the bodies. Assured that none of them were faking, we walked back out into the sunlight. Faces watched us from the doorway of the hospital, a few of Royce's men standing just outside, their firearms held tightly.

"It worked," Avian said loudly as we crossed the street. "The Bane are dead!"

That was all it took. Everyone started pouring out of the building in a stampede, rushing out onto the street. Cries of joy echoed off the buildings, laughter emanating from everywhere. I couldn't help but smile too. Avian turned his face to the blue sky, a laugh shaking his entire body. He pulled me into his arms for a moment and gave me a tight squeeze.

"This probably wouldn't have been possible if it weren't for you," Royce's voice came from behind us. He struggled to coordinate himself on the crutches. "We owe you a lot."

"You would have found some other way if I hadn't come along," I said, giving him a small smile.

"We would have lost a lot more people," he said, clapping a hand on my right shoulder. "Thank you."

"Thank you," I said as I watched him hobble down the street after his people.

"They did it," Tuck said, his hands pushed into his pockets as he walked up to us.

"We all did," Avian said as he glanced at me.

"Just imagine Eden's surprise when our messages lead them into a cleared city," he said with a smile creeping onto his face.

"They were planning to leave in just over a week," Avian said. "We should be seeing them in less than two."

"How different Eden is going to be," I breathed.

"Not so different," Avian said as he slid his hand into mine. "We'll always have each other. As long as we have that, it will always be Eden."

And as usual, I knew Avian was right.

FOURTY-ONE

Not a single trace of glass was to be found as the roof of the hospital was flooded with its occupants. The Pulse sat in the middle of the expansive space, a gleaming trophy for every single one of us. It was a testament to mankind's will to survive. To live.

Twinkling lights were strung around the area, the only light to see by beside the huge moon that loomed in the sky. Music filtered through a box that was plugged into one of the many electrical cords that ran back into the building. I watched as people moved in time with it, saw their smiling faces as they held each other close.

The rest of the members of Eden had arrived only six days after the Pulse went off. When Hunters had been spotted every day for three days straight they decided they had no other choice but to leave early. Their truck had run better and faster than ours had and they found us quickly.

I had felt like my insides might burst from the joy I felt as we explained to them the bodies they saw lying everywhere. We were finally safe. Hopefully for a good long while. Nearly every one of them had tears in their eyes.

I hesitantly hugged Gabriel when a sob escaped his chest. "Thank you," he had simply whispered. I pulled Bill into my arms next. To my surprise, he didn't let go for quite a while. Even though I knew it made him uncomfortable, I pulled Graye into a hug as well and gave him a tight squeeze. It felt so good to see my brothers again.

Their joy was crushed though when we told them about West. Their tears of joy quickly turned to tears of sorrow. Victoria broke down into sobs. I didn't think West ever realized just how loved he had been in Eden. He had been accepted as a family member, even if he didn't realize it.

What was unexpected though, was seeing the way Wix looked at Victoria, the way he consoled her tears. I didn't anticipate seeing her slide her hand into his. And to see Brady grab Wix's other hand and call him "daddy." Apparently I'd been *way* off the marker thinking she and Avian were falling for each other.

And so there we were, three days later, watching as Wix and Victoria stood before the one-hundred and thirty-six residents of Los Angeles. Gabriel stood with them and spoke of love lasting beyond death. And wearing the white dress she had picked from one of the long forgotten about shops, she and Wix spoke words to each other I finally understood.

Maybe I should have waited to have Dr. Beeson lessen my emotional blockers. Ever since the rest of my family was reunited, I've felt everything was going to overwhelm me. One little bit at a time, he said, and someday I'd be normal. As normal as I could be anyway. Now I had to decide if I really wanted to be normal. Already at times I felt everything would consume me, all the joy I felt, all the sorrow I experienced for the billions of lives that had been lost.

But mostly I felt an overwhelming sense of hope for the future.

We'd slowly been clearing bodies out of the city in the days since the Pulse went off. Even though we knew everything was dead, most of us didn't trust having them all lying in the streets and in buildings. There was enough live tissue left in most of them for there to be a risk of disease spreading. We were never going to be able to clear all the hundreds of thousands of bodies out, but we would clear the areas we inhabited. The floor of the Pacific Ocean would be littered with bodies.

I pushed the plate of food away from me as I brought myself back to the present, feeling fuller than I could remember ever feeling. Avian walked over in his recently picked out suit, two cups filled with some kind of liquid. He offered one to me and when I shook my head, he set them down on the table. I couldn't help but smile at him as he held a hand out to me. I took it and stood, the green silky fabric of the dress I wore sliding around my body in an alien way.

My hand in his, Avian led us to the area of the roof where people danced, moving in time to the music that wove around us. He slid his hand around my waist, pulling me close, resting his cheek against mine.

"You look amazing," he said quietly as we moved in a slow circle.

"You clean up pretty nicely yourself," I said with a smile.

We danced slowly, our hearts slowing to the same rhythm.

"I can't believe you asked me if I was in love with Victoria," Avian suddenly said with a chuckle.

"You're bringing this up now?" I said defensively as I backed away from him just a bit.

"I just think it's funny," he said with a chuckle, pulling me close again. I just shook my head and rolled my eyes, even though he couldn't see.

"She looks really beautiful tonight," I said as I watched her and Wix dance together. Their red hair nearly glowed under the twinkling light. Brady danced by himself next to them in his own little suit.

We slowed a bit as Avian turned to look at her. The fabric draped around her thin frame in an almost dreamy way, shimmering in the lights.

"Would you wear one?" Avian asked quietly as he looked at me with his burning blue eyes. "Someday. For me?"

My eyes widened a bit as I realized what he was really asking. My insides swelled, my heart picking up in pace. A smile crossed my lips as I leaned forward, pressing my lips to his. "Only for you," I whispered.

Avian smiled as I pulled away, giving me a small squeeze. His eyes still on mine, he took a step away, keeping my hand in his. He led me through the crowd, through the door, and back down the stairs into the hospital.

As we walked past the door to the Extraction room, I gave a hard swallow. It was hard to fully enjoy the wedding party when I knew West was sitting unconscious in that room.

We continued to watch West on a daily basis. His vitals remained stable, his wounds completely healed from that awful day. Every night someone would go in to sweep up the cybernetic scraps that worked their way out of his skin. They were melted down and transported away.

I asked the doctors every few days what they thought would happen to West but they only said that they still don't know if he would recover or not. We could only hope.

Things had escalated between Avian and I the last few days. Even though West still didn't know what had happened, things feel whole. Maybe it was the nights we'd spent together, sleeping in each other's arms. Maybe it was the hunts we'd gone on. It didn't matter. It only mattered how right it was, how perfect.

There were a lot of things that I didn't know about the future. I didn't know if West would ever wake up. I didn't know how I would deal with it if he never did. I didn't know if the Bane would ever travel here from another city, if we would ever have to fight them off again. I didn't know how everyone in Eden would adjust to our new way of life.

I didn't know if we would ever reclaim our planet or even just our country, whatever that meant anymore.

But there were a few things that I did know.

I knew that I would continue to take care of Eden. I knew I would help till our new gardens come spring. I would continue to do everything in my power to keep my family alive.

I knew that I could count on Avian to be by my side until the day my heart stopped beating.

And I finally knew what love was.

I woke the next morning just an hour from dawn. I felt the cold sheets next to me, realizing that Avian was gone. At the same time, the door to my room opened, letting in a little sliver of light.

"Where were you?" I asked as I pushed my hair out of my face.

"Come on," he said through the dim light. Even with how dark it was I could see the smile on his face. "I've got a surprise for you."

I pulled on my boots and followed Avian silently through the sleeping hospital. We came out on the ground level and exited through the front doors. Sitting on the sidewalk was a beautiful two-wheeled red mass of machinery.

"What is it?" I asked, running my hand along its glossy surface.

"It's called a motorcycle," Avian said with a smile as he walked over to it.

"Does it still work?"

"Royce had it saved in the basement of the hospital. Do you want to go for a ride?"

I couldn't suppress the smile that spread on my face as I nodded.

Avian straddled the motorcycle and a moment later had the engine roaring to life. I sat on the seat behind him, wrapping my arms around his chest. "Hang on," he said over his shoulder.

The beast ripped to life, the pavement falling behind us as the hospital faded away. The night air caressed my cheeks as we sped by, my hair fanning out behind me. This was a freedom I had never experienced, one I vowed to live over and over again.

We drove for nearly an hour and I realized where we were going when I smelled the salt in the air. Avian parked the motorcycle in the middle of the road and looked out to the west.

I didn't wait for him to follow me as I slid off the back of the motorcycle. My eyes fixed in front of me as I crossed the pavement and then my boots sank into the sand. I walked to the edge of the water, staring into the horizon.

There was nothing but water and sky for as far as I could see.

I understood then what West had said about the ocean being scary and beautiful at the same time. I felt so small, so helpless. It could claim my life in just a moment if it were to awaken with fury. But it was beautiful. The slowly fading moon gleamed on its surface, an endless dance of celestial skill. Mankind could never hope to have that kind of grace.

And then I noticed something at the edge of the sand. My old tent had been pitched, waiting there like an old friend.

"Welcome home," Avian said softly.

As I looked back out over the water, his thumb brushed across my cheek. I realized there were tears streaming down my face.

Maybe I was more human than I thought.

ACKNOWLEDGMENTS

My how this story has evolved! It has come through quite a journey to be the story that it is today and there were many, many people who helped along the way.

Thank you to those who were there in the beginning: Mom, Jenni, Alex, Crystal, Halley and Kim. You read it in its early stages and gave me the direction I needed to make this into a readable stack of pages.

Thank you to my dad who took me shooting and who answered many random, bizarre questions that helped to create the world of Eden and the Bane.

A huge thank you to Kami Garcia, a woman who I consider my mentor, good friend, and amazing author.

And the biggest thank you to my readers. You loved Eden enough and kept pestering me enough to turn this story into a trilogy and gave me the courage to finally do it. Thank you for your support and enthusiasm. I love you all!

KEARY TAYLOR grew up along the foothills of the Rocky Mountains where she started creating imaginary worlds and daring characters who always fell in love. She now resides on a tiny island in the Pacific Northwest with her husband and their two young children. She continues to have an overactive imagination that frequently keeps her up at night.

Please visit **KEARYTAYLOR.COM** to learn more about her and her writing process.

Made in the USA
San Bernardino, CA
01 November 2013